Sung Home

Laura Ramnarace

Cover art by Ben Rico, "*Dancing Woman*"

Illustrations by Diana Ingalls Leyba

ISBN: 13-978-1-0771-1977-2

DEDICATION

For Amber, Anand and Bianca (in order of appearance):
You will always be my most treasured creations.
You hold the seeds for the future of which I dream.

Laura Ramnarace

What Readers are Saying about Sung Home

"As Covid 19 begins its journey through our world, Sung Home comes to be. Ramnarace's depiction of humanity, her willingness to seek grace through the worst of behaviors and her ability to keep a reader in a constant state of wonder make Sung Home a beacon of hope in these uneasy times.' -Curtis Michaels

"A timely, adventurous work of art. Given our current global situation with COVID19, this story isn't at all far-fetched.– Soraya

"...the narrative sweeps you along." -Hayra Nur

"...intriguing, thoroughly engaging...page turning...timely." -Paul Westcott

"Laura Ramnarace has a beautiful writing style. This is a superb piece of literature." -Linda Friedman

"You won't be disappointed ...vivid and true ... engaging and real. I can't wait for the sequel."
-J. E. Foster

"This is a superb read. ... a journey that you won't forget. Engaging, exciting, enrapturing." -B.A. Gordon

"Could not put it down." -Augustine Verciglio

"Enthralling, thought provoking story. I could not put it down and eagerly look forward to the remaining books in the series!" -Heather Gorder Nutt

ACKNOWLEDGMENTS

To the Apache people and all indigenous people on every continent of our precious mother earth. You are on the forefront of the struggle for justice, healing of past wrongs and a return to balanced living. Today and in generations past you have served as an inspiration to peoples of all cultures who believe that all people should be allowed to live in dignity, following their own traditions and life-ways. All of us need these things if we are to live in a world where the word "humanity" is not synonymous with "destroyer.".

To my mother, Bette Jean Boykin, for instilling in me a love of the written word and good storytelling. I imagine you reading this story in the Elysian Fields, surrounded by wildflowers.

Great appreciation to Soumyajeet Chattaraj at Rebelle Society for his initial encouragement of my writing, and for his patience and unflagging support of the serialization of the first version of Sung Home.

Thank you to my formal readers, Susan Rice, Diana Ingalls Leyba and Roberta Hunt, for their invaluable critical feedback and encouragement as I sought to hone Sung Home for print publishing.

Deepest gratitude to Ben Rico for the painting, *Dancing Woman* and permission to use it on the cover, and to Diana Ingalls Leyba for drawing the maps.

Special thanks to the readers who responded enthusiastically to the serialized version on Rebelle Society. Your response gave me the confidence to publish this story in print.

1

It's gotta be tonight. Can't stand one more day. No matter what. Tonight.

My arms trembled as I lifted the massive black cast iron cooking pot filled with hot water off the grate over the cooking fire, flaming high out of the fire pit. I stepped gingerly sideways, scorpion like, a few inches at a time, the fine desert dust forming tiny dunes over my sandaled toes, until I could set the pot on the thick rough-cut wooden counter several feet away. I rubbed the fat gray bar of homemade soap in the steaming water until it clouded slightly, then placed the bar onto the rough stone wedge that served as a soap dish. Piñon Jays chattered excitedly in a nearby mesquite thicket, springing from branch to branch, as if already anticipating the sweet and sour bean pods which wouldn't be ripe for months yet. Normally their behavior would make me smile but that day I just tensed irritably. As I eased the pots and metal plates into the dishwater I glanced around to see if Darian was nearby. I saw no sign of him.

Just one more night.

I hoped fervently that he remained well occupied elsewhere.

"Pretty fast with the dishes tonight," commented Robert with a forced casualness, coming up behind me so suddenly I nearly launched straight out of my sandals. Robert cocked his eyebrow at me, trying for humor, although his mouth remained tight. "Kinda jumpy too."

"Yeah," I said shortly, "guess I am." I looked hard at the plate in my hands and scrubbed as if it had personally insulted me.

Robert's voice turned suddenly gravelly, eyes darting to make sure no one else heard. "Yeah. I don't blame you. I'm kinda jittery myself, since...well, you know...." He swallowed hard.

I stopped scrubbing and looked up at him. His large brown eyes turned watery for just a second. Eyes as big as a Kodiak bear's. He took a deep breath, looking towards the mountains in the west, and I wondered if he suspected my plan.

Robert was seventeen, just a year older than me and Sylvia. His mom died in the epidemic but Emma, Sylvia's mom, took him in without a moment's thought, as she had done with me a few years later. He had been like a brother to me and Sylvia. Until now. I didn't dare ask Robert to go with me. Robert was big and lumbering, strong, but not fast and quiet like me. If he decided to come, he might get us both caught. If he decided *not* to come, he'd probably try to talk me out of it. His father and mother both gone, and now Sylvia. Just what he needs, to lose someone else. But I had to do it and he couldn't know.

So I said nothing.

The stark reality of leaving Robert and Emma, the closest thing I had to family, leaned like a boulder against my chest. I turned away from the dishwater and towards Robert, grasping him tightly, startling him so much he stepped back and we both nearly fell. Still clenching him, we staggered upright again and he returned my hug with equal fierceness. It would have been funny, real-life slapstick, if it weren't for the surrounding circumstances. Robert's big chest shook and a short sob escaped his mouth and found refuge in my ear. I trembled a moment myself, just a moment. But I couldn't handle a sob-fest right then so I disentangled myself from his hold and clasped my hands around his shoulders, looking him right in the face.

"We're going get through this. It's going to be okay – some day!"

Robert's head hung forward. "Yeah. Okay. I know," he whispered.

I turned back to my dishes like nothing had happened and Robert ambled away.

What a liar I was. I just spoke to him as if we were going to get through this *together*.

My luck had held through the week, as I planned and collected the things I would need. I hadn't wanted to leave right after Sylvia died because Darian and his men knew that Sylvia and I were practically sisters, and I figured they might expect me to act out somehow right afterwards. And

I needed time to collect the things I would need for the journey. Two days after Sylvia left us, Darian and his men mounted their horses and rode off in a hurry. Robert had said that he overheard them saying that one of the scouts had spotted a caravan on the old highway and they were riding off to raid it. I breathed a little easier, knowing they would be distracted for at least a few days. They had returned the day before, horses walking slowly, heads down, laden with booty from the caravan. One horse even pulled an improvised travois made of agave stalks, stacked tall with rattling cloth-covered bundles.

If Darian just kept his distance for another few hours I might make it out of there. I knew if I saw him up close I would shake so hard with hatred and fear that he'd surely notice, and suspect something.

A cool spring breeze sprung up and the sun bobbed above the skyline, as if reluctant to end the day. Hands flying fast out of habit and anxiety, I rinsed the last of the dishes in the large battered aluminum pot filled with cold water that sat beside the hot soapy one. I stacked the dishes carefully so they wouldn't fall clattering all over the counter and let anyone else know I had finished the dishes early. I heard the clang of the hoes in the garden as the gardeners banged the hard soil, coaxing it to receive a few more seeds before dark. On the other side of the outdoor kitchen wall the baby goats baaaaaa-ed for their mamas. The burro, named Burl, moaned fitfully.

I had always liked working in the kitchen because so much of it I did by myself, away from the others. Emma – sturdy, unflappable Emma – usually led the cooking while I chopped meat and vegetables, but I always did the dishes: breakfast, lunch and dinner. Since Sylvia died though, Emma laid in her bed staring at the wall. It was all I could do to get her to take a little water and little bites of cheese and bread a few times a day. Face fixed, staring hard into nothingness, Emma had turned into some kind of zombie, not alive, but not dead either. I didn't know if she'd ever be whole, really alive, again. After the virus hit, there had been a lot of people like this, too stunned and grief stricken to care for themselves. In the wake of the virus there were three kinds of people: the dead, the living dead, and a few, very few, living, fully functional people. I was trying really hard to stay in the last category.

Dishes done, our own star Sol shimmered golden, coaxed downward by the horizon. I snatched my favorite carbon steel knife from the large wooden knife block, and grabbed the sharpener as well. Poor Robert. With me and Sylvia gone, and Emma catatonic, he'd have to get some of the other, younger ones, to do the cooking and cleaning with him, along with the gardening and other chores they normally did. What a grim way to rise amongst the ranks.

I hadn't had the heart to sleep in the casita with Emma like I usually did, so from my napping cot in the closet beside the kitchen I lightly dozed while waiting for the night to deepen. A couple of hours later the half-full moon light glimmered through the boards that covered what used to be a window, signaling my departure time. Snores from the nearby gardener's casita punctuated the desert stillness.

As I lie drowsy and fully clothed under the covers,

waiting until it was late enough to risk leaving, I saw Sylvia wearing the colorful, flowing dress she had sewn together from bright scraps cut from discarded clothes. Since the virus took most of the people, and clothing didn't exactly go bad, there was more than enough fabric to use in sewing. Even years after the virus, most of us dressed pretty much the same way as we had before.

"I'm going to be a fairy princess in this dress!" Sylvia had proclaimed in an exaggerated, dramatic tone, head thrown back and twirling so the skirt spun around her curving hips.

My body trembled as I thought of Sylvia and her effervescent fantasy. Was it fear that shook me? Anger? Grief? It didn't matter. Thinking back, I hated that beautiful dress as much as I had once loved it, and Sylvia, before. Before Sylvia found out that Darian was no prince charming

Darian's compound had been the only home I had known for the last seven years, almost half my life. But after burying Sylvia, I had felt like a rabbit trying not to bolt straight into a coyote's mouth. It took every bit of self-control I could muster not to run screaming out of that compound that day. I must have slept that first night after her death somehow, because the next morning I awoke, arms and legs tangled in the sheets, with a dream of my mama's singing echoing in my ears. I realized then that staying wasn't a given, and leaving didn't *have* to mean death. I would risk anything to escape, but I'd rather live.

So that night, six days after Sylvia had departed, I left too. Riding a burro, not death.

A couple of hours after everyone else went to bed I

slithered out from under the rough wool blanket and slid my feet into mama's worn ankle-high leather hiking boots. I carefully shoved the kitchen knife into the sheath I had sewn to the outside of the right boot, snapping it snuggly into place. Setting one heavy wool sweater and a pair of blue jeans into the middle of the blanket, I rolled them together and tied them with a piece of home-made yucca fiber twine. I grabbed the leather satchel containing dried pinto beans, mesquite powder, pecans from last years' crop, and a large piece of goat cheese. Another satchel held full water skins made from goats' bladders. I would need to stock up well on water any chance I had along the way.

Stopping to listen at the doorway I heard coyotes yipping querulously nearby. The light from the main house still shone through the windows into the darkness, lighting up the lilacs blooming against the tan stucco wall, their smell floating sweetly on the air. Darian's brash laugh rang out from the house and I heard the rumbling voices of his underlings as well. My bowels hollowed and for a few long seconds I trembled so hard I couldn't move. If they caught me who knew what they would do to me? In the seven years since Mama and I were captured by Darian and his band, when I was nine, only two people had tried to escape, both in the first year, and both gruesomely memorable.

One, a grey-haired man named Sammy Jiron, had snuck out on foot one night and was noticed missing at dawn. Darian's men had run him down just a few miles away and drug him behind a horse all the way back. They tied his bloody body, still alive, to a post and whipped him to death, forcing the rest of the captives to watch. They left his body there for a week before they finally cut him down and buried him. I remember the reek of his rotting corpse, as much as the blood, and flesh like a large bundle of torn rags. By then the coyotes, ravens and other opportunists had chewed most of the flesh off of his skeleton and the stench made even Darian's men retch if they walked too close.

The second escapee, a thirtyish woman named Naomi Martinez, was discovered after many days missing, curled up beneath a creosote bush, thin and dry as an ocotillo, dead of dehydration and hunger. After that everyone resigned themselves to making the best of it, including me and mama. Our village, Columbus, had always been remote, far from any population center since before the days of the explorer for whom it was named. But now, since Before, even El Paso and Juarez were more ghost towns than cities. No one had any idea what was happening elsewhere, except that the virus had scoured the entire planet of about 90% of the human population before civilization as we knew it collapsed.

Satchels slung over one shoulder, and blanket rolled beneath the other arm, I took a deep breath before walking, as Daddy had taught me to when hunting rabbits. I padded carefully through the talcum-like dust, pausing between steps, ear cocked towards the stock pen. Before Burl the burro could huff at my approach, I thrust a handful of the sweet and sour mesquite powder beneath his nostrils. He snuffled it up so eagerly it puffed out in tiny tan clouds around his snout. Mama had chided me for spoiling Burl when he was young but right then I was glad I had disobeyed her. Burl loved me. Or at least he could be bribed into cooperation.

"There you go boy, no need to say anything. This is just between you and me. Our little secret," I whispered soothingly into my four-footed friend's ear as I first fitted my homemade bridle onto his nose, and then pulled myself up onto his back. I startled momentarily at a colorful flash, seen out of the corner of my eye. Rainbow colors, impossible in the dark. I glanced wildly all around me, heart nearly knocking a hole in my chest, but I saw nothing but the gently lit desert landscape. Creosote bushes crouched like animal ghosts in the darkness but not a beetle stirred. The sound of shattering glass rang out in the main house, and I froze. Then, limbs thawing moments later, I kicked Burl in the sides and off we trotted. The compound's dogs took no notice of the familiar burro and the girl they had known since they were born. The guard dogs were trained to attack strangers.

My strategy was to *not* get as far away as possible the first night.

Darian and his men had fast horses and they would expect me to try to flee as far and quickly as I could right off. I knew as well as they that I wouldn't stand a chance that way. They would assume I was stupid enough *not* to understand this, and they were not smart enough themselves to imagine any reasonable alternative. Darian's gang had reigned supreme in this region through brute force and not brains. There was not enough competition for this territory to require more. My plan was to only go about half as far as I could comfortably, hide well away from any logical, more traveled route, and sit there while Darian and his boys wore themselves out riding hard and long, looking for me where I wasn't. When they gave up, I would head north. To the place where the songs began.

Once Burl and I were about a mile away from the compound I slid off his back and walked beside him, knowing the trip would be challenging enough without me on top of him the whole time. We weren't in a hurry anyway. We easily avoided the prickly pear and cholla cactus stands, their distinctive shapes, squat and rounded, and tall and narrow respectively, easily identifiable even in the faint light. Stars crowded the cobalt desert sky like dragon's treasure, augmenting the light from the rising moon. A couple days before, I had spotted the area where I could best monitor Darian's hunt for me while keeping enough distance to feel safe. We would head into the hills west of the compound, and camp on the east-facing slope of a high rise. Surrounded by piñon and juniper trees we would be sheltered from view, while the compound sat open to my scrutiny in the midst of low scrub oak, and sparse mesquite and ocotillo. From there I could safely keep an eye on the comings and goings at the compound and know when they had given up looking for me. I doubted they would think to search those hills because they were so close, and Darian would know it would be slow going there for someone trying to put distance between themselves and the compound.

Dawn arrived at my campsite in the hills and the sun

tossed its pastel palette of muted coral, turquoise and amethyst across the eastern horizon. I stirred lazily, reaching for the water bag beside me, then sat in my bedroll nibbling some pecans, watching the compound. About an hour later I was stretching myself more fully awake when I spotted Darian and his men emerge one by one from the main house and make their way to the joint kitchen for breakfast. As I expected someone must have told them I was missing because it wasn't long before Darian and his gang mounted their horses, leaned forward in their saddles, and rode north along the old highway, now rarely used by automobiles. They must have assumed I was heading towards the closest towns of any size, Deming or Silver City. I assumed they were grimly smug in their conviction that they would find me soon. I imagined them planning my punishment and my skull and stomach swam with fear for a moment. I shook the images from my head and turned my mind elsewhere.

My daddy once told me, when I hesitated to cross a hefty log over a rushing stream, keeping me from the wild raspberries I knew ripened on the other side, "move toward what you want, not away from what you fear."

I hummed the song, mama's song, that I hoped would take me to my new home.

As the men grew smaller in the distance a covey of quail skittered quickly by me in a curvy line, mama and daddy leading, four little ones rushing to keep up. The black topknots protruding out of their foreheads like wobbly question marks made me smile. I had tied Burl to a tree with a vigorous bunch of new grass at its base which he contentedly munched as we waited.

Nibbling just enough provisions to keep my stomach from growling I napped off and on through the day, head cradled in my crooked arm as I lie in the pine needles, bits of bark and old piñon nut shells strewn at the edge of the overlook. I checked between dozes for signs of Darian and his men's return to the compound. It was nearly sundown when I saw them, moving slowly now. Darian in the lead still and the others straggling behind. I felt a thrill of triumph that I had outwitted them so far, and entertained a moment's temptation to sneak back down and listen at the window to their conversation about the day. They had kept us all cowed for so long, they believed as much as we had that we *couldn't* escape.

Even tyrants can be dumb-asses.

The next morning they set out again, hunched in their saddles against the brisk spring wind. They first clustered together on their horses just outside the compound, apparently debating which direction they should go. To my dismay they headed off in pairs in four different directions, including one pair coming west.

Straight towards me.

My breath felt taut in my chest, as if my ribs had suddenly shrunk two sizes. I had been careful to drag a branch behind me and Burl, sprinkling sticks and leaves now and then so that we could not be tracked. The seasonal morning gusts obscured our trail still more I was sure. And yet seeing the two lean, rangy men headed straight for us caused my stomach to clench and dried my mouth. The horsemen threaded their way through the creosote and mesquite, closer and closer. I perched like a wary squirrel, high enough in those rocky hills that there was little chance they would come up exactly the way I did. Then, realizing I may have to get out of there quickly in case they came too close, I darted through the sparse dry foliage locating two possible escape routes to the west that I could take, just in case. I returned to my roost to check their progress.

The two men ambled along, still heading my way. They were moving pretty slowly for guys who were supposed to be hunting someone. The sun was high in the sky when they finally arrived at the foot of the hill. I hadn't realized I had been following a faint wash as I traveled here. My efforts at covering our tracks had not kept their horses from following the natural indentation in the soil, the easiest route, just as I had. I felt like such a fool. Dangerously foolish.

It was Lem and Jeff, two scraggly brothers who Darian had picked up a few months ago. Although they were many yards below me and Burl, they were still close enough that a well-aimed spit could have hit one on the head. I looked again at my escape routes, calculating which would be the best to take. I decided on the path that dropped over a sharp western ledge right away instead of the one that crossed the flat first. It would be good to step below sight as soon as possible. I quickly tied my bedroll onto Burl's back, cinching it firmly, patting Burl encouragingly then hoisted my satchels onto one shoulder. I took one more peek over the edge and saw to my surprise that the men had stopped.

The pair had tied their horses to a tree and sat down in the shade of the granite hillside. In the dry mid-day stillness I could just hear their voices drifting up to my perch. Alarm bells rang in my head, urging me to make my getaway but I was transfixed, fascinated. What were they doing?

"He's such an idiot, sending us here," said Lem.

"Like that 'lil gal would come up these hills. She wouldn't get nowhere this way. She probably ain't that bright but probably not that stupid either. She's gone and why does he even care? What a waste of time!" said Jeff.

"You know, we could do a better job leading this gang than him. He don't have no ambition. We could be raking in way more than we are now," Lem agreed, nodding his narrow head vigorously, white blond hair bobbing heavily with grease.

"I know, I know. It's a good gig for now though. Let's just take it easy. Later maybe we can get our *own* compound."

Jeff, stockier but just as tow-headed, pulled some jerky and apples out of a worn leather saddle bag and they had their lunch. Then they sprawled out in the dirt and granite gravel and fell asleep, Lem snoring loudly.

I found it hard to believe, and felt a little insulted, that they would just stop looking for me like that. I squelched a brief impulse to toss pebbles down at them. Then, scared by that impulse, I watched them more anxiously than ever for a couple hours while they napped, convinced that if I relaxed even a little bit they would be upon me minutes later. Burl contentedly munched fine spring grass, oblivious to the specter of danger.

The men didn't stir again until the sun was halfway down the sky. Lem and Jeff were just humoring Darian. They didn't care if I were caught or not, and just took the day off. Breathing more easily, I slept a little myself after seeing them pack up and head east again.

When the sun hovered low in the west, behind me, I saw Darian and his other men coming in from their expeditions as well, converging just outside the corral. From the horses' slow pace and the men's slumped postures it seemed like their mission had lost steam. I decided to sit quietly for another day just to make sure.

"Well Burl, it looks like my plan is working. At least so far." Burl blinked his long thick lashes at me, then closed them drowsily.

The third morning after my escape, I peeked over the rocky eastern edge of our campsite but I didn't see anyone leave the compound. All was quiet. I slept much of the day, so as to have as much energy as possible for the evening's travel. Though I had only nibbled at my food supply, Burl had eaten so much spring grass I could've sworn I saw a few more pounds around his middle. I was glad he had the extra food, because for sure he'd wear it off soon enough. Now that it appeared that they would not search for me again, I wanted to put as much distance as I could between myself and that place as I could, for real.

The molten magenta sunset illuminated our way as we gingerly picked our path down the rocky slope, irrationally concerned as I was about making noise. By sundown Burl and I had turned north, roughly paralleling the weathered, north-bound road out of Columbus from a safe distance. Darian's men nearly always went east for their raids because there were still more people between Columbus and El Paso than any other direction. To the west there had been practically no people even Before, so they had no reason to come my way now that they had given up on finding me.

I fixed my gaze upon Cooke's Peak, dead north, noting its relationship to the surrounding terrain so that I could head that direction even in the gibbous moonlight.

Burl and I trudged across the sand and gravel desert for the first couple of hours, now angling slightly east, until we intersected with the disintegrating north-bound highway that would take us towards Cooke's Peak, also called Standing Mountain by the Apache. Even though there was a small chance of crossing paths with other travelers it was easier going on the pavement, and I didn't want to leave any tracks on the off-chance Darian's men came looking again.

The southernmost end of the Florída Mountains loomed darkly to the east, on my right. Bats flocked and dove before us, and an owl hooted nearby, perched in a tall piñon pine. Burl seemed unconcerned, though he would stop for a second and listen hard when we occasionally heard coyotes in the distance.

I felt relieved to be free of the compound even as I felt its threatening presence at my back acutely. Running away from danger. And the only people left on earth who loved me. I wondered what Robert thought of me now, and of our last conversation. *We're going get through this,* I had told him. Offering reassurance just before abandoning him and Emma. I wondered if Emma would ever pull out of her grief-stricken stupor. If Robert would ever forgive me for leaving just when he needed me most.

The sharp coolness of the early spring night air filled my lungs and I looked up for the millionth time in my life at the stars strewn across the sky like bits of glass glittering near a campfire. The owl hooted again and a moment later it swooped down upon a scurrying in the brush. Every so often I turned to look back the way we had come for some sign that we were being followed, as unlikely that was. As much as adrenaline and the elixir of freedom spurred my steps early in the evening, my feet were heavy and my mind dull by the time the soft welcome glow of dawn whispered its presence in the east. We had reached the northernmost tip of the Florídas, the Cooke's Range filling the view ahead. I looked around for a bush or rock big enough for Burl and I to rest beside without being seen and, finding a largish mountain mahogany that would suffice, I curled up on top of my blanket, soothed to sleep by the warmth of the rising sun.

2

Mama had said, "That's where the songs start, and show the way back to Grandma's house. She's not there anymore, but the house is."

She had pointed to Cooke's Peak directly to the north, "If we were to walk from here we would keep the Florídas on our right and go towards Cooke's Peak. After going under the overpass, we'd turn a little west and have Cooke's Peak on our right." When I was little and my mom pointed out Cooke's Peak to me one time as we drove by, I thought she said, "Crooked Peak" because it was hooked over, not straight. So she called it that in the song.

City of Sun behind you, Crooked Peak in front,
Florída's rocky flowers, slow the rising sun
Clap your hand's to-ge-ther, now you've walked day one!

Since being captured by Darian and brought to the

compound, Mama sang this to me at bedtime every night and sometimes we'd sing it while cooking or washing dishes or weeding the garden together. Singing, Mama's face softened and her hands moved more like fish in a brisk stream instead of like small flickering machines, in the wash water or garden soil. I felt lighter and happier too, maybe just because she was, or maybe because some part of me sensed the hope she still had for the betterment of my own lot.

She never said, "If anything happens to me, follow the song lines," but I just sensed she would want that. I'm sure she never imagined I would go alone, without her. Maybe she had it in her mind for us both to go together when I was old enough, fast enough, and strong enough to make that journey. I'll never know now what exactly was in her head then, just that after what happened to Sylvia, the place in the song, Grandma Sita's house, was the only one in which I could imagine feeling good again, maybe even safe. I knew the song by heart. I believed mama must have carefully composed it to describe the way to Grandma Sita's house by using easily identifiable landmarks and so that each stanza was a gentle day's walk. As sad as I was that she would not make this journey with me, I still felt confidence in her and in myself.

I only slept a few hours, wanting to keep to the stanza-a-day plan, so up I got, four hours into daylight.

Deming city to your front, Crooked Peak beyond

Pecan grove where the sun sets, keeps you safe and sound

Rest well now my dear-er one, two days now are gone!

It was easy going for me and Burl, with no sign of anyone else on the road or off, though I kept my ear cocked sharply for any sounds nevertheless. I hadn't been this far down this road for years, since before we were rounded up by Darian and his men. I still felt a burning sensation of the compound at my back, and often glanced around, fearing that Darian might have gotten a clue about me and come looking again. But before I knew it, the now ill-kempt pecan grove materialized on my left just as the sun sat down on top of it, pressing its late afternoon rays between the thick branches. Deming sat directly ahead, the first few buildings just in view.

Sneak careful through the city, please do not get caught,
Go under the overpass, onward straight ahead
Once you've made it safely past, rest in Diaz fields now

Unlike before the virus, towns and cities were a danger, not a place of safety. They were filled with the self-appointed lords and their sad servants, just the rulers and the ruled. Not so different than at the compound, except we had plenty to eat at the compound, and plenty of clean well water to drink and bath in. Why more people didn't try to escape the towns was beyond me, but I guess maybe it was all many of the residents knew. I didn't want to take a huge detour all the way around Deming, so I'd have to be very careful.

Up a hill we climbed, Burl and I, scoping out the whole

town in one glance. Some sections of the town were pretty well kept up and then there were whole swaths of burned out and tumbled down brick and frame buildings. I guessed that the petty tyrants lounged in the nicer areas, keeping them up. The burned and broken areas had probably been destroyed during the panicked rampages immediately following the sweep of the virus. So that's where I would go. I noted one destroyed street that wound from the south end of town to the north, bisected by the freeway overpass. I headed for the southern, nearest, end.

Burl had never been particularly vocal, but he seemed quieter than usual, and more watchful. His huge brown eyes swept left then right with his head as he lumbered along. Maybe it was because he had never seen a town before. Crows circled low to the west, possibly having found kill remains left by the coyotes I had heard shrilling excitedly that direction just before dawn. A dry, steady breeze fluttered my unbound hair like a black flag along my right ear, absorbing the sparse morning dew before the sun had fully risen. I chewed roasted pecans for my breakfast, washed down with precious water.

As we made our way closer to Deming I kept a sharp eye out for any sign of movement. Even though we were going through an area least likely to be occupied, it didn't mean there couldn't be someone rummaging around in the debris. We picked our way along the crumbled remnants of a street entering the edge of town, looking left, looking right, looking left again each step of the way. Bombed, burnt and weather battered homes lined the streets, the smoky tang sometimes punctuated by the smell of long rotted flesh. I didn't see one window that had survived, just empty frames. A front door swung in the breeze held to its frame by one nearly disintegrated hinge, the dingy remains of sage green paint hung in thin strips, also fluttering in the wind.

We came across a large house that had crumbled eastward, right into the street. As we picked our way through the boards and glass shards I glanced over to what had been the interior. Probably the living room since a rotted couch sat in it. Then I saw some whitish looking sticks piled together, looking weirdly familiar. I peered a little closer trying to figure out what they were. I spotted a skull a couple of feet away from the "sticks" and was shocked nearly out of my shoes. The skeleton was spread across decomposing carpeting in a jumble of boney disarray, but the skull was unmistakably human. The person must have rotted completely before the house fell, since it had not attracted carnivorous scavengers. My heart thumped in my throat, racing with adrenaline, and I picked up my pace.

I noticed a water spigot at the base of the front wall of the next house we passed and had regained my wits enough to take advantage. I felt grateful that it still produced water. Crouching next to the battered brick façade I turned the stiff knob and let the water run in a cool stream for several long seconds to clear the pipes before filling each of my water bags in turn. Water is life as they say, so I was glad we had it. Several wary but uneventful blocks later we came to a large cross street, lined east to west with what had been businesses.

Halfway through, I thought, feeling a little more confident that we would get out of town without incident.

Across the street we came to an area with much larger buildings, mostly brick, and more intact. The only sounds were the occasional skittering of some small animal or another but no people.

I had just spotted the shift from the business district back to residential buildings ahead of us when I felt the solid sensation of a gun pressed against my left temple. Burl startled, eyes wide, too late for both of us. He had never been trained for security detail after all. My knees went soft and my breath stopped.

"Hold on girl. You ain't goin' nowhere." The voice was male, gravely, but also young. I couldn't tell for sure, but I thought I felt some trembling coming through the gun's barrel. It occurred to me that if the gunman didn't do this often, it *could* be a good thing for me, but not necessarily. I stood granite-still and forced myself to take a deep, quiet breath, to get my brain working again. His body pressed so close behind me I could smell that this guy had not taken a bath in a very long time. I repressed a gag, then tried to breathe through my mouth.

"You're gonna come with me."

I didn't argue. In fact, I didn't say anything.

Slowly he eased the gun off my temple, one hand clamped onto my arm like a dog on a freshly killed rabbit. He turned me back towards a building Burl and I had just passed and marched me towards it. I didn't dare look right at my captor, but I could see out of the corner of my eye that he didn't look much older than me. He had long straggly brown hair, and a thin, downy beard forming on his chin.

"I'm not trying to move into your territory, or cause you any problems. I'm just passing though," I said, trying to keep my voice low and steady despite my breath trying to come quick and high in my chest.

"It doesn't matter what you think you're doing. You're coming with me."

For a moment I considered dropping Burl's lead rope and giving him a smack on the behind, which was our signal for him to bolt, but I worried this guy might just shoot us both. I held Burl's rope as I was half-led, half-drug by Stinky Boy. We clambered over a low wall of brick rubble and into a shadowy building, Burl stumbling on the uneven surface, his hooves clattering loudly. The room we entered through now disintegrated glass double doors must have been the lobby of a hotel or bank or government office complex, spacious, with smooth granite floors throughout, though covered in dulling dust.

As my eyes adjusted to the darkness, I saw arrayed around the edges of the room about fifteen overstuffed, battered but still comfortable, chairs with people in them. All looking at me. Each one appeared to be as filthy as Stinky Boy. There were three small children, a couple of older children and adults up to about middle age. I wondered why they were so dirty. I knew there was water around and plenty of clothing, like I said. Were they also escapees from somewhere terrible? Was this just a rest stop for them? One of the older women rose from her chair and strode over to us. Her hair was stringy and greasy like Stinky Boy's but she looked strong and confident. Just a few inches away from me, she looked long and hard into my face. I looked her direction but kept my gaze soft, not threatening, like when encountering a bear in the forest.

"What're you doing here?" she demanded.

"Just passing through."

"From where to where?"

"South of here. Goin' northwest."

"You one of Darian's scouts?" She said Darian's name like DAR...ee...AN, all drawn out and with a look of utter clenched-jaw hatred the likes of which I had rarely seen before. I guessed it was the same look I would have if I said his name.

"No. I have no interest in helping Darian." I took a risk, trusting what I had seen in her face, and added, "Probably for the same reasons you don't."

She stepped back a bit, relaxing some. She still watched my face but seemed to have read the truth there. "Well he came through here a couple of days ago with his men and roughed some of us up demanding to know if we had seen someone, a girl, someone looking a lot like you."

Asking if I was one of his scouts was a kind of test, to see if I would acknowledge even knowing him, as she knew I must. She gazed at my face some more, as if making calculations. I started trembling and breathing faster than I wanted. I dared a look into her eyes, trying to decipher her intention. Had he offered her some kind of reward? There were a lot more of them than of me, plus at least one gun. I couldn't help wonder what Darian would do to me if he got me back. Tie me up and whip me to death in front of the others, then leave my body tied to the post as it rotted, as he had with Sammy Jiron all those years ago? Take me into the gang's house and use me as they had Sylvia?

Leader Lady broke our stare down, turning to look at the group seated behind her. "What do you think?" she asked no one in particular.

"Kill her!" yelled a stout middle-aged man, who sported a fresh-looking black eye and an apparently broken nose, which I assumed must be the result of the roughing up Leader Lady had mentioned. The man then laughed abruptly and loudly, a high pitched, manic edge to his voice, causing some of the others to either snicker or squirm in their seats. I didn't know how to read this. Was he serious? Were they?

Through all this Stinky Boy had kept the gun against my head, of which I was suddenly more acutely aware. Glancing sideways at him I could tell by the sad look in his eyes and rigid set of his chin that he didn't want to shoot me, but he had shot people before and would do it now if told to.

A younger man standing near an interior doorway across the room, possibly Leader Lady's son or nephew from the similar auburn hair and green eyes, said with an exaggerated sigh, "But then we'd have to dispose of the body, and you know how much I hate that. I'd be the one to have to bury her, and that means hauling her out of town, and that means risking being seen by one of the Roamers. And *that's* never good."

A skinny, dishwater blond, thirty-ish looking woman said matter-of-factly, "Don't shoot her. But DO take any food she has. And anything else we can use."

In the end they took all my food, all the pecans, mesquite powder and jerky I had so carefully scavenged for this trip. Gone. But at least they didn't take my knife or other gear. I would be able to hunt, collect and prepare food along the way. Someone suggested they keep Burl, but another pointed out that he would have to be fed, so really would be costing them more than he would help. And he was still so skinny from the long winter that I guess they figured he wouldn't make good eating, thank goodness. Burl and I had been friends since he was born, five years before, and I would hate to lose him like that.

Stinky Boy and Thirtyish Woman were given the task of escorting us out of town, as the sun began its slide down the western sky. We walked in silence, Thirtyish in front, me and Burl behind her, and Stinky Boy bringing up the rear, following some winding route through the residential area on that side of town, which no doubt held some strategic advantage invisible to me. We were taking a different route than Mama's song said to take but I could see that there was just one paved road heading the direction we needed to go so I didn't worry about it. In fact, I figured Thirtyish knew the safest route through this part of town, so in a weird way, being captured by them might have saved us from being caught by one of the warlords, which they called "Roamers." I wanted to know why the group who caught me lived where they did, how they managed to stay out of the clutches of the warlords, but didn't dare ask a thing. I figured I had gotten off a lot easier than I might have and didn't want to push my luck by seeming too nosy. Finally, at the last broken remnant of concrete sidewalk, Thirtyish stopped, turned to me, looked me in the eye much as Leader Lady had and said in a tone of finality, "Keep moving. Don't come back." Then she and Stinky Boy wound their way back the way we had come.

"Oh BURL! That was a close one!" Burl huffed in agreement. Glad for the cover of the fast-darkening sky, we stuck to the road for a couple of hours until we came to the remains of Diaz Farms. The once spacious, open-ended processing building had long since succumbed to weather and scavenging. The roof had caved in and the wall boards collapsed down upon one another in a slow-motion journey to join the level ground. The adjacent fields sat overgrown with now wild chile intermingled with tenacious weeds and native wildflowers. The ghostly red imprint of the business name on what had been the front overhang of the store entryway, now set on edge against the ground by gravity, was all that indicated we had arrived at our intended location. After tying Burl to a still steady post, I shooed some rats from beneath an impromptu lean-to formed from the boards of the decrepit overhang and unfolded my bedroll for the night. My empty stomach growled and I still felt the echo of the cool metal gun snout against the side of my head.

3

Morning find Crooked nipple, sighted right at first
Beware and keep it there, leave twin peaks behind
The cottonwoods will tell you, where to quench your thirst

The next day I crawled out of bed at the first hint of dawn, anxious to head out, and get as far away from Deming as we could. Even Burl seemed a little more alert than usual, large brown, soulful eyes reflecting the glittering sunrise as he chomped contentedly on some spring grama grass. A fine layer of fresh-smelling dew covered everything, including my hair, making it fluffier and wavy. I pulled it back and tied it in a knot to keep it out of my eyes. Jays and finches squawked and chirped in the fields but I heard no sounds of the human kind come from the direction of the road. I relaxed a little even as I still kept a sharp eye out. The last thing I needed was another surprise encounter.

The rising sun warmed the stiffness out of my legs and

the sound of Burl's solid steady footfalls provided soft percussive accompaniment to my own, quicker, steps. Trekking north of the highway and parallel to it, the low sparse forest shielded us from easy viewing from the road. It would have been easy enough to follow the roads roughly along most the song's route but after the Deming encounter I didn't want to take any unnecessary chances.

The twin peaks loomed companionably together against the southwest sky to the left of the road, dropping behind us by mid-morning, sooner than I expected. As promised by the song, a cluster of cottonwoods appeared slightly to the north of our path. Burl and I came upon a small boggy area, fed by a spring that trickled steadily from a crack in a rocky hillock. I filled my water bags and sipped the crystal clean fluid from my cupped hands until I was full. Soon after we resumed our trek a staggered row of smaller peaks emerged ahead and to our left. Ready for the next day's song verse, I felt relieved at this evidence of distance between ourselves, Deming and the compound.

Spot itty bitty mountains, to the left all day
Crooked Peaks are on your right, one more night you see
End the day white pond in view, right turn just before

I took a break to collect early purslane and lambsquarters nestled in small clusters on the north side of large rocks, for a nutritious if not exactly filling meal. Once I had eaten a few mouthfuls I tied more onto a length of cordage to hang onto Burl's sun bathed, southern, side, to dehydrate as we continued. As disappointed as I was to lose my food to the Deming group, I felt grateful for the wet winter and spring and for the food that we would find along the way as a result. More water meant more plants, and more plants meant more game. I'd probably lose some weight along the way, but I doubted we would starve. I scanned for signs of rabbits and birds as we walked, rabbit stick clasped lightly in my hand.

The sun shone bright and strong, but there was a steady, cool breeze coming from the west, creating the perfect temperature for a day's walk. Tiny chickadees, too small to eat, chirped excitedly in the branches of the thorny mesquite bushes as small spikey lizards skittered about the sun-warmed rocks. If I got hungry enough I *would* eat them.

Burl stopped suddenly, staring wide-eyed at the ground in front of us, then pedaling awkwardly backward. A large bull snake slid, smooth and quick, across our path. I considered killing it to eat, but thought better of it. Bull snakes kept the rattlesnake population in check. The whole world seemed to be busy and full of purpose, right along with us. I patted Burl on the back and scratched behind his ears as we walked. I felt grateful for his sturdy company.

Around midday I spotted a female Gambel's quail. Springtime for quail meant eggs. I wrapped Burl's rope around a handy piñon branch and crept low through the brush after her. Sure enough, she disappeared into a stand of young mesquite. I sidled up and spotted my prize. A clutch of small eggs, each one containing a bit of much needed protein. I felt bad stealing the mama quail's eggs, so I left a couple for her. I set the handful of eggs carefully inside my big jacket pocket before retrieving Burl.

Burl's rope in one hand I ate each egg one at a time, much in the way I had eaten M&Ms from a bag as a small girl. Crack it open across my knife's edge, drop the egg into the back of my throat, swallow, toss the shells, and pull out another one. Not the most flavorsome fair—they would have tasted better scrambled—but they relieved my hunger well, and I felt the boost from the energy they provided. Mentally I thanked the mama quail.

And I thanked my now dead daddy for all he had taught me, which at the time just seemed like play.

During the summer, when mama was teaching long classes at the university, Daddy would take me and Seth camping in the Gila Wilderness. Daddy had been teaching wilderness living skills when he met mama. She had attended one of his classes so she could write a paper about it for a class she was taking. He didn't teach much by the time I came along, being so busy with his carpentry business, but on these trips he would tutor us. We learned to track animals, catch fish with hooks made from plant thorns, and how to skin any game we caught. He showed us how to make fire by friction using a bow drill, or solo hand drill, or a team hand drill. He showed us where the wild strawberries and raspberries ripened, which kinds of greens were edible. He demonstrated how to prepare prickly pear cactus leaves and make syrup from the fruit. Every night we had at least one kind of wild food to add to our dinner while on these expeditions. If there was any leftover booty, we brought it home to mama, preparing it for her to show off our newest cooking skills.

One day, when I was 8, I walked proudly into camp carrying a small dead rabbit by its long ears. Daddy stared at me in shock.

"Where did you get that rabbit?" he asked in a rush, "Did you find it dead, because if you did then you've got to get rid of it..."

Before he could continue I declared happily, "No Daddy! I got it with a Rabbit Stick, just like you showed us! I saw the rabbit, picked up a stick and threw it hard at its head!"

Daddy's eyes opened wide for a long second then crinkled up as he burst into laughter. He laughed so long and hard, loud guffaws erupting from his lungs and tears collecting in the corners of his eyes, that I felt irritated and hurt. Seth and I had practiced throwing any short thick stick we could find at nearby targets – a tree trunk, a large rock or whatever – and I had gotten to be a good shot. What was so funny about the fact that I had finally hit a rabbit with a Rabbit Stick? Isn't that exactly what a Rabbit Stick was for?

"Oh, Lakshmi honey, you are the best daughter a man could ever have!" he declared between paroxysms, "I taught many people how to use a Rabbit Stick to bring down small animals, but I never, ever, saw anyone actually get a *rabbit* with a Rabbit Stick!" He sat for a moment on a stump wiping his eyes. It still seemed to me that he thought I had done something wrong and I started to cry.

"No sweetheart, I'm laughing because you did better than anyone I ever taught. Even me!" He pulled me up into his arms, rabbit ears still clasped in my hand and rabbit body bumping against his leg. "From now on I'm going to call you 'Rabbit Girl' because I'm so proud of you!"

And he did. I became known for my skill at using a rabbit stick. Since then I made it my mission to maintain my right to that name, and by the time Burl and I headed off into the desert in search of our new home, I had lost count of the rabbits and other small game that I had brought home for supper. My chest hurt, thinking of those days with Daddy, Mama and Seth, when life seemed safe, comfortable and predictable. When, if I didn't bring home a rabbit for dinner, we would still eat well.

With any luck at all, we could make at least a day's progress per stanza and be back to Grandma's house at Gila Hot Springs in less than two weeks. There were so few people who had lived in that area when Grandma Sita was alive, and it was so far from a town of any size, I imagined it would be less dangerous than other places. Maybe some of Sita's neighbors I had gotten to know as a child would be there, and welcome me as her granddaughter. Maybe I would be helped by people who genuinely cared about me, if only because of her.

As I lie in my bedroll, gazing up at stars thick as bees in a field of flowers and listening to Burl snuffling grass comfortingly beside me, my heart expanded and I exhaled long and deeply. For the first time since mama and I lived in the community at Columbus, before Darian and his men captured us, I felt hopeful, as if there might be something to look forward to in life again. I had been so desperate to get away from Darian that I hadn't considered much what I was running *to*. How great it would feel to be a part of a real community again instead of a warlord's compound.

I hadn't been asleep for more than an hour when the sound of men's voices awoke me. They were coming my way. I curled up as small as I could, pulling my sleeping bag tightly around me, wriggling in the gritty desert sand till I was snug under a nearby bit of scrub oak. I was painfully aware of Burl's bulk looming nearby and prayed he wouldn't startle at the sound of the men. I held my breath as I listened. I heard the men dismount about 30 yards from us. A lightning bolt of recognition pealed through my body – it was Lem and Jeff! Did Darian send them back out to look for me? After six days? That didn't make any sense. I wasn't that important to the running of the compound. I didn't have any irreplaceable knowledge or skills. Robert knew farming, and Marianne, the mechanic, understood any machine she saw like a mother knows her own baby. But me? I mostly cooked and cleaned and weeded.

Fighting to quiet my breath, bit by bit I calmed myself. Peering through the oak leaves I could see no more than vague shadowy movements. I heard the sound of saddles sliding off their horses and laid on the ground.

Centuries later, when my heart slowed to a human rhythm again, I resolved to find out what they were up to. I shot Burl a warning look that said, "Not a sound!" But he returned a sleepy gaze without as much as a snuffle.

I crawled as slowly as a stink bug, belly low, on my hands and knees, careful to keep my feet lifted a little so they wouldn't drag noisily in the leaves and other debris. I settled on my stomach near a dense prickly pear cluster, hoping the men would be disinclined to relieve themselves near the forbidding thorns.

"... better off without Darian, Lem," said Jeff.

"Yeah, yeah. I know. I didn't like getting *run off* though," replied Lem, shaking his head.

"We can do like we planned before, just find a house of our own and start our own gang."

"Yeah, yeah. We can head towards Silver City and find some place around there. Not too many people lived between here and there before so there'll be something, someplace we can live I bet. It pisses me off he blamed us about that girl leaving though. Just cuz we started it with that other girl, he weren't complaining then. He joined in."

"We was the new guys, right?"

"Yeah, yeah. I guess so."

Lem's words trailed off to silence, soon followed by the sound of the deep breathing of sleep. My blood had frozen at the mention of Sylvia. So they had "started it" with her? I lie in the dirt shaking like I had when I first saw her body. I had hated all of them before but now I hated Lem and Jeff even more, which I had not thought possible. I didn't just want to run from them. I wanted to kill them. Chances were though, that the best I could do, the very best, would be to kill one before the other got to me. I could choose vengeance and death, or worse. Or I could choose life and stick with my plan.

I crawled back to my bed, where I had no intention of sleeping, knife clutched in my hand. I must have been more tired than I had realized because I startled awake at first light, almost giving myself away with a fearful gasp, looking blindly left and right before the scenery came into focus. All I heard were crickets. I saw the silhouettes of the men's horses against the starry sky. I so feared being caught asleep again, I lie steel-limbed under my blankets until I heard them rouse. I wanted to bolt out of there like a rabbit trying to get hit by a truck but they *would* hit me unless I kept still. To my infinite relief the two packed up immediately after awakening and headed west, towards Silver City.

Thank goodness I'm turning north from here!

What a stroke of luck that my song wouldn't take me the same direction as they. I was glad that at least Lem and Jeff weren't looking for me.

Turn north onto the new road, sunrise to the east
March on between layer cake, fam-ly hills on right
Look out for the rattlesnakes, when the weather's warm

Eyes sharp, I ambled along with Burl, me picking and eating greens along the way. About midday we came to the intersection the song mentioned. The "layer cake" butte jutting up to the west, striped tan, reddish brown and beige. Facing north again I could see the "family hills," two looming hills near the road, then three smaller peaks, the "little sisters," set just behind them, to the east. We walked along the base of the "parents," keeping just out of sight from the road.

The day continued uneventfully except for the

occasional whack of the rabbit stick on some unsuspecting squirrels we happened upon, which seemed to be in great abundance along the towering, creaky cottonwoods.

My mind wandered to my mother, father, brother, and the virus that changed a pretty good childhood into a nightmare.

Daddy curled up in his and mama's bed, skin turning a strange mottled rust color and his eyes only seeing inwards, even when they were open. He died in that bed as my brother Seth did in his own.

During the days of the virus mama kept glancing anxiously at me, eyes wide and hunted, searching my face for the spots, as she tried to comfort daddy and Seth. So many of our neighbors were dying and news of the virus was all that was on television, even as wide-eyed commentators kept disappearing, replaced by others, so we knew what to expect. Mama barely spoke to me, except to ask for more damp washrags to cool their foreheads as they seemed to sink more deeply into their beds, like emaciated sloths that had fallen asleep in quicksand, descending ever farther away from us, into the greedy arms of death. Seth died one morning and daddy the afternoon of the same day.

Mama carried Seth to the car alone, face as stony as our concrete driveway but tears falling fast, squeezing his body so hard against her it was as if she was trying to press her own life into him, hoping one last time to revive him. Mama and I carried daddy together. Back seats laid flat, we arranged Daddy on his side, legs bent towards his chest so he looked like a fetus, like he hadn't even been born yet, much less having died. Seth she set next to daddy, curled so he looked like he and daddy were having a friendly cuddle.

We drove them in silence to the mass grave. The giant grave had been dug in an empty lot in our neighborhood by a big yellow, bulldozer which roared and huffed like a demon. We carried Seth and Daddy, laying them next to those who would be their companions for eternity. Mama wept uncontrollably, fat tears pouring one after another down her pale, gaunt cheeks, streaming onto the grimy Gila River Festival t-shirt she had been wearing for days.

I didn't cry right then, though I would make up for it later. I felt like I was watching one of those apocalypse movies, so popular then, hoping that pretty soon the heroes would save the right people and we'd feel hope again. My chest felt like it was stuffed with cotton and my brain with spaghetti instead of brains. I just couldn't sort it all out. How could life be one way for so long, and so suddenly be a completely different thing? It wasn't like it was just a personal tragedy either, as can happen in any family. This was happening to everyone. Everyone on the planet. No exceptions. The scope was literally unimaginable to me then, and it still was. Billions of people dead in a matter of weeks. The stench of death alone was almost enough to kill the rest of us.

Mama mumbled quietly, as she sniffed and rubbed her running nose absently against her sleeve, "We should bury them properly, not throw them in a pit! They deserve more.... It just shouldn't happen like this!"

But later, after Seth and Daddy were covered by a thick

layer of dirt by the bulldozer, Mama told me in a flat monotone, "Every person can't have their own grave. There's too many dead people. Not enough room, or time, for individual burials."

It was just too much. So, wrapped snuggly in their blankets, daddy and Seth were lowered down by parallel ropes into the big hole along with all the other dead people from our neighborhood. Mama explained to me when I was older, and asked about it, that every neighborhood in town had had a mass grave after the virus. Some version of this happened all over the world, at very nearly the same time. Was this what the meteor striking the earth had been like for the dinosaurs, all those millennia ago? One day, life is fine, lots of plants and other dinosaurs to eat, balmy weather just right, then – BOOM! – things get dark and cold and everyone around you is dropping dead?

Once the virus had made its way through town, fast as a runaway forest fire before gale winds, mama and I drove out to Gila Hot Springs to check on Grandma Sita. Sure enough, we found her lying in her bed, dark brown eyes open to the ceiling as if she could see right through it, but still, still, still. Her gray and black hair had been fixed in one long graceful braid down her back, and she wore her newest blue jeans and favorite tie-dyed t-shirt. Everything was neat and tidy in the house as if she had seen death coming and made an effort to welcome it. I had never seen a dead person before the virus, since I was only nine years old, but in the short time between the virus coming and the virus going, I had seen so many that I wasn't shocked to see Grandma dead too. Still, she had always been so much fun when we visited, reading to me and Seth at bedtime, teaching us to grow and eat her garden vegetables, and teaching us animal yoga poses for fun, seeing her lying empty as a shell in the desert shook me to my core. Daddy, Seth and now Sita.

Later, as mama gathered Grandma Sita up in her arms, carrying her to her newly dug grave, I finally cried because I knew that I would never get to do those things with her anymore. I was named after a big batik that grandma Sita had on the wall of her bedroom of the Hindu goddess Lakshmi, busty and smiling mysteriously in her red and gold sari, bangles on her arms, seed pot, gold coins and lotus flowers in her many hands. My mother had always loved that batik and hoped that I would love the earth and all life the way the goddess Lakshmi does. Mama took the batik down from grandma's wall to take home with us.

Mama could hardly stand to be in the house after daddy and Seth died. Everything was very chaotic then I'm sure, with so few people to run businesses, the government, maintain roads, and teach in the schools.

Things just fell apart.

Mama had been teaching English literature at the university but all she could think of was going someplace where we might be safer in the long run. Outside of Columbus, a couple hours drive south of Silver City, and lower in elevation, there was a community where many people who had built "off the grid" houses – houses that didn't need to be hooked up to the gas, water and electrical systems for people to live comfortably. There were houses like that in and near Silver City too, but I think mama also needed to get away from the things that reminded her of daddy and Seth, and all the other dead people we knew. In any case, Mama said it was important that we buy a house in Columbus before everyone else realized how valuable houses like that were and bought them up. As soon as the bank opened again mama withdrew all our money and off we went.

Life in Silver City with Mama and Daddy and Seth seemed like one that I read about in a story, or dreamed of long ago. It was as if I had died when daddy and Seth died and been re-born with mama in Columbus. Gone forever was our cozy, noisy home.

4

Mimbres River is calling, welcoming you back
Trick-ling lightly in the fall, rushing in the spring,
You'll see it from the distance, cottonwoods tall green

The next day was so uneventful that I relaxed a little. I had gotten into a routine of picking greens and bopping the plentiful rabbits or other small game on the head for roasting, sometimes cooking a few at a time. My waistband was a little looser than when I left but I truly can't say I went hungry. I was walking farther before needing to rest, and it felt good to be gaining strength as we traveled closer to Grandma Sita's.

Sure enough, as that day's stanza predicted, Burl and I came upon the Mimbres River, just as the sun dropped behind the hills to the west. Cottonwood trees lined its meanders, great crowns bowed over the waterway, weighted by the sweet, gentle emerald of new leaves. Gnarly old branches littered the ground beneath them, dropped there by the forces of snow, wind and gravity.

New grass and other greens sprung cheerfully besides the flowing stream.

I picketed Burl next to the water and the tantalizing new grass, both of which he enjoyed in his usual, understated manner. I shed my coat, resting on it under a cottonwood, listening to the musical murmur of the river splashing beside me. Yellow and black butterflies flitted about, dancing in the air from one dandelion bloom to another. After a short doze, I filled my water skins, then dipped my cupped hands and gulped the fresh icy beverage until I could hold no more. The cattle had proved easy hunting in the early days after the virus, after the grocery stores been ravaged to emptiness, so I did not worry about being eviscerated by giardia, a parasite that had been commonly carried by cattle and manifested in vicious diarrhea in humans.

Munching a handful of dandelion greens I thought about whether to gain some more ground or settle in for the evening. The question was answered for me, in the form of voices in the distance, towards the road. Popping up from my spot, I grabbed my coat, tossing the water bags into the satchel tied to Burl and led him hurriedly across the creek, farther away from the road and deeper into the thicket. I cocked my ear in the direction of the voices and heard that they were indeed nearby, between the road and the river. Thank goodness that Burl was not a talkative guy. His taciturn nature had saved us a lot of trouble so far, and I counted on this valuable personality feature keeping us both safe as we continued.

Soon, the forms that belonged to the voices appeared

between the branches that hid me. A tall middle- aged man, wearing a worn, flabby cowboy hat and stained leather jacket, and a woman about half his age, similarly attired, strolled side by side, bundles perched on their backs. Naturally it made sense for all traveling in this area to gravitate towards the river which provided water for drinking and young plants for eating.

After they were well past us, I took Burl's lead rope and marched us still farther away from both river and road to find our camp site for the night. The last thing we needed at this point was company.

Relieved that Burl and I had turned away from the highway I slept peacefully. Wrapped in my thick wool blanket, wearing all my clothes in layers, I felt cozy and safe and free. I didn't really know how caged I had been at the compound until then, sleeping outside Darian's control.

Follow Mimbres curving path, to the Frog boulder
Then dirt track to the east, leave the river now
Turquoise house they are our friends, happy to see you

Burl and I had settled into a companionable rhythm and our tenth day of travel started out predictably enough. Rise, eat leftovers from dinner for breakfast, load up Burl, and follow the instructions in the day's stanza.

The sky was clear and sunny but a chilly steady wind kept me bundled up, scarf wrapped double around my neck. The new leaves rustled so hard they sounded like heavy rainfall as we made our way back to the waterway. The narrow river bubbled briskly over the volcanic rocks that had made their way into its bed and the birds chattered madly, hopping from one rock to another, heads turning to and fro, searching for breakfast. Amidst this busy conversation I paused now and then to gather greens, eating some and tying the rest in loose bundles over Burl's back.

Eventually we came to a spot in the river where it took a particularly sharp turn and I could see the water hit the bank hard enough to turn back on itself, forming a deep, slow-moving whirlpool. I perched on a large flat rock beside the pool searching its depths and was rewarded with the sight of shadowy flickering movements along the bottom. I pulled a fishing spear from Burl's back, one that I had made from river cane in hopes of finding such a treasure trove.

It had been years since I had speared fish with daddy, but I did remember that I had to hold very still until the very last instant before thrusting it into the water. It was also important to adjust one's aim for the way water distorts things visually. A lovely large Gila Trout wandered into view and of course I missed, spooking the other fish in the attempt. A warm up period always seemed necessary when spear fishing after a long hiatus. I was hooked though, even if the fish weren't just yet. I settled myself in for as long as necessary, shutting my eyes, face upturned, feeling the continuous breeze caressing my face as I waited until the fish forgot I was there. It took several rounds of this before I had four fat trout strung onto cordage and wrapped in a large bandana to keep the flies off. By the time I had built a fire and cooked the fish it was nearly noon, but I was glad to lose a little distance for such good food. I ate two of them right away, scorching my fingertips a bit at first, so eager was I to taste that tender, flavorful flesh. The other two I wrapped up for later.

I found the frog-shaped boulder set above the somewhat overgrown but deep parallel ruts of the dirt track that we were supposed to take east. I walked up the rise to the frog boulder to see where the road would take us when a loud buzzing sound erupted next to my right foot. I leapt so suddenly I landed awkwardly in the loose scree, twisting my ankle hard and falling to sit hard upon the sharp stones. I spotted the rattler several yards away, sliding fast as it could away from me, into the undergrowth. I hadn't been in any danger after all. Rattlers are not particularly aggressive, preferring to slither quickly away if threatened. But they will strike fast as lightening if you suddenly box them in somewhere, and they *are* deadly. A rattlesnake buzz always sounds close.

I sat in the gravel holding my ankle, Burl still looking wide-eyed and skittish. The snake continued its way through the underbrush, so I knew we were safe from it. My ankle was another matter.

Carefully I raised myself upright, first keeping my weight on my uninjured left foot. Gingerly I put a little weight onto my right foot and was rewarded with a sharp shooting pain that felt like it went from my ankle straight through my head. I leaned panting against the boulder surveying the situation. By this time it was only a couple of hours to sundown and there was a cluster of trees that, combined with the shelter of the frog boulder, prevented any passersby from seeing us easily. Discouraged from the little distance we had made and stunned by the pain of my sprained my ankle, I figured it would be best to just hunker down there for the night. I managed to get the packs off of Burl's back and picket him next to some tall grass. I sat on the ground, tossing my wool blanket open and rolled myself inside. I figured we would just get a good night's sleep, then a fresh start in the morning.

But I figured wrong.

The coyotes whined just a little too loud and a skunk wandered just a little too close. My ankle throbbed so much I started worrying that I may have fractured it instead of just spraining it. Morning finally came and Burl looked like he slept as badly as me. Both of us the worse for wear, I loaded up Burl while standing on my good foot, slung my bad foot across him and shimmied up to ride.

Burl was not happy about this arrangement at all, since I had walked almost the entire way, only burdening him with water, my satchel, and my bedroll. He huffed and rolled his eyes at me, and I could have sworn he was actually dragging his feet in protest. I hoped the rutted old road would take us to the friend's house as promised. I wondered how many of them survived. I couldn't remember who they might have been. Even if there were people there, they may not be happy to see me, especially injured as I was.

Following the dirt road we finally came upon the turquoise house. The sun still rode high in the sky since we had split the stanza between two days, but I liked the idea of a safe place to rest while my ankle healed, friends or no friends. As it happened there was a giant "V" painted in red on the side, against the fading bright turquoise, indicating that the whole household had been struck by the virus. When the virus was burning like a wildfire before a gale wind across the land, people started painting these Vs on houses to warn others not to enter and risk exposure. That danger was long past now so I directed Burl towards it.

The house was a classic "ranch style" design, frame and stucco exterior, all on one level, sporting a generous covered wood plank porch along the long front side. Several colorful pots as big as barrels sat along the front edge of the porch with thick tangles of weeds spilling over the edges. Likely they had been filled with pansies or carnations or something equally cheerful and tame before the virus.

My stomach sank as I approached, anxious about what I might find. I didn't hear any sounds coming from inside the house, just the front screen door flapping in the wind, held to the door frame by just one hinge. I could see that the place hadn't been lived in for a long time. Dead grasses lie thick around the house, leaves and other debris had piled up along the base, especially on the north side, where the wind blew strongest.

I slid off of Burl cautiously, and limped to the door. I pushed past the flapping screen door, turned the weathered knob and stepped inside. My skin rippled with goosebumps, up my legs and across my arms. Other than the dust that had accumulated over the years and a lot of cobwebs, the place was eerily neat and tidy. The throw pillows on the couch were arranged perfectly. The dining room table was set as if for dinner, for four. Placemats, plates, glasses, silverware, napkins, and a floral centerpiece that must have been nice before it dried up and died. Coincidentally, and very conveniently, I spotted a cane in a tall umbrella stand by the door, and gratefully made use of that to save my aching appendage. The kitchen was as well ordered as the living room and dining room. Dishes neatly placed in the cupboards, dish drainer cleared. Pots and pans hung on the rack above the stove. There was even a red and white checkered dishtowel draped over the handle of the black oven door. It was as if someone cleaned the house especially well before the arrival of their special guest, Viral Death. Or perhaps, soon before its departure.

I hobbled down the hallway with my cane to investigate further. The bathroom in the hall was just as orderly as the rest of the house. Had someone removed the dead inhabitants and buried them, then cleaned up as a show of respect?

It was the bedrooms that proved disturbing. The first was the children's room. I knew this not only from the décor – stuffed animals on a long shelf, cartoon character toys, colorful jungle wallpaper – but there were also the long-dead corpses of two children, carefully tucked into their perfectly made little beds. Their small skulls nestled upon their pillows, grinning horribly up at the ceiling. One looked like it might have been about 8 years old, the other somewhat smaller. I had seen a lot of dead people when the virus struck but these somehow struck me as more horrible. It looked like someone had lovingly tucked them in and read them one last bedtime story before they drifted off into permanent slumber.

I continued my limping exploration and found the rest of the family, dad and mom, in the next bedroom. Dad looked much like the children, tucked in under the covers, head on the pillow, face staring at the ceiling.

Mom was another matter. She was draped askew, across the other side of the bed, on top of the blankets, a handgun still tangled around her finger bones and a big jagged hole blown in her head, long congealed blood spattered in a grisly halo across the pillow. Then I spotted the dog, a small desiccated Corgi from its size and markings, in the corner next to an overstuffed chair. He curled as if napping except there was a hole in his head too.

The mother had watched her whole family die. Tucked them in, cleaned the house, shot the dog, and killed herself. As awful as it was, I could see the sense in it. What had she to live *for*? And it would have been cruel to leave the dog amidst its dead family, to soon become dinner for a pack of coyotes.

It was going to be hard traveling with my sprained ankle, for both me and Burl. As gruesomely unnerving as it was to have four dead people in the house it seemed like it might be a good place to hole up for a bit while my ankle healed. And I could use the rest anyway. No one had disturbed this house in the years since the family died, tucked as it was away from both river and road, so it should be safe from unsavory travelers. It didn't hurt that the cupboards still contained a fair amount of dried and canned goods too. There was even a functioning can opener.

I led Burl around to the back of the house where sat a serviceable, if rickety, covered wooden pen that I imagine had been used for goats. I found a scythe in the adjacent shed and cut some of the tall, tender spring grass, putting it into the feed bin inside the pen. I tried the hand pump and to my delight found it still worked, though I had to press the lever hard at first before it loosened up and the water flowed easily. After tossing a couple of buckets of rusted water aside, the faucet finally ran clean. Another luxury – clean, plentiful water for us both.

I returned to the house and shut the bedroom doors vowing to forget about the corpses for the time being. The day was still young so I hobbled around dusting the kitchen and living room, wiping down the kitchen counters, table and chairs with a freshly rinsed dish rag. I wished the electricity still worked so I could vacuum the floors, the couch and overstuffed recliner. Instead, I swept the floor and wiped the couch and recliner down with the damp rag.

Basic cleaning done I rummaged eagerly in the cupboard, examining the selection of canned and boxed goods for my lunch: instant mashed potatoes, a large, unopened can of oatmeal, various sizes and shapes of pasta, jars of pasta sauce—marinara and Alfredo—canned beans and a variety of soups lined the shelves. I chose a can of Amy's Chili, "spicy," because it seemed the most immediately gratifying and set to work on it with the can opener. I picked a slightly dusty tablespoon from the selection of flatware that sat comfortably in their assigned slots in a drawer, swishing it briefly under the faucet before sitting at the table with my culinary treasure.

I drew the chili from the spoon into my mouth a little at a time, savoring each bite and the sharp smell of red chile and tomatoes. The red beans were firm but tender. Perfect. Even cold, it was the best thing I had eaten in a very long time, as well as the most I had eaten in one sitting since I left the compound. I sat immobile in a satisfied, plump-bellied stupor for several minutes, feeling dizzy from the nutrients and calories rushing through my veins. I rinsed the can in the sink and deposited it with a thud into the big blue bin labeled "Recycle"—as if there was still a recycling center to take it to.

Hobbling over to the couch, I curled up atop its incredibly soft cushions for a long nap, listening to the rhythmic flap-flap sound of the screen door against the door frame and enjoying the soft swishing of the cedar scented breeze as it flowed through and around the house.

5

I awoke just before dusk, disoriented. For a few seconds I couldn't remember where I was. I even had a moment before I opened my eyes when I thought I was at home, before the virus. I used to take naps on the living room couch a lot. I stretched my leaden limbs, shaking my head to clear the fog. My ankle twinged, reminding me of my injury.

I shuffled out the front door and made my way around to the back of the house from the outside, not wanting to walk down the hall by the bedrooms to the back door. Burl napped contentedly in his pen. I cut more grass for him and topped off his water, the cool sturdy metal pump handle in my hand, watching the clear clean liquid pour in a gush into the galvanized steel trough below. The sun glowed low on the horizon; the breeze had slowed since mid-day. The rustling new leaves on the hunched cottonwoods sounded like the excited whispers of children at a slumber party when they're supposed to be asleep.

For the first time since I had left I gave myself permission to just rest. It was going to be awfully hard to make much progress with my sprained ankle, and it wasn't really fair to Burl to have him carry me for the days it would take to heal. Plus, being in the open while injured made us both more vulnerable so I decided we were going to take a little respite from our journey. We had come at least half way so I felt optimistic that we would get to Grandma Sita's house soon enough no matter what.

Burl and I spent the next week or so mostly sleeping and eating. Aided by my cane, I led Burl with me around the property as I looked for game and wild edibles, so he wouldn't descend completely into a slovenly condition while on our vacation, and I could save more of the packaged foods I had found for the rest of our journey. I discovered a round metal grill in the back yard which I used to cook the foods that benefited from cooking, fueled by the abundant cottonwood deadwood droppings. I ate hot pasta with the sauce du jour several times, and oatmeal with raisins and nuts I had found still sealed in their cellophane packs. Except for the Amy's chili I saved all the canned goods for my journey, since the cans couldn't be penetrated by curious rodents along the way.

After ten days my ankle had steadied up enough that I could put my full weight on it without pain, though I did continue to favor it a bit. It was time to leave, but there was one more task I had to attend to, as much as I dreaded it. I had managed to forget about the dead people in the bedrooms for the most part, quiet as they were.

I found the perfect spot for the family cemetery a little

uphill from the garden. It was a beautiful site under a towering ancient alligator juniper with reasonably soft, loamy, soil. It took me two days to dig all five graves, including the dog's, since my ankle was still a little sensitive. I didn't make them a full six feet deep, but only about four, just hoping that would be enough to allow them to continue rotting peacefully without being assaulted by bears. Life had been hard enough on them while they were alive; I'd rather they not suffer further insults in death.

I carried each one wrapped in blankets and once they were lined up neatly in their respective final resting places I shoveled the soil I had removed on top of them, starting at one end of the row and continuing to the end. I had found birth certificates in a drawer by the desk so I was able to figure out the names of the parents, Lionel and Melissa, and both children, Duane and Kirstin. Their last name was Gunderson. Using a Philips head screwdriver I had crudely carved each name into scraps of two-by-four lumber and pounded each into the ground at the corresponding grave with a mallet. I didn't know the dog's name so I made one up: Hero. I figured that any dog that had to watch three family members die before being put down by the fourth deserved an honorable name.

The sun had nearly set as I placed the last shovel-full of dirt atop the last grave, Hero's. I stood for a long moment, imagining what their lives had been like before the virus. Lionel and Melissa maybe worked jobs at the schools, running a store or supervising a construction crew. The kids probably went to the small school in San Lorenzo, nearby. I figured that mama had put them on my route because she must have known them, but I had no memory of them, and it was doubtful that anyone else alive did either. A fat tear slid down to my chin before stopping. I wiped my nose and turned towards the house, for one last soft night's sleep on the couch.

The next morning I finished washing the last dishes I had used. I lugged the satchel, densely packed with canned and dried foods, to Burl standing glumly by a post in the front where he was tied. Clearly he would have been perfectly happy to live there forever.

I packed a small canvas duffle bag I had found in the shed with tools I thought might come in handy: two hammers, flathead and Philips head screwdrivers, a file, a foldable hacksaw, a sturdy gardening spade and a small shovel. I even found a hand-powered drill and bits to match. The other tools required electricity so there was no point in bringing any of those.

In another big bag I packed other useful kitchen items – a couple of large metal mixing bowls, a ladle, some flatware, a set of four wooden soup bowls, a grater, serving spoons and of course the can opener. I also brought an assortment of kitchen knives, wrapped tightly in kitchen towels. I had found a hefty length of medium weight canvas fabric, along with heavy scissors, thread and needles so I packed them too. A five-pound bag of salt was perhaps the biggest treasure. Not only could I season my food with it, but it would prove useful for jerking meat for winter use.

I rolled up a large blue tarp I had found in the shed, still in the package, and tucked it into one of the larger straps holding everything onto my trusty, living, truck. Burl was not happy about the hefty load but I promised him he wouldn't have to carry *me* anymore.

My pants no longer hung like limp sacks on my hips and legs. I had filled out during our stay to almost the same weight as before we had left the compound. I felt refreshed and strong. Optimistic. We hadn't had too much trouble along the way and had made good progress. After enjoying our long break, I now felt a surging eagerness to be on our way.

On our way home.

Leave our friends now, say goodbye, more than halfway there!

Follow road that brought you here, farther north you go

Two track winds but don't you fear, rest at the crossroads

The daytime weather had turned from cool to pleasantly warm since my retreat at the Gunderson's house. We followed the same two-track that had taken us to the house, winding through the thickening woods. The piñon and juniper forest began to include more ponderosas and a greater variety of wild flowers, which swayed in the breeze and shined brightly in the clear sunlight. Jays scolded us and the woodpeckers pecked industriously, high in the pines. A small brown lizard eyed us from the side of an oak tree, skittering suddenly up the trunk as we passed, tail whipping as it went. As overgrown as it had become the ruts of the dirt tracks had been deepened by runoff so were easy to see.

I ate lunch then slept through the middle of the day, waking at mid-afternoon to continue our trek. The sun set somewhat later now so I knew we could still make good progress by the day's end.

The wind picked up an hour or so later, blowing in thick, dark clouds that settled low overhead. A short sprinkling prelude began then the rain came in earnest, wind whipping the fat drops nearly horizontally into our faces. Sheltering on the lee side of a large cedar I unrolled the tarp and wrapped it around Burl and I. The rain rushed down, forming rivulets, then small streams, cutting pathways through the decaying forest floor detritus. The sun cut a hole in the clouds, even as the rain still rattled heavily onto the tarp. I spotted a shimmering rainbow, first slight, then brighter, on the horizon. We continued once the rain had spent itself, the air thick with moisture. There was still a couple hours of daylight left when we came upon the dirt road crossing the one we had been following, as described by the song. I staked out Burl then set about gathering greens to add to my jerky for dinner.

To the left at the crossroads, follow the track west
West at the sentinel stones, leaving track behind
Hear the Mimbres call again, take it gently up

The track that crossed the one we had been on proved very similar. Deeply rutted and easy to follow. As the song predicted we came to a point where the track turned south just where a large cluster of enormous stones stood. Staying west we wound our way through the stones for about a half an hour before I could hear the river in front of us. We crossed a low, slightly boggy meadow before arriving at the banks of the Mimbres, rushing over the river rocks in its cheerfully brisk springtime manner, as if it were excited to get where it was going too.

Spring had fully sprung by this time and tiny purple and yellow wildflowers nested in delicate freshly sprouted grass in the meadows and hillsides we passed. Brilliant red penstemons waved excitedly in the breeze. The rich, light smell of the spring flowers filled the air. Oftentimes I could see the paved road from the riverside path we walked. It was late afternoon when I selected a pleasant camp site out of view of the road. I unburdened Burl just as the sun hesitated upon the western hill before sinking behind it.

Stay along the river, watch now, others may be near
Last full day on the Mimbres, fill your water bags
Two more days and you're home, journey almost done

On the third day from the Gunderson's I spotted a cluster of houses along the river so we hiked up the ridge, staying behind the tree line for cover. A couple of houses had gardens and laundry hanging outside. Once I saw a man with a small child. The man was hammering on a shed, making repairs I assumed, while the curly headed toddler looked on. I hadn't heard a sound that loud since I left the compound and it made me nervous, like it might alert someone to our presence, even though we weren't making the sound. I stood watching the man hammer as if hypnotized by such a normal activity. Something one just does when at home. Home. I wished I could walk up to one of these houses, knock on the door, and go in for a glass of tea, chatting with its inhabitant. Of course I didn't dare. Loneliness ached in my chest like a wounded squirrel, chittering and anxious. It had been more than three weeks since I left the compound, and the only friends I had in the world.

The last verse of the song.

After this we would just follow the road until we reached Grandma Sita's.

See the highway turn northward, stay close to it now
Leave the river you will climb, the road takes you high
Twist and turn be careful now, before you drop down

The next day the song took me away from the river and back to the road, winding in steep, tight curves up the rocky canyon. The ponderosas grew more plentiful and the piñons and junipers thinned as we trudged higher up the steep slope. The shimmering mid-day light shone in dappled rays through the trees. The high mountain air smelled piney and clean. We kept just inside the tree line as much as possible but there were many places where there was a plunging drop-off on one side of the road and vertical stone wall on the other. That, combined with the sharp curves, around which I couldn't see, made that day almost as anxiety producing as going through Deming. I strained my ears listening for any human-like sound, glancing about constantly.

I was glad that I had filled every possible container with water now that I couldn't take it for granted. I huffed and puffed and sweated so much moisture from me that I would have dried up like the jerky I chewed if I hadn't been able to drink as much as I needed.

It seemed like it had taken me forever to get this far, much longer than I had guessed to begin with, but now that I was only a day or two from Gila Hot Springs it felt like we had suddenly leapt forward.

While I had been in a state of hopeful anticipation since leaving the Gunderson's, now I began to worry. What would I find there? What if some awful bandit like Darian ruled the place? Where would I go then? My lungs stiffened at the thought. My mind grew foggy. I could not think of any other options, except maybe to go back to the Gunderson's. I wracked my brain for memories of other family friends who might live in the area, who might take me in but couldn't remember anyone. I had been so young when the virus came. I never paid attention to the routes we took when visiting friends. If it didn't work out at Gila Hot Springs I *would* go back to the Gunderson's I decided. With the dead people now buried it could make a pretty nice home.

I *did* remember the route to grandma Sita's house from this point, though from my low, child's vantage point in the backseat of our Honda. Now, I remembered the particular curve I now climbed, the colorful striations in the hills off to one side and the cluster of three ponderosas right next to the road on the other side.

When I was little we'd come around this curve in the road just as the long hill topped off. The combination of steepness and the curve, gave the illusion that we were headed right off a cliff towards the grey and purple mountains in the distance. I'd let out a shriek of terror, then Seth would take my cue and wail even louder than me and Mama had to turn around in her seat to reassure us. Then we'd see the towering ponderosas rise into the frame of the window again and know we were safe. When I was finally tall enough to see clearly out the windows I told Seth as we rounded this curve, "It only *looks* like we're going over the edge but we're *not*, okay?" Seth would look back at me, eyes wide with fear, nodding his head, trusting my word over his own senses, but just barely.

I chose a camping spot at the top of a hill with a view to the north, the direction we were headed. Only two or three more hills to climb between where we were and Grandma Sita's.

After tying Burl to a scrub oak and eating half a roast rabbit for dinner myself, I bedded down with my head full of wondrous speculation about what lie ahead. I remembered the winding road through the mountains to Grandma Sita's, Ponderosa pines reaching tall and straight through the washed-out blue sky. Purple asters, red Indian Paintbrush and golden poppies grew in clusters or swaths along the way.

Grandma Sita always had craft materials set up for us in the stout adobe studio where she made soap and mosaic tables. Laid out across long work tables were paint and paper, buckets of clay, overflowing bins of colorful yarn, clean, new popsicle sticks, glue, tape and a riot of colored markers.

"It's all for you my little ones!" Sita would exclaim, almost as excited as we were to be set loose on the riches she provided. "As long as you keep the mess in here, you can pretty much do anything you want."

And we did. By the end of our visit Seth and I each had collections of paintings, drawings, bowls or mugs ready to be fired in Sita's kiln, and collages of magazine pictures, accented with yarn and glitter. Each time, Sita would be given some to keep, and we'd take the rest home for display on our refrigerator and walls.

We got to know most of the people living in the settlement of Gila Hot Springs because Grandma Sita welcomed everyone enthusiastically, old and young, rich or poor, all shades of skin and speaking in all kinds of accents and even languages.

There was Dane and Jeanne, owners of a rustic bed and breakfast, who had two boys and three girls that they homeschooled. The elder two, Hallie and Noah were teenagers last time I saw them, the other two girls, Lilly and Miriam, were a little older than me, and Liam was Seth's age. When we visited, Seth and Liam would disappear for hours fishing, collecting interesting stones or doing cannon balls into a deep spot in the river, where an eddy-formed whirlpool had dug the riverbed downwards. During colder months they would make up stories together, drawing illustrations and writing the stories neatly on lined paper.

Sometimes the whole lot of us, their five plus me and Seth and a couple of parents, would ride together downriver on giant overinflated inner tubes. Another parent or two would drive their large van down to the take-out point to haul us all home at the end of our ride.

Broad, jovial and always bustling, Jeanne was like a second mother to me on our visits, despite the multitude of children she had already. Smiling and attentive, she was quick to praise or comfort, and slow to criticize. On top of it all, Jeanne was an avid herbalist, cultivating a vast herb garden and dragging us children, each put in charge of a gathering sack, on expeditions to collect roots and other plant medicines to be processed into tinctures, powders and salves. Her customers visited frequently to sit for a consultation and buy her wares, including Grandma Sita and mama.

Grandma had a man friend who I suspected was really her boyfriend but the adults never spoke about him that way. He was a tall, rangy Apache man named Joe Swift, a horse outfitter. Joe would take us out sometimes on the horses, along with his grandson, Victorio, who was a couple of years older than me. I loved those horses and cherished every moment I was allowed to ride.

Victorio didn't talk much, at least around me. I figured that he thought of me as just a baby when we were kids. Now we would be close enough in age to be friends. I looked up to him for his easy confidence with the horses, even as young as he was. I admired the long, neat, black braid he always wore down the center of his back to the point of envy. I had never been able to grow my own hair out as long.

Several times when Seth and I stayed with Grandma

Sita, Joe and Victorio joined us for dinner. After one of Sita's legendary abundant and delicious meals us kids would cluster together on the big couch in the living room and watch a movie. Victorio was so quiet and serious most of the time I was always surprised by how he laughed so hard at the funny movies. I guessed his sense of humor must have been mostly on the inside. Once I noticed him blinking back tears during a sad part of a movie about a boy and girl who were friends and played in the woods together, when the girl died at the end. I figured Victorio must have kept his other feelings to himself mostly too. He treated Seth like a little brother, patiently showing him how to brush the horses and giving him riding tips. Even though Victorio mostly ignored me, I liked him for being so nice to Seth. He had lived in Silver City with his parents so it was unlikely he would be at Gila Hot Springs, even if he had survived.

A retired couple, Inez and Benjamin, lived a couple doors down from Sita's, and they took turns having dinner or tea together throughout the year. Another guy, Beto, ran a hot springs retreat nearby, renting small cabins and camping spaces to visitors, who enjoyed the wooded setting and cool river in addition to the several graceful pools that Beto had built to capture the naturally occurring hot water.

Another lady across the way, Kate "the goat lady," kept a huge pen of goats and chickens. In the springtime the place would be a riot of tiny springy baby goats bounding around happily and greedily suckling at their mamas' teats. They were so cute I begged mama and daddy to let me take one home every single time we saw them but I could never get them to say yes. Kate lived with her daughter, son-in-law and three small granddaughters all of whom helped with the goats. Kate's roasted piñon nut goat cheese was the best cheese I have ever had; the creamy cheese dissolved in my mouth and I relished the smoky piñons that provided a little crunch as well as flavor.

Whenever any of these friends and neighbors arrived at her house Sita shrieked happily and threw her arms upward in welcome with each arrival, as if each one were a long lost cousin, no matter how recently they last visited, which made most of them smile broadly or laugh. She'd ply them with a glass of tea, homemade cookies or cake or pie and a comfortable chair at the table. Stories were traded, favors asked and agreed to, garden harvests exchanged. All this set beneath the towering sandstone cliffs, like undulated beaches set on end, dotted with scraggly brave flora. To the front of the property, just across the road from Sita's driveway, coursed the Gila River, swollen and rushing dangerously in the springtime and quietly meandering the rest of the year.

6

Never in my life will I forget the view as Burl and I topped the last rise before dropping down into the valley where the village of Gila Hot Springs sat. In the distance spring green mountains grew stoutly upwards from the valley floor, topped with broad stands of towering ponderosas. Piñons and junipers perched on the nearby hills that jutted high and plunged low on either side of the road we walked.

How many of Grandma Sita's former friends and neighbors would still be there? Any of them? Had a warlord like Darian taken over the place and imprisoned the locals? Or killed them all?

A blackened burn scar along a south-facing slope threw the surrounding green of new growth into brilliant relief. A bald eagle floated forward far ahead, yet level, with me, and soon overtook its mate, small against the horizon. I stopped, standing paralyzed by the bliss of wild beauty, as the avian couple settled into a ponderosa stand a mile or so away, presumably to attend their nest of hatchlings.

The sun hovered just above the craggy skyline by then so I set up camp there for the night. We would make our final descent in the morning. I tossed around in my sleeping bag so much that night that I awoke halfway out of it well before sun up, shivering so hard I thought I'd crack my teeth against each other.

I forced myself to cook a big hot breakfast of oatmeal heaped with nuts and dried apricots before loading up Burl and heading, I hoped, home.

There had been no houses from the point where I left the Mimbres River until now. I became extra vigilant as we stepped down, down, down the steep road to Gila Hot Springs. As we came nearer and lower I spotted what appeared to be home sites but before I could see them clearly we dropped behind the hills between the village and us. The voluptuous Gila River, swollen with the spring runoff, rushed by us in its winding spring urgency.

So far we hadn't seen any sign of other humans and I began to wonder if that was because there were people there who didn't want me to see *them* or because there wasn't anyone to see. Then, as we came around the last curve to the village, I saw the reality of the place I had walked so far to see.

My skin crawled as I looked around, ears abruptly attuned to any unusual sounds. It would be too terrible to be captured by another slaving tyrant like Darian. As bad as he was, someone else could be a lot worse. I glanced down at the knife strapped to my boot, just to be sure I still had it. Stepping quietly, I led Burl off the road, just inside the tree line.

The first house I saw had been burnt to the ground, apparently years before. The charcoal timbers lie tumbled together like a giant's campfire. Grass and thick, furry mullein sprang up where the living room had been, judging from the couch carcass there—springs and a metal frame. A bird's nest perched atop the one post left standing in the whole place, and its resident startled at our arrival, twittering in alarm as it sought a high branch in a nearby ponderosa.

My breath tight, head swiveling left, right, back, forward, I kept a slow but steady pace, taking in the village as it arose before me. All the houses I could see had been burned. Some completely, some just enough to render them uninhabitable. Grandma Sita's place was at the far end of the village, and I clung to a tiny precious hope that her house had missed the conflagration that had caught the others. As I rounded the last familiar bend before her place, I saw it.

Or what remained.

No more stanzas left to the song. Nowhere else to go, and Grandma's house was virtually obliterated. Her home had been built in front of a looming butte of beige and tan striated sandstone and the blackened skeleton of her two-story house stood out starkly against the pale background. The second story had collapsed into the first in a charcoal jumble. I made out the remains of a few things I remembered, including a pile of broken and charred ceramic plates and mugs, once bright with scarlet flowers and green leaves, now peeking faintly between a charred crust. The heat-warped stainless steel sink slumped, and a cluster of partially melted flatware slumped in a prickly bundle, on what used to be the floor of the kitchen. The woodstove stood in the center of the living room, edges drooping, legs sagging. The stovepipe lie disintegrated into a pile of rusted metallic leaves.

I stood, gripping Burl's lead rope tightly for support, staring at the extinguished hope before me. After weeks of moving forward, towards the vision I had held of friends and home, I now stood staring at the one sight that never, ever entered my imaginings. I had imagined someone else might be living there. Or that most useful things might have been stolen. But I had never envisioned it not existing at all.

No home. Nothing.

As I stood staring, paralyzed in the moment, time stretched and contracted for seconds or for hours. I couldn't tell. My head felt like it was full of fog or cotton, or foggy cotton. No thoughts, no ideas. I had not the slightest notion of what to do. My whole sense of self had coalesced around the thought of this place, Grandma Sita's place, being *my* place, my refuge. I had told myself not to expect too much, but I had also lied to myself when I promised not to. I had expected much more than what lie before me. I didn't even have an enclosed place for shelter, much less Grandma's comfy kitchen in which to cook and soft bed in which to sleep.

Not knowing what else to do, Burl and I walked around the property. I wasn't conscious of my direction but soon found myself standing before Grandma Sita's grave, a simple mound with large rocks piled high on top of it, as Mama and I had left it. The two by four post that Mama had carved and hammered into one end of the grave site still remained:

Sita Kamala Sriprasad
1970 – 2034
Always loved, never forgotten

I laid down on the ground next to Sita's grave and closed my eyes, as if we were taking one our naps together as we sometimes did on our visits. I wished so much that I could awaken soon to see her smiling face looking into my own, the promise of some watery adventure or special treat on her lips. I opened my eyes and stared at the pile of cold rocks. Burl chomped the nearby spring grass contentedly, oblivious to the change in our shared fortune.

Well I can't just stay here, I thought, pushing myself up off the ground. I took Burl's lead rope and continued my tour of Sita's property.

An intact shed sat tucked just inside a cluster of trees between the house and the butte, about the size of my bedroom back in Silver City, years ago. I remembered that Sita had kept some tools and machinery in there before—shovels, rakes, two hulking generators, a mower and the like. But when I creaked open the door nothing but dusty shadows and cobwebs filled the shelves and lined the walls.

How odd.

Was she cleaning the shed out for some other use when the virus came to claim her? I opened the door a bit more.

It was pretty tightly built for a shed, although there were some mouse droppings on the counters and floor. No insulation.

It's funny how our reactions to things have so much to do with the expectations we have. I had come here expecting to find a house in which I could live, and felt devastated to find it burned to charcoal. My original expectation having been reset, finding a small shack felt like a consolation prize, enough to take the edge off the initial loss. This outbuilding could at least protect me from the elements. Once the mice had been driven out, it would provide a reasonably safe place to store food. It would provide suitable shelter for now, until I decided what else I could do.

The loneliness was the worst. Other than very specifically missing Robert and Emma, and of course Sylvia, I hadn't felt too lonely so far because I kept imagining that someone I knew, some of Sita's neighbors and friends, would be here. It never dawned on me that not one other person would be left alive in the village.

How was I supposed to start a new life with no one else at all? Was I supposed to live out my whole life, alone here?

I figured I could survive well enough, at least in the warmer months, on local game, seasonal plant foods, and fish from the river. But the winter was another thing. I would have to insulate the shed somehow, then figure out how to heat it, then also collect and dry enough food to not only feed myself now, but through the whole winter as well. I remembered reading *Little House on the Prairie* and did not like the idea of twisting dried grass for a fire with my raw, starving fingers. Nevertheless, when I thought of my earlier resolve to return to the Gunderson's if it didn't work here, I found myself unable to even consider leaving this place, however it had failed to meet my expectations.

I thought of Robert and wished I had given him the option of joining me. I couldn't afford to go back for him this late in the season since I needed to use every day for hunting and gathering food, so I pushed that thought hard from my mind. If I was going to stand a chance of making it through the winter I would have to set aside my regrets and get busy.

As late spring turned into summer, the months passed quickly. I hunted, fished, and collected greens, berries and roots. I ate what I needed and dried the meat by hanging it on tree branches held by strips of homemade cordage. Berries and greens I spread out on the shelves inside the shed, which I had first meticulously cleaned. It was a constant battle keeping the mice, packrats and miscellaneous other rodents out of the food, even after it had been dried and tied up in pieces of the cotton canvas, coated with a mixture of beeswax and pine sap. I constructed a rectangular latticework rack from wood scraps and some nails I had found in a drawer in the shed, then tied the bundles from these to hang in the air above my head. As my food cache grew I had to find a more substantial solution. I finally gained what I thought was the final ground when I constructed a hanging shelf that I suspended high above the floor but below the rafters of the roof. Four sturdy ropes held my aerial pantry aloft.

While clambering around the rafters I came upon a truly valuable find: a crossbow and a thick bundle of aluminum arrows. I had only shot one a few times, one that daddy had, which required a lot of help, but I knew I could figure it out if I had enough time, and I certainly had plenty of that.

I insulated the walls of my shed bit by bit, using the tall thick grasses that grew by the river and held in place with small branches that I wedged into the spaces between the framed two by fours that formed the walls. I heated pine sap to patch cracks between the outer boards, both to keep it warmer and to further outwit the pesky rodents. I still had no idea how I would heat the place. It seemed a shame to cut a smoke hole in the corrugated metal roof that did such a great job keeping the rain out.

The next morning I grabbed my canvas rucksack and headed out to gather some edible plants. Roasted rabbit and fish were very satisfying and they *stuck to my ribs* as Grandma Sita would say, but there is nothing like greens in the summertime. Fresh watercress bobbed cheerfully in bright green clusters at the edges of the cool, trickling, east fork of the Gila, the reflected sun blinding me momentarily now and then. Lambsquarter sprouted in narrow tongues along the shaded game trails and the small hearty rounded leaves of purslane carpeted large sunny meadows. I felt like a thief who has come upon a jewelry store with the door swinging wide open, the help gone, after hours. Soon my sack was nearly full and I decided to see if I could find some prickly pear along the base of one of the sandy hills that stood sentinel high above the restless waters. I was rewarded with a large stand, with paddles twice the size of my hand.

Another day, sack on my back, I trudged flat-footed up the loose slope of a nearby hill, one that I hadn't yet explored, careful not to slip. I reached a narrow flat band at the base of the hill and made my way around its curve, counterclockwise, scanning for plants to forage. As I came around the sweep, I suddenly found myself walking into a rare raspberry bramble—full of ripe raspberries! I couldn't believe my luck. Immediately pressing the greens deeper into the sack, I made room for the delicious haul I planned to take. I hadn't had a raspberry of any description since Before but they bloomed bright in my memory as jam, syrup and fresh, the last on top of a heaping bowl of homemade vanilla ice cream. Saliva flooded my mouth at the thought. As worried as I was about how I was going to fare through the winter, for the moment I just knew I had died and wound up in a largely undeserved heaven of some sort. The first several handfuls went straight into my mouth. I continued picking, carefully setting each treasured handful into my sack, cradled by the tender greens. Once home I mashed the remaining raspberries and spread them in a thin layer on some clean canvass, to dry into crumbly raspberry flakes to add to other dishes as I wanted, or even eat a little straight, as a special treat.

At the end of the day I often soaked in the spring-fed hot tubs built by the residents long ago, or in the natural springs that bubbled up directly from the river. Seth, mama, daddy and I used to sit in the luxurious lined pools that several residents of the area had built on their properties, piping in the naturally occurring hot water from the various places where the hot springs rose to the surface. Then and now, the water drew the soreness from my body and brought peacefulness to my mind.

Burl loved our new home, munching contentedly between the shed and the river, or the butte and the shed. He seemed to instinctively understand that venturing further was a bad idea, and I was glad for his good sense. I didn't want to have to defend him against coyotes, cougars or wolves, who would rather avoid humans, even now that there were so few of us to bother them.

I worked to survive, hoping even to thrive, but the loneliness deepened in my chest and churned the pit of my stomach daily. I remembered mama reading the book *The Island of the Blue Dolphins* to me when I was little, a true story of an Aleut girl left alone on her home island after her people were slaughtered and kidnapped by invaders. She lived her entire life alone there and was only found when she was a very old woman. With most of the population dead from the virus, the little village that had been here burned down and abandoned, it was possible that no one would come here for a very long time. Like the girl, I could probably figure out how to stay alive, but how much was that worth, to live alone from now on? It was also likely enough that someone would come, but they could be people like Darian and his gang, intent on dominating and using others. Still, the drive to live is fundamental to all life so I did the only thing I could do, hunt and collect food, and continue to make my shed winter-worthy.

7

Summer faded as fall descended and the nights turned chilly again. I decided to spend a couple of days hunting in the higher elevations, hoping to bring down a deer or elk. An elk, along with the smaller game and fish I had already dried and stored, would give me enough meat to last through the winter and probably well into spring too, especially if I could hunt some fresh meat now and then too. I had been practicing shooting the crossbow for several weeks, since I first found it, and I was eager to test my skill on something that moved and could make a significant difference in my winter diet. Early one cool morning I packed up Burl and we headed out.

There were plenty of deer and elk fairly close by but I kept going deeper into the mountains, following the east fork of the Gila River, enjoying a vacation from the valley. We stood high along a ridgeline, the mountains undulating to each horizon like a giant's chenille blanket tossed carelessly down. The high-altitude conifers created a soft fuzzy effect, making the whole world seem more comfy and welcoming to me than it had in recent memory. The high desert fall sun shone gently down now, no longer the harsh burn of August. I reclined in the thick meadow grasses that were already wilting some from the cold nights, and napped while Burl browsed. I didn't even bother looking for elk or deer sign after I woke from my nap. I decided I would just take the rest of the day off for a change.

The third day out we headed back towards home and though we did cross paths with a herd of deer in the morning and spotted some elk just before dusk, I decided that the closer to home I bagged my prey, the easier it would be for Burl and I to carry it home. The excuse I had made to take a trip had worn through and I knew I had just gotten a little cabin fever, despite the lack of a real cabin.

On the fourth day I hunted in earnest and was rewarded for my practice by bringing down a buck on my first try. I could hardly believe my luck. Burl and I had been hunkered down in a stand near a lot of deer droppings, and the buck just walked out right in front of us as if it had never heard of a predator. I wish I could say I got that deer because I was such a great shot, but it was so close and stood so still I would have had to try to miss to not hit it. Right through the heart. It just dropped like a sack of grain, eyes rolling and legs thrashing for a minute. Then it went still. It was nearly dusk so after a prayer of thanks to the deer for giving its life to me I worked fast to get it gutted, skinned and cut up into pieces for the walk home. I packed the meat onto Burl and we made our way by moonlight a couple of miles so we wouldn't be too close when the scavengers came for the entrails and other remains. Once we found a place to camp I hoisted the canvas bag of meat high up a branch by first tying the rope to the bag, then tossing the rope over a sturdy branch, then pulling the load up, well off the ground. I built a fire underneath the meat too, not close enough to cook it but close enough to discourage any interest from other animals. I slept fitfully next to my treasure, occasionally hearing some rustling in the forest, but nothing came close enough for alarm.

I awoke to the realization that we were closer to home than I had thought. High above our valley I saw the Gila River snaking its way down and around the curves of the hills. I saw the burned-out village so I knew my little shack was there too, tucked into the trees. As I ate a bundle of lambsquarter and some dried rabbit for breakfast I saw something moving down there, near the village, just past where my shed would be. I was too far away to see for sure but it looked a little like a person. I stared, trying to make it out but it disappeared in to the trees before I could see it clearly. I decided it must be a bear, though the bears in the neighborhood usually stayed farther upstream.

It was early afternoon when we rounded the curve in the road near the shed. The sun was high and hot and I looked forward to taking a quick dip in the river before taking a nap in my shed home. It wasn't much but I had grown fond of it. I felt secure and comfortable there. I smiled to myself at the realization that I did think of it as *home,* not just a fixed up shed.

I turned the knob and knew something was wrong even

before I opened the door. The smells were wrong. I had cleaned the cabin thoroughly before leaving, using soap and vinegar I had brought from the Gunderson's to scrub the counters and floors. Now I smelled animal urine and feces. I heard scurrying sounds and squeaks. In the two seconds it took for me to sense that something was wrong, to standing in the open doorway, I knew exactly what had happened. The stacked suspended wooden shelves I had built to hold my precious hunted and gathered stores slumped, askew on the floor. One edge of the shelf unit had caught on my table so the whole thing lie partially propped, slanted so that the contents of the shelves had slid onto the floor. I looked up at the one rope that connected the four corner ropes and saw the bit that remained at the top had been chewed through, dropping the whole unit down where it could be easily reached by the many rodents and other scavengers who had burglarized an entire summer's worth of hunting, gathering and drying.

I had worked hard to make the cabin fairly animal proof and except for the occasional mouse had mostly succeeded. I examined the walls all the way around and then saw it on the south side, under the counter top, at the base of the wall. Something, perhaps an industrious badger, had dug a hole under the wall and chewed and scraped its way through a bit of loose flooring, making a hole big enough for a medium sized dog, and of course, anything smaller than that.

All my carefully constructed bags were strewn all over the floors, torn and chewed to uselessness. Every bit of food had been eaten or taken and many of the marauders had left excrement in its place. So not only did I have no food, but I had a lot more cleaning to do before I could even go to bed. I saw tiny marks in the debris, signs of scampering animal feet. I imagined mice, packrats, skunks, squirrels and at least one badger partying for all they were worth here. They must have gotten in on the first or second day to have absconded with so much before I got back.

I walked over to my bed, shook out the top blanket, sat on the edge, took off my shoes, pulled my feet off the floor, curled up into a small ball, and cried myself to sleep.

I awoke an hour or so later, groggy and puffy eyed*. I'm dead*, I thought. I think I would have filled my pockets with stones and walked into the river to drown if it had been deep enough to do so. I remembered poor Burl, tied up outside the door, still bearing the deer meat. Feeling like a human shaped bag of sand, I drug myself out to unburden the poor burro, who stood with resentful patience, awaiting my return to my senses.

Feeling as if I was watching someone else instead of doing it myself, I set the meat on the table and commenced scrubbing the counter with the precious vinegar. By sundown I had the meat cut into strips and hanging from the latticework drying rack, which still remained suspended from the ceiling. I stuffed some rags into the hole in the floor and wall for the time being. The animals were usually disinclined to harass me as long as I had lit some of the bee's wax candles I had made. I would keep them going all night and repair the hole more carefully in the morning.

That night I dreamed of daddy, mama, grandma Sita and Seth. We were sitting around Grandma's big round kitchen table the way we had countless times before the virus. The table was piled high with all our favorite foods. Green chile cheese enchiladas, jicama salad, and pinto beans cooked to near disintegration and topped with a thick layer of melted cheese. There was vegetable korma, saag paneer, basmati rice and a large plate holding steaming hot garlic naan covered with a clean dish cloth. Assorted garnishes and condiments—chopped onions, tomatoes, lettuce, cilantro, and mango chutney in a small ceramic dish—sat tucked between the larger dishes of food. We were all smiling at each other and taking turns dishing out the delectable offerings onto our plates. The smells alone were nearly intoxicating. Around us sat all of Grandma Sita's friends from the surrounding area, each with a big plate in front of them and reaching in turns to serve themselves too. They were also lively conversation and laughing. There was so much love in that big kitchen, so much happiness, and most of all, so much food.

I awoke with the contrast between the dream of abundant love and food to the reality of loneliness and the specter of starvation. While I thought it was possible, not likely, but possible, that I could survive the winter, I couldn't think of why I would want to. Still, lacking the will to actually kill myself, and having Burl to think of in any case, I did the only thing I could do. I started gathering what plant foods were still available this late in the season and set snares for rabbits.

Two weeks later the first freeze came. A thin layer of ice lie like a crystalline spider web atop puddles near the river and I could see my breath come in tiny cloud-like puffs as I exhaled. Soon the high desert sun warmed the air and melted the ice, as I grimly set to work again, gathering, drying, packing, skinning and jerking meat.

I had contrived a less than perfect solution to the problem of heating: I used the hand drill to drill small holes in the tin roof in a circle, then hammered the circle out, making a small smoke hole. I built a stand out of large rocks placed in a circle on the floor then set a large wok I had brought from the Gunderson's on top of that. It wouldn't make a big fire, and wasn't the safest way to heat a wooden cabin, but I wouldn't freeze and if I was careful, I probably wouldn't burn it down either. Like everything else, it would have to do.

Bit by bit the nights got colder and the days warmed less. Shadowed puddles froze and never melted. The ice rimming the edges of the river thickened towards the center. I had replaced enough of my previous stash of food so I knew I wouldn't die any time soon, but I also knew it was not anything close to what I'd need to survive the winter. All I could do was take things one day at a time, just like after the virus. When you don't know what to do then just focus on what's in front of you and keep stepping forward into life. What other choice did I have?

Fall turned into full winter and the snow came down like I had never seen it do there before. Day after day for an entire week the big fluffy flakes rained down, softly, silently, potentially deadly. Even though I kept the fire going constantly I still had to wear my coat inside. I awoke about every hour through the night to feed the fire but by morning I could still see my breath inside the cabin.

I had collected firewood all summer and stacked it roof-high along one wall, but I doubted it would last the whole season. To postpone the day that I had none I collected some from the dead branches of surrounding trees, breaking the smaller branches off with my hands, or using the saw for thicker limbs. I had to clear the path from my front door each morning and again before sunset, to the series of trees from which I gathered the firewood or I would soon be unable to leave the cabin at all. I also filled every available container I had with snow to melt beside the meager fire. I scraped through the snow around Burl's shelter so he could eat the dead grasses there but I didn't know how long I could keep that up. Burl looked at me with a resigned expression, accepting whatever I did or didn't do for him, as usual.

"Hang in there buddy," I said, rubbing his head and neck affectionately. He nuzzled my hand signaling his trust in me. I hoped I deserved that trust.

Around noon I cooked myself a daily stew of jerked meat and the vegetable of the day. Other than my chores, I slept as much as possible, to conserve calories. I never ate enough to feel truly full and satisfied but I had to make the little I had last as long as possible. As I watched my food stores dwindle and the days dragged on, I felt increasingly sure that I would in fact starve before spring. I knew that many people in that situation would have considered it a sad necessity to kill Burl and eat him but Burl was the closest thing to family I had now. I would literally rather die than kill him.

During the seventh night of snow I decided I would bring Burl into the cabin with me as soon as the sun rose. It had gotten harder to get out to him and the snow had piled up to the top of his corral. I had no way of knowing when the snow would finally stop falling. The makeshift roof on his enclosure creaked and groaned with the increasing weight. I doubted it could take much more. I awoke as the first light of dawn filtered through the cracks in the eastern wall and I heard a pack of coyotes call and yip excitedly from near the butte and upstream a bit. At first I figured they had located a deer and were closing in for the kill, but then they grew louder. They had never ventured very close to my cabin before, I guess because they were wary of humans. But this time I could tell they were coming our way, and fast. I had just made it to my feet and reached the door knob when I heard them hit.

Burl let out a bray like I'd never heard before, so loud and panic-filled that it shredded my heart. I stood frozen at the door, shaking with horror, adrenaline demanding action and terror telling me to stay put. A pack of coyotes hungry enough to attack a full-grown burro wouldn't think twice about going after a small human, even one wielding a shovel.

I didn't stand a chance.

My hesitation made the decision for me. I heard a sharp yowl from one coyote. Burl wasn't going to go down without a fight. But he was outnumbered and the coyotes were designed for killing. Burl was not. Burl screamed and thrashed a few moments more, then fell silent. I heard the sickening sound of tearing flesh and happy growls as the pack tore into my only, my last, dear friend. It had been nine months since I had spoken to another human.

I curled into a knot on my bed, staring numbly into the flame flickering in my makeshift fireplace feeling the full weight of my failure squeezing my chest like a giant, angry hand. I sobbed into my blankets and covered my ears, trying to shut out the sound of the triumphant coyotes.

They would live through the winter.

8

The weeks came and went.

I continued my very simple routine: rise, collect firewood and snow to melt for water, cook my one meal of the day, eat, tidy up and sleep an awful lot. A semi-hibernation. I dreamed of my long dead family and friends, better days and how those better days came to an end. Sometimes I awoke startled and confused about where I was, and when. Then it would come back to me.

It was probably about mid-January and I just had a few packets of jerky and even less dried vegetables left on the shelves suspended above me. The snow had continued to accumulate at a regular pace but it had not snowed so heavily as that first week-long deluge, so it had partially melted in the sun and compacted to a thick layer of ice over the entire ground. I could no longer tell for sure where the river course began or ended.

As bad as was the prospect of simultaneously starving and freezing to death, the fact that I was so completely alone made it much worse. What if I had made this trek with Mama? Well, for one thing, we probably wouldn't be starving to death. More hands meant more to do all the work of creating this little home as well as finding food. The loneliness crushed me bit by bit into a small, hard, brittle version of my former self. The image of finding others here who knew me had staved off the feeling of isolation on the way here, but I had no such hope of good company now, even if I did live.

I thought of Daddy, Mama, Seth, Grandma Sita and Burl, and just wanted to be wherever they were. At this thought, the pressure on my chest eased. I felt light and peaceful. I found that I didn't mind the notion of dying nearly as much as I expected I would, so close to its reality.

So be it.

I would die here and join them. In the meantime, I figured I might as well use up the food stores I had. As much as I now looked forward to death I didn't really like the idea of starving any sooner than I had to. Being dead I could accept but I wasn't in a hurry to experience starvation.

About two weeks later the weather warmed unseasonably and the snow melted in earnest. I knew winter wasn't over, that this was just a break and probably a short one before it resumed its course. Winter wouldn't retreat for real for many weeks yet.

I had only enough jerky for another few days if I was careful. I had eaten the last of the vegetables a week before. I took my gathering sack and shovel to dig some roots. I had ceased feeling much hunger but felt instinctively driven to keep eating at least a mouthful once or twice a day. By then I was so thin that I had to cut another hole in my belt. My jeans hung loosely on my hips and I could see my ribs in sharp relief against my shirt. My hair came out in clumps on the rare occasions I brushed and re-braided it.

I decided to search around the base of the butte upstream, opposite the direction I usually went, behind my cabin. I hadn't looked that way until now because plant foods had been so abundant nearer the river during the summer and fall, but I had noticed some agaves clinging to the gently slanted base, surrounded by clusters of live oak. I knew the Apaches had roasted the roots of the agave, though I had never tried it myself. Agave roots were also supposed to be very big too, so it gave me a mixed-feeling of hope and dread that I might survive another couple of weeks.

I looked for one that was big enough to be worth the trouble but not so big that it would be too hard to for me to dig up and carry back. I found a healthy specimen with a base about the size of a car tire. Thick, triangular, waxy leaves nested inside of each other, getting smaller towards the center, leaves opened upwards, like a giant overripe artichoke. I set my sack down and started to dig, slowly, making my way around the plant a bit at a time, in circles, digging a little deeper with each round. I had just dug deeply enough around the tuber to see it start to loosen from the sandy soil when a muted flash caught my eye.

Something had reflected the rays of the descending

sun.

I scanned the side of the sandy butte, trying to spot what had briefly sent the sunlight my direction. I moved my head from side to side until I caught the flash again. Walking uphill to that spot, a few feet off the ground and partially conceal behind a small stand of live oak, I saw a flat piece of what used to be clear plastic, but was now obscured by dust. I reached towards it through the tangle of thin, crooked branches of the oak and touched a gritty, round, flat piece of plexiglass set vertically into the side of the butte.

Plexiglass, such a rare reminder of the so recently past era of humankind, about 10 inches in diameter. I rubbed the surface first with my hand, then my handkerchief, until I had cleared most of the dust away. I tried to pry it loose but it was set as if glued into place. There was something on the other side of the slab of plexiglass. Donning my work gloves, I pressed apart the foliage enough to get my head and shoulders farther between the oak branches to have a closer look.

My face now just a few inches away, the object came into focus. A candle on a candle holder, sitting on a window sill. I felt slightly dizzy, confused by this thing that appeared to be something it couldn't possibly be. Was the hunger making me delirious? Was I hallucinating? If so, I was in worse shape than I had realized. My hands trembled.

I looked again, sure that it was a mirage, or maybe a photo glued to the plexiglass. But it wasn't. I could see the dimensionality of the candle and its holder. The curve of the candle, the flat base. There was no mistaking it. The candle and its holder were *inside* the butte. My breath came high and fast and I shut my eyes tightly in an effort to slow it down. I opened my eyes again and saw past the candle holder into a room.

A room.

How could that be? My head spun.

Panicked, I backed out of the oak as fast as I could. I shifted myself away from the window and plastered myself against the side of the butte so as not to be visible to whoever used that room. I slid down to the ground and sat shaking, arms clasped about my knees, gasping in shock and then fear, glancing wildly about, terrified of suddenly meeting that room's inhabitant. Whoever it was wouldn't be happy to be found for sure, and I had no way of guessing the temperament of such a person.

As my breathing slowed my brain began to function again. I had never seen any tracks around here, and there certainly would be tracks if someone were staying there, at least anyone living. My stomach clenched at the thought of yet another dead body lying in yet another home. Shaking off my remaining trepidation, I finally stood, slowly. A person couldn't get in and out through that window. There must be a door somewhere.

I walked around the base of the butte, poking my gloved hands into stalwart stands of scrub oak, and brittle long-fingered ephedra, pushing them aside, searching for an entryway. I was about a quarter of the way around the butte when I found it. Hidden by two rows of mountain mahogany, each with barely enough room between them to get through without getting scraped up, I found it. A small arched door, made from mountain mahogany branches, attached to flat boards on the inside. The perfect camouflage. I scraped away some plant debris and dirt that had collected at the base of the door. Holding my breath, I pulled the mahogany handle. I am not particularly tall but I still had to stoop some to get through the doorway.

Once I was through the entryway the ceiling rose and I could stand upright. A narrow staircase descended before me, with steps long enough for a man's feet but not wide enough for anyone with a lot of extra weight. The sandstone steps were set with tile. For a moment I feared the darkness ahead of me. What might I encounter here, I wondered? But then I realized it wasn't dark, or not very dark. As my eyes adjusted, an unseen source of light made it possible for me to see several feet in front of me. Slowly I traveled down the steps a story or so into the earth.

The walls were smooth, flowing sandstone. Someone had carved this stairway. Hearing no ominous sounds ahead I was starting to enjoy the journey when a giant snake appeared before me, eyes glaring and mouth open, ready to strike.

I shrieked high and loud, and stumbled backwards as fast as I could, back up several steps. Then I realized that the snake had not struck after all, and indeed had made no sound and not moved. For the second time that afternoon I fought to slow my breath. My hands shook with adrenaline and my legs turned watery beneath me. I sobbed briefly, so scared and angry I was with myself.

Mincingly I crept forward, one slow step at a time, until I came once again in view of the snake. It was enormous. Carved beautifully into the sandstone wall, the snake's tail curled twice around what appeared to be a fireplace, the head coming down one side, engraved in deep relief and fine detail. The scales had the slightest depth, the bared fangs fearfully sharp, the rattles on the tail each articulated exactly as they would on a living specimen of a diamondback, although, like everything else, much bigger. The topmost section of the snake's body rose higher than my head. A large niche had been carved into the sandstone next to the snake, holding neatly cut pieces of firewood.

But that wasn't all.

As I stepped further into the room, because it *was* a room, as large as our living room had been in Silver City, more light came in and I saw that this was not just a room with walls and windows and seats, though it had all of that.

This room was a work of art.

The external walls had been carved with clusters of oversized flower blooms—roses, sunflowers, dahlias, and lilies—set atop sturdy sandstone stems. The centers of the blooms held round plexiglass windows through which I could see dusty sunlight and the branches of mountain mahogany and scrub oak, shielding the windows from outside view. Small seats emerged from the walls, set beneath this mineral bouquet. Small niches nestled between the stems about head high, holding dusty candle sticks atop simple, smooth, wooden candle holders. Cheerfully painted pounded tin wall sconces held electric lightbulbs. The floor was paved in hefty pale burnt-orange

Saltillo tiles, accented with colorful smaller tiles set artfully between, in counterpoint to the surrounding tan stone.

I felt like Alice, walking through the looking glass, or more likely, down a really big rabbit hole. Or into a Hobbit home.

A large central pillar flowed in rippling waves from floor to ceiling, carved in the shape of a sturdy Alligator Juniper, rough offset squares running up the trunk, the underside of branches expanding overheard and melting into the stone ceiling. The base of the trunk took the shape of raised roots forming a circular banco-style bench complete with cushions, as dusty as everything else, for guests no doubt.

Slowly, feeling pretty sure that I was dreaming, I walked around the pillar, spotting a large platform carved into the sandstone, topped with an equally large mattress. Carefully folded blankets lie at the bottom of the bed. Pillows, all very dusty, rested at the head of the bed. Small shelves had been carved into the wall that bound the bed to the outside wall, holding books and still another candleholder. Past the foot of the bed were long, broad wooden shelves, set right into the sandstone, presumably for clothes or other personal items. Above these larger shelves three small round windows sat in a row, beyond which I could see some dormant raspberry bushes, also hiding the windows from easy view, but allowing in plenty of high desert sunlight. As I walked slowly by I ran my hand over the top blanket, feeling the grittiness of the sand that had sifted onto it from the low ceiling over the years that this place must have lain empty. I stared at the blanket, a dim memory tugging at the back of my brain...Sita! This was a quilt Grandma Sita had made. I remembered that it had been on the bed in which Seth usually slept when we came to visit.

I stood stock still, mind whirling in an attempt to make sense of this. Could this be Sita's place? No! We would have known. She would have told us. She must have given the quilt to a friend, who made this place.

Then I noticed farther ahead, to the left, a passageway leading farther into the hill. I stepped into the short hallway and it split in a V, into two other rooms. I bore right, into a gently lit, curving space, this one even larger than the first.

The kitchen.

Several more small, round windows stood in deeply set window sills, above a long wooden counter top. An old-fashioned "ice box" sat to the right of the counter, a bulky metal box with a handle at the front. I pulled the handle and the door swung open. It was empty but for the thickly insulated walls and several shelves. At the bottom was a full-length drawer, presumably for ice or cold water, to slow the decay of fresh foods.

Most astonishing was the sink. An actual deep-set stainless steel sink, complete with water faucets. Water faucets. Under a hill, in a carved-out cave. I reached towards the faucet as timidly as if it might strike me. I turned the "cold" knob. And out came water. Cool water. I tentatively cupped my hand below the flow, sipped the water and found it delicious. I turned off the faucet.

Wooden cupboards set above the windows contained mugs, glasses, plates and bowls. Drawers below the counter held silver ware and cooking utensils. The lower cupboards held pots, frying pans, measuring cups, mixing bowls and assorted baking pans. A small two-burner electric stove and oven sat daintily to the right of the sink. Behind me, opposite the counter and sink, stood an expandable kitchen table, with room for four but could, when the leaf was in place, seat eight. Four chairs were tucked in, as if awaiting company.

Beyond it all stood deep-set floor-to-ceiling shelves, loaded heavily with canned and boxed goods. Stuffed. I even found an unopened gallon jar of crystalized honey. I couldn't even remember when I had anything sweeter than raspberries. Eyes like a giant panda's and jaw dropped to the floor, my mouth watered. Canned pinto beans, red chile powder, pouches of heat-and-serve Indian food, rice, oatmeal, baking powder, salt, pepper and a whole corner of spices of all kinds, double bagged sugar...and on and on. Another set of shelves on the adjacent wall, much deeper and sturdier than the others, contained sealed five-gallon buckets of oats, rice, several kinds of beans, flour, sugar, salt and cooking oils, two deep. It was a massive amount of food.

Moving like a zombie I pulled out one of the chairs and lay my head on the table, trembling again, tears running down my cheeks, sniffing wetly. I could survive for a year on what was on the smaller shelves alone. If I couldn't make it here, starting from this place, I didn't deserve to live.

Slowly I lifted my head, wiping my nose on my sleeve, remembering the other room, as yet unexplored. I floated back towards the entryway room and made a right. This room sported a wooden door made of cross set one-by-fours, which I tentatively pushed inwards.

Bright tiles of all colors covered nearly every surface. It was as if kindergarteners were asked to make the ones that covered the floor and counter. They were all blobby, uneven shapes, though flat on top, like amoebas pressed into microscope slides, or sloppily poured pancakes. From small as a quarter to twice the size of my palm, they flowed across the floor, up the side of the tub, which was shaped like a gigantic porcelain clamshell and tipped up on one end, then ran up across the counter and down into the sink. An underwater scene of fish and water plants covered one entire wall. Sturdy heavily speckled Gila trout, the narrower, graceful Loach minnow, the gawky, narrow Longfin dace with its cartoonish, oversized fins, all swam with the river's waves, around tile rocks and water grasses.

The style was definitely Grandma Sita's. I began to think she may have had more to do with this place than I had first thought. Then I vaguely remembered making oddly shaped tiles with her, when, in fact, I *had* been a kindergartener. She had rolled thick slabs of clay through the large "clay smoosher" as we had called it, and she said Seth and I could cut them however we wanted.

The only thing that was not covered in tiles were the fixtures and the most surprising piece of equipment of all—the bidet. While just short of full in-door plumbing, it looked like one could at least take a pee indoors in a pinch. And wash up besides. I turned the knob, and water flowed through the faucet. Small shelves were carved into the wall just above the sink, each one edged in fine leafy, sandstone vines. A tall, broad cupboard with glass windows sat at the far end of the bathroom holding sheets, towels and blankets. Next to it sat a hand powered washer and an old-fashioned clothes ringer. Drawers and a small cabinet under the sink held incidental first aid supplies, nail clippers, tweezers, an oral thermometer and something I literally had not seen in years, store-bought shampoo, conditioner and soap. Along the tops of the walls water nymphs and mermaids frolicked happily, carved in relief in the sandstone. I guessed the sun was probably barely bobbing above the horizon now. It seemed like I should go back to the cabin and sleep on the implications of my discovery. But I didn't want to leave. I was sure that if I left now, I would wake up in the morning and find this *was* all a dream. At the very least I wanted to sleep inside this dream. And I desperately wanted it to be real. I *needed* it to be real.

I had spotted some matches in one of the drawers.

Matches.

Imagine that.

I lit a few candles, in the bedroom and in the kitchen.

I pulled some deer jerky out of my pocket for my dinner. I just couldn't bring myself to eat any of the canned or packaged foods in the pantry. Like a greedy dragon with a hoard of gold and precious gems, I wanted to have it, not use it, at least not yet.

After my meager dinner I lie awake for a long time on the soft elevated bed, grains of sand that had resisted my attempts to shake them out making their way under my shirt and down my pants. The smell of sandstone was so thick I had a moment where I imagined myself in a tomb, if a beautiful one. Maybe I was really dead. Or dying.

It was incredibly quiet inside the hill, and I found it unnerving not hearing the usual night sounds—the trickling of the creek, howls of the wolves, hooting of owls and skittering of small rodents. But when I finally slept, peace settled deeply into my bones. It was as if I hadn't slept in years.

9

I awoke slowly to the dim light, though it was already mid-morning. The room wasn't particularly cold, despite the lack of a fire. It made sense since the rooms were set deep into the butte. The sandstone interior maintained a fairly consistent temperature a couple of feet from the outside air.

I would bring my food stores and other belongings here. Whoever made this place hadn't been here in a very long time and likely wasn't coming back. Not only was I going to survive this winter, I was going to do it in this lovely, comfortable *home*.

I spent the morning hauling my supplies to the cave, setting my clothes on the wooden shelves next to the bed, the meager food onto the kitchen shelves. I considered the risk of someone spotting the door as I had, but thought it would be unlikely that anyone would be traveling here in the middle of winter. I would worry more about security matters come spring.

I would live like a queen. At least a queen from before inter-continental trading and grocery stores.

No more water to haul. A table with matching chairs and cushions at which to eat. I didn't have to worry about mice or rats or other unwanted scavengers in the well-sealed cave. It wasn't until I decided to try out the bathtub that I found out what royalty I really was.

I had assumed that only cold water came out of the faucets and out of habit I used only the right-hand knobs on the sinks. But when I went to use the tub, anticipating a rather chilly bath, I held a bottle of shampoo in my right hand so I reached for the left knob to release the flow of water. A few moments later I saw steam rising from the clear, flowing liquid. I blinked twice, then put two fingers under the steaming stream. It was hot! Like the hot springs.

I couldn't believe my own stupidity, and luck. Of *course* there were hot springs in this area. They were too far upstream or downstream from the cabin for me to make use of in the winter so I hadn't given them a lot of thought. Whoever built this place must have piped the water into the cave. I said a silent prayer of thanks to the builder again, this time for the genius of providing hot running water indoors.

I filled the tub full and sank into it like a stone, up to my chin in the precious brew. I soaked until the water started to cool, then scrubbed the filth of the last few months away. For the first time since I arrived at the burnt down village, I knew beyond a doubt that I had done the right thing by coming here, following Mama's song.

That night, I ate something from the pantry. I was nearly

out of my own food and winter would soon return full force, probably until spring broke for real. I stood in front of the densely packed shelves, scanning the offerings, most of which I hadn't eaten since before the virus. Then I spotted it. The one thing that made me think of home, of the life long past, more than anything.

Peanut butter.

My breath felt thick and my hand quivered as I opened the jar set on the thick wooden countertop. It felt almost sacrilegious. Once opened it couldn't be sealed again. The oil sat in a thick shimmering golden layer on top of the gravity-densified pulverized peanuts. Holding my breath, I poured the oil into a bowl carefully, not wanting to waste any of the treasure. Then I pressed the tip of a sharp knife into the peanut clay at the bottom, scoring it over and over until chunks of it could be pried out and deposited into the oil. Then I used a metal potato masher to coax the peanut chunks into smaller pieces, blending those into the oil bit by bit. Straining with each depression. I stared down at the smooth, dark, oily mass, and inhaled the intoxicating scent of roasted peanuts. I reached for a spoon in the drawer and scooped up a miniscule amount, lifting it to my nose for another deep huff. My tongue reached out, no longer under my control, and I licked the spoon.

My brain blazed with a frenetic swirl of memories:

Grandma Sita spreading peanut butter onto one slice of bread, and thick, shiny strawberry jam onto another. Her wrinkled hands brought the two slices together and she set the whole thing back on the plate. Carefully she cut the sandwich diagonally and handed me the plate, smiling broadly, no doubt in response to my own happy grin.

Daddy spooning a blob of peanut butter into a metal cage, a live trap, to catch a skunk that had taken up residence under our house.

Seth standing on a stool, just barely raising him enough to reach the peanut butter jar on the counter. He grasps the jar, strains until his five-year-old biceps bulge, then triumphantly sets the lid on the counter. Eyes wide, he dunks his fingers into the jar, brings them up dripping and starts licking as big blobs fall onto the counter, the floor and the stool. I hear my own voice saying sternly, "You're going to get us into trouble!"

Mama pulls a slab of solid peanut butter out of the refrigerator. It has been mixed with a little sugar and she will cut the confection into pieces which we will later dunk into melted chocolate, as a special treat.

I set the now cleaned spoon onto the counter and sank to the floor, my face in my hands. I trembled and gasped. I worried that I was actually going crazy.

Made crazy by a jar of peanut butter.

This is what we had lost. Once such an ordinary thing and we couldn't ever have it again. It was gone, all except this little jar, which I had so impulsively opened. How much else was gone forever?

Gone were the trips to the cavernous grocery store with its multitudinous aisles, row after row after row of shelves towering high above my head, packed with a seemingly infinite number of foods. Shelves so high that mama had to ask for help reaching things on the top ones. Row after row after row of breakfast cereals, pickles, salsas, canned beans and vegetables, boxes of pasta and sauces to match, enormous freezers with every kind of meal imaginable, frozen in neat cardboard, ready to POP! into the microwave for just a couple minutes and voila—a whole meal! Too many pizzas to even decide which one to pick so mama always picked the 5-cheese and we'd add our own favorite things on top— green chile, bright red bits of bell peppers and whole black olives that me and Seth would stick on the ends of our fingers for fun before we ate them.

Gone were the stacks of ice cream cartons of every flavor anyone could ever dream up, and nearly all of them I thought were so heavenly good that I couldn't even say so in words, just "yuuuuuuuummmmmmmmmm!" Never again would we have ice cream. Never again would we sit in front of the television and watch Sponge Bob Square Pants or Dora the Explorer. Or documentaries on global warming, or the health care crisis, that mama and daddy watched after Seth and I were supposed to be asleep but we'd watch from around the hallway corner until we fell asleep on the floor. Somehow, we always awoke in our beds.

Gone were the fiddle lessons, and Saturday mornings nervously playing for the customers at the Farmer's Market—another place overflowing with fresh, miraculously varied foods. Gone were the camping trips all over the west—the Grand Canyon, Chaco Canyon, the Rio Grande at Orilla Verde, the Sand Dunes of southern Colorado and White Sands Missile Range. No more going to Puerto Peñasco to kayak, snorkel and fish.

Gone were the airplane rides to Costa Rica to hike in the

rain forest and swim in the ocean, to San Francisco to see daddy's parents, and to Seattle to see mama's best friend Serena, who was also mine and Seth's godmother. After the virus, only on rare occasions did we spot an airplane in the sky, high, high, above us, and mama said those were military planes and not ones that people like us flew in. But after a while even those had stopped appearing in the heavens above.

No more trips to Grandma's as a family, to hike in the forest, clamber through the rocky cliff dwellings that sat watching the west fork of the Gila River far below, or soak in the hot springs, lined thoughtfully with gravel while the snow fell onto mine and Seth's outstretched tongues. We giggled at the notion that we could be outside, naked, in the middle of winter and be steaming warm at the same time.

Gone were too many friends, too many husbands, wives, sisters and brothers, aunts and uncles and cousins and next-door neighbors. Death had stunk up every building, room and open space with rotting flesh and grief.

On my third day in the cave I noticed a vertical strip of wood embedded in the wall behind the large cupboard at the back of the kitchen. I hadn't seen it earlier because it was almost perfectly aligned with the right edge of the back panel. It looked as if someone had built something wooden into the wall behind the cupboard, which seemed odd to me. Starting at the top, about six feet up, I ran a finger down it while looking behind the cupboard, trying to see how wide the board was. When my finger descended to about waist high it crossed a black button about the size of a quarter set into the wooden strip. I pressed the button and heard a low humming sound that startled me so much I sprang backwards. I stood gawking as the whole cupboard opened like a door, as if the whole thing was on hinges. Which, as it turned out, it was.

A large doorway stood open, wide enough for two people to easily walk through side by side. An arched passageway a couple of yards long led into a big bedroom, similar in style to the entryway sleeping loft but much larger and fully furnished.

Inside I found a queen-sized bed with dark wooden nightstands on either side, each topped with identical floral lamps. Two matching dressers flanked a tall double-doored wardrobe standing against the far wall. A graceful freestanding mirror set in a beautifully carved wooden frame stood beside one of the dressers. A large trunk sat at the foot of the bed, which, upon opening the lid, revealed linens, bedspreads and quilts. Gentle light flowed downward from a clean metal tube in the ceiling that extended upwards for several yards. Floral and landscape paintings and exotic woven textiles adorned the walls.

On the wall at the head of the bed, towering over anyone who would sleep there, was the vivid, colorful batik of the Hindu goddess Lakshmi. Grandma Sita's batik. The one that inspired my mother to name me after this earth-loving deity. I lay myself down in wonder on the bed allowing the beauty of this place to engulf me. I felt held and comforted under Lakshmi's gaze, as if my grandma and mama were there with me. I felt like I was in one of those stories of portals into enchanted realms. But there was no evil witch or queen, no fauns or living chess pieces or smiling, talking cats. Just the magic of love and vision, surviving the abyss of death. I drowsed dreamily for a long time allowing the soothing feeling of being loved and embraced across the dimensions to seep deeply into my flesh and to marinate my bones.

So gradually that I hardly realized what I was seeing, an arched doorway slowly came into focus. It stood opposite the foot of the bed, set with a perfectly matched arched door made from two layers of two by fours, simple but well sanded and varnished. I rose from the soft bed and walked through the doorway, standing open-mouthed once more.

The immense room before me, a room at least three or four times larger than all the rest of the cave house, was lined with metal frame book shelves from floor to ceiling, all filled with books. There were thousands of them. Grandma Sita had built a hidden library. I wandered down each row, which were neatly labeled "fiction" or "non-fiction" and numbered in the Dewey decimal system exactly like the library on Cooper Street in Silver City. Standing near the entryway I found an old-fashioned paper card catalog to facilitate one's search for particular subjects or authors.

The books were raggedly old, shiny and new, hard back, paperback, small and large. Every topic I could think of was represented in this collection. History, mathematics, philosophy, books on nearly every country, region and culture imaginable. There were large sections on building and on solar, wind and water generated electricity and equally large sections on permaculture, and local plants for both food and medicine. There was an arts and crafts selection covering everything from drawing to basket making and weaving to pottery.

The fiction section was just as extensive, holding every genre from hundreds of years ago right up to the year the virus hit. Along one wall sat a neat row of tables, and at each of these were comfortable sturdy wooden chairs with thick cushions. A giant chalk board ran the full length of the wall next to the tables. You could easily have a school here if you wanted to. Or use it for planning. But who would I teach or learn from? Who would plan anything with me?

The most tantalizing thing of all my discoveries was the old fashioned, hand operated printing press inside a large alcove at the very back of the library. Huge rolls of newsprint stood like sentinels against the wall next to the press, along with at least fifty 1-gallon bottles of ink. I had a hard time envisioning wanting to print anything, much less multiple copies. Who on earth would I print them *for*? Still, just the thought that I *could* stirred my imagination. What would I want to tell subsequent generations, if indeed there were ever to *be* subsequent generations?

After my complete investigation of the library I pulled a copy of *The Lion, the Witch and the Wardrobe* from its shelf and returned to the large comfy bed in the beautiful bedroom for a read. Mama had read me and Seth the story Before and though I couldn't remember the particulars I remembered enjoying it. It seemed like a logical place to start, considering.

The weeks passed peacefully. Dreamily. A full year had gone by since I had escaped from the compound and I knew I wasn't going to die. At least not of starvation. At least not yet. I had become so accustomed to the loneliness that ate a fresh hole in my chest each day that I hardly noticed it, much as I hardly noticed how I still favored the ankle I had sprained. Coping becomes a habit. But I had found refuge, safety and comfort. And plenty of food. As winter gradually eased its grip on the land I soaked up the luxury of my home and enjoyed regaining some of the weight I had lost.

Another delightful discovery I made, was that of the heating system throughout the cave complex. The floors held pipes cleverly set inside a wooden framework under the floor tiles. Knobs to release the flow of water were placed periodically, causing water from the hot springs to circulate beneath the floors, gently warming them and therefore the rooms. I didn't even have to make a fire to stay warm, unless I felt like it.

Much of the snow had melted and I heard the loud CRACK of the river thawing as slabs of ice broke loose and drifted downstream. Tiny brave shoots lifted their heads skyward in the patches of ground that lie in the sunlight most of the day. The days were pleasantly cool but not cold now, though the nights were still often below freezing.

I had resumed my hunting and gathering activities as soon as practical. Although I had enjoyed stuffing myself for a while with the dried goods from the cave's pantry while the winter still held the land tightly in its grip, I didn't want to deplete those reserves any more than necessary.

I felt thrilled by my triumph of surviving the winter. Who knew what challenges next winter would bring? Maybe I could make my way back to the compound to rescue Robert. Together we could make it here. But would my luck hold? Could I sneak in again and sneak out with Robert? Could I make it away a second time, especially without Burl? My heart sank like a stone thrown into a deep well at the thought of Burl. I missed his steady, comforting presence, and his perennially unflappable demeanor. I felt searing guilt at my failure to save him from those coyotes.

Each night I curled up with my latest book where I was transported to an imaginary world, or a city on the other side of the planet where a savvy yet vulnerable detective sought to solve a difficult but compelling murder case. Or I read about the local edible plants in order to better supplement my diet. I found in the library stacks of spiral bound notebooks and loose-leaf paper and binders. Clusters of pens sealed in their original plastic wrappers were piled inside a deep drawer. Maybe one day I would have something to write for the collection myself.

10

I was hiking up the west fork of the river investigating the plants that grew in that area and checking for animal sign, my tattered canvas gathering bag slung over my shoulder, when I smelled smoke. Not a forest fire smoke. Cooking fire smoke.

Someone was cooking venison.

As well fed as I now was, my mouth instantly watered. And I froze, instinctively pressing myself against a nearby piñon tree for cover. Just the thought of seeing another human being sent lightning bolts of anxiety throughout every cell in my body. Whether or not such a person might want to do me harm, the prospect of seeing another person, much less speaking to them, felt like a tidal wave roaring towards me from the distance. My loneliness had shielded me, even as it enclosed me from all sides like a cage. And what if it *was* someone who would wish me harm? Another warlord looking for more workers? I quickly realized that this would not be the first place someone would go to find more people. After all, it had been only me here for a year and I hadn't seen anyone else. Still, it could be someone dangerous, whatever their purpose in coming here. A lot of people went kind of crazy after the virus.

What if I needed to speak with the intruder? How did I know my voice still worked? I forced myself to breathe deeply for a few breaths. When my breathing finally slowed to close to a normal rate I peeked carefully through the branches of the piñon at the trespasser.

Instantly I knew him.

The sharp straight nose, long-limbed grace and the hip length black braid snaking down his back. Appearing close to my age, it could only be one person.

Victorio Swift, grandson of Grandma Sita's outfitter lover and my own childhood companion.

The shock of seeing someone I knew, and believed I could trust, was almost as hard to bear as confronting Lem and Jeff again. My mind reeled with questions. How long had he been here? What was he doing here? He looked healthy. How was he surviving? Were there others? Where?

I clasped my hands over my mouth to quiet the sound of my gasping breaths as I sank slowly to the ground, back pressed against the tree which shielded me from Victorio's view. I clenched my eyes shut, as if seeing what I saw again would give me away. Tears streamed down my face and over clamped hands. I braved a glance up only to see a fully-grown version of my childhood horse-riding friend looking down at me.

His eyes glistened with moisture, which surprised me a

little, but he didn't seem at all amazed to see me, which surprised me a lot.

Still frozen in place yet shaking like a tree in a storm, now weeping and wide-eyed, I watched Victorio crouch down before me and gaze at me for a long moment. He reached out one hand, palm up. I held out one hand, now wet with tears, and took his. Victorio slowly stood and guided me up as well. Standing a full head taller than me he pulled me into his chest, wrapping his arms firmly and gently around me, palms clasping my shoulder blades, holding me for a very long time while I cried into the plaid flannel shirt that covered his chest until it was thoroughly damp.

When my sobs had subsided to hiccupping gasps and my shaking had eased to lighter tremors, he said quietly into my ear, "You're okay now. You're safe. You're with friends."

"Friends?" I squeaked, rubbing my nose on my sleeve and looking around.

Victorio led me as if guiding a spooked horse until we reached the fire where his venison cooked in an old cast iron frying pan set on a metal grate. He eased me down on a tree stump then turned the meat in the pan. I sat staring into the low flames, feeling drained. He pulled out an enameled metal plate from a saddle bag on his horse, deftly cut the piece of meat in two, placed them both on the plate and crouched next to me, offering me one of the pieces.

We chewed our venison in silence and I felt more grounded in reality with each perfectly normal, and yet extraordinary, bite. By the time I finished my piece of meat my body had stopped quivering and I felt like I could refrain from crying, at least for the time being. I licked the grease from my fingers.

Victorio rinsed the plate and pan with some hot water in a pail he had above the fire then stacked them on a flat rock. He turned towards me with his large, serious, hazel eyes, casting his gaze directly into my face for several long moments, as if gauging how much more I could handle.

He must have decided I could handle more because he asked, "Do you want to see the others?"

I didn't know how I felt so didn't answer.

"I could go with you to your place if you want until you're ready to see them."

How did he know I had a "place"? Why did he assume I had been here for a while, instead of just now arriving? He saw the questions, and then the answers I deduced, dawn on my face in quick succession, and his eyes opened wide in helpless apology. I started to shiver uncontrollably again. He quickly strode over, leaning down to where I sat, wrapping his arms around me, pulling me against him once more.

I didn't cry this time, just shook with the magnitude of the betrayal this man had already wrought against me. I could have died. I very nearly *did* die, and he knew it. He knew it at the time and he hadn't come to help me.

I wanted to run, to run as far and fast as I could. I wished I could lift myself off the ground and fly from this impossibly disappointing place forever. But my legs felt so wobbly it was all I could do to stay upright on my stump. I had no strength to fight him, just a blossoming, cold, utterly impotent, rage.

He spoke urgently, quickly, pleading, into my hair, as if the faster he spoke the less I would hate him. "I wanted to come, to get you, but we had all agreed that we couldn't take in anyone who couldn't survive on their own. I even snuck down to your cabin one time but you weren't there and the mice and rats had gotten into your food. I thought maybe you had left for good. I got into a lot of trouble for risking being seen by you. They told me if I did that again, they would banish me. We can't risk anyone from the outside knowing about us. And we already have kids and old people to care for. We'd risk the whole group if we took in someone who wasn't strong enough..." I felt his arms tighten around me holding me up, and felt his desperation for me to understand.

"I almost died. My burro was killed right outside my door. I nearly starved *and* froze!"

"I know. I – I mean, I don't know it all, but I knew it had to be horrible," He paused, then swallowed hard, forcing the words from his mouth, "I knew you could die."

His grip loosened on me and I stepped back, looking him in the eyes.

My voice rose to a full-lunged yell, "*I could have died because you let me die*!"

"I know. I'm sorry," his voice flattened in resignation as he looked down at the ground, arms now hanging at his sides.

We stood in silence facing each other, me glaring, his eyes brimming with sadness, just like when the girl died in the movie we watched together when we were kids. My mind reeled a thousand miles an hour in every direction.

I knew him. I needed him. Or I needed *somebody*. I had finally found someone I knew, someone I had been friends with and he had already broken my trust. Victorio, one of the people I had dreamed about seeing again as I journeyed here had been willing to let me die alone.

"I was on my way to check on you, to see if you had, well…made it," he said limply, looking away.

"What were you going to do, come collect any of my bones the coyotes had left? Rifle through my belongings to see if there was anything you could use?"

His face froze as if I had slapped him and I felt a small thrill of satisfaction.

I walked away from him, pacing in big circles around his little camp. Fear and loneliness and hatred and grief roiled within me like flowing lava, scouring and searing my innards. There were others with him. Others who had thought about how to survive long term. But they had been willing to let me die. I felt like a ponderosa tree being tossed every direction by a violent storm.

"I don't want to leave my home," I said.

"You don't have to. We don't have to go there, to the others, now. You don't have to go there ever if you don't want. I mean, please just come tell them all you won't tell anyone else we're here."

"I will tell them that. But I - I can't go today."

Suddenly, after a year completely alone, I felt an inexplicable terror at the thought of meeting others *and* of going back home by myself. Like when I found the cave and I didn't want to leave that first night because I was afraid it would cease to exist. As much as I hated him right now, I really needed Victorio to continue to exist. I looked at him. So familiar, dressed in the kind of denim jeans and plaid shirt he had always worn, topped with what appeared to be a home-made deer skin vest. He represented home to me as much as anyone I remembered from the village, despite his horrifying duplicity.

My voice felt heavy in my chest. "You can come with me. If you want." I turned and started home.

He nodded, throwing his cooking gear into a saddle bag before leading his horse behind me.

I couldn't speak the whole way back to my cave home and, wisely, he didn't push the matter.

He did, however, stop for a moment with a puzzled frown when I turned from the path that would have taken us straight downstream to the cabin and turned up towards the butte instead. I repressed a smile at his confusion, despite my unhappiness with him.

"Tie your horse," I said, pointing to a juniper.

I led him around the curve of the butte to the cave entrance. His eyes lit up in delight when he spotted the door, mouth twitching with a cautious grin. Once again though, I did not see *surprise* there.

I opened the door and gestured for him to go in before me, watching his reaction as we made our way down the stairs. Victorio paused to run one hand admiringly over the surface of the carved snake as he entered, then stopped a moment to scan the room with all its sandstone floral glory before sitting with me on one of the long bancos.

"Looks like Grandpa Joe's carvings," he said.

"You're not surprised at this place," I said gesturing around the room.

"No." Forearms resting on his knees, he leaned forward, looking down at his feet.

"Then either you've been here before or there are others like this."

"Yes. No. I mean... No, I haven't been in this one before. I didn't know exactly where it was. And yes, there are others." He looked up at me, meeting my gaze.

I sat dumbfounded, the implication of this sealing my lips and freezing me to my seat.

After a long pause I asked, "How? Who? Where?"

Victorio took a deep breath.

"Sita, my grandpa Joe and others here believed that something bad was going to happen. Catastrophic. That civilization would collapse somehow. Most thought it would be climate change. Some thought nuclear war. A sculptor named Ra had built caves like this up north, near Taos, and others here picked up on the idea. They knew that things could go really bad pretty quickly and knew that right away a lot of people would be desperate. They figured people would find their way here and take our food and maybe kill us."

"The houses in the village..." I began.

"Yes. Only a couple of families—what was left of them—stayed long enough for the raiders to get them. Kill them. Burn everything to the ground. Right after the virus passed through, the rest of us left alive packed up and got into the caves as quick as we could. Before we left I saw you come get your grandma Sita and bury her, when Grandpa was still sick. He was always grateful you did that. Before the raiders burned her house down. Grandpa got sick but survived."

I had never heard of anyone who had gotten the virus and not died.

"The raiders didn't find you?"

"No. They didn't look. I guess they figured everyone else in the village died or left to Silver City or Deming or something. The cliff dwellings, the ancient ones, wouldn't hide anyone. No reason they would look for caves. Even I didn't know about them until After because I lived in town with my folks and the cave builders kept them secret. But I was visiting Grandpa Joe when the virus came through. I kept thinking my parents would come if they had survived but they never showed."

"Who else made it?" I asked. My throat hollowed, eager and scared at the same time to hear the answer.

"Noah, his mom Jeanne and his older sister Hallie made it. Ben, Beto and the goat lady, Kate. Some of the Forest Service people, Devon, Frank, Gavin and Yazmin. There're a few people who were camping when the virus hit, who we took in. Tochuku, Ching Shih, Olga and Patricio Nunez, and three kids whose grandpa died while camping with them—Zoe, Walter and Thomas. With the three new babies we have twenty-two people. Plus you. If you want."

Dane, Liam and the other boy and two girls gone. Inez, Kate's son and daughter in-law and all their kids gone. It seemed silly to feel their loss so keenly, after seeing most of the people I knew die, but I did. They had been a part of this place too, part of my memory of this place, and the feeling of belonging. Then there were all the households with no survivors at all. So many that I had never even met. Now there was just a handful of people to start over here. It was impossible to tell what was happening elsewhere, with other survivors.

After a dinner of some more of Victorio's venison and some greens I had picked on the way home, I showered and then offered Victorio a fresh towel so he could also wash up. As he bathed I made up a bed for him on the banco bench, just below my own bed set up on its platform. I didn't feel like showing him the big bedroom and the library, not yet.

As I lie there staring at the sandstone ceiling, listening to Victorio's breath deepen into full sleep, I thought of those he had named as part of the community. I had hesitated when he first mentioned "others" but now my heart pounded at the thought of seeing people I had known as a child, my grandmother's familiar friends and their now grown children. They were the reason I made this journey. Of course I would go meet them. Of course I would want to be part of their community. I felt thrilled and terrified. And a thick-throated fury heated my veins at the thought that they had been willing to let me die.

11

The next morning we walked upstream again towards where the others lived. Victorio said, voice low and steady as if scared to set me off again, "We have a few babies, well, toddlers now, and a couple of older people who can't do much. So we really need people who are strong enough to work. We spend a lot of time caring for the older ones and kids, and hunting, gathering, gardening and the like..." he said, as if trying again to explain why they had left me on my own so long.

I shrugged, not knowing what to say for a while.

"I understand. I get it. Still, so many of them knew me...."

"Just for the record, I did tell them that you would be a huge help. How you as a little girl you would bring home rabbits and other game for Sita to cook, your knowledge of edible plants.... Others argued for you too. But too many didn't know you, just that you were a girl, not fully grown."

I stopped dead in my tracks and glared at him.

"A girl? Not fully grown?"

"Hey!" he said raising his palms defensively, eyes wide at my outburst, "I *said* I stuck up for you. *I* knew you'd help!"

"Okay, okay," I said, walking again. "You said it was people who didn't know me...." Who was I to criticize their choice when I had left Robert and Emma and the others the way I did? Who knows what harsh reaction was triggered by my escape? Did I make things even worse for those I left behind? Probably.

We hiked a couple of miles or so before we came to the next cave, Victorio leading his dun mare to walk beside me. Apparently the one I found was farthest downstream, nearest to Sita's incinerated house at the edge of the blackened, leveled village. According to Victorio this was not a coincidence. The first cave built was Sita's, waiting for me and my family. Others picked up on the idea and worked together to formulate a plan for a system of caves. The entrances to each cave were separated by at least a quarter mile, for the purpose of security. They were all built into the curve of a hill on the left side of the river as it gradually gained in altitude, upstream.

After securing his horse to a juniper Victorio led me by the hand up a steep rise to a doorway, partially shielded from view by stands of mountain mahogany. Victorio put two fingers in his mouth and whistled shrilly. Moments later the door flew open and before me stood Jeanne, mother of my now dead childhood friends Lilly, Miriam and Liam, and their surviving older siblings, Noah and Hallie.

"Eeeeeee!" she shrieked in delight, flinging her strong arms around me and squeezing me so tightly that I thought she might fracture my ribs. When she finally loosened her grip and stepped back from me I saw happy tears glistening in her eyes.

Her words came in a long torrent, "My god I'm so glad you made it. I was *furious* that we couldn't come get you as soon as Frank and Ching Shih spotted you last fall! But we had agreed in the beginning that we could only bring in someone new after they had proven they wouldn't be a burden—an agreement I now regret of course! I was so worried about you honey I just don't know what to say. Of course those of us that knew you knew you'd do fine, with your great hunting skills and all. We knew you had found the shed too. Then Victorio said it looked like maybe you left, that your shed had been trashed by vermin, so I felt so bad we had missed you, but I hoped he was wrong and you were still around.... I knew you'd make it one way or another, and you sure have. I've been so anxious, hoping Victorio would bring you back to us, I could hardly think straight!"

Not knowing what else to do I submitted to this furious and affectionate outburst. When she finally ran out of steam I croaked tentatively, "It's so good to see you...." My words felt completely inadequate. How could I explain in a sentence or two what it had been like to be alone for so long, to live nearly a whole year without knowing they were there? "I almost didn't make it. The rodents got into my food, I mean, while I was still living there. It was my winter stash..." I added, looking at my feet.

Her face fell and she paled despite her naturally ruddy complexion, taking in my thin form, perhaps realizing how bad it had actually been for me. I didn't know if her lack of awareness should make me more mad, or less. Still, her warm arms around me had felt incredibly good. Her enthusiastic affection made it hard to be as angry as I had intended. I could nestle inside that embrace for weeks. Mama and Jeanne had always been good friends.

"Well let's get inside and we'll get caught up," as she turned, leading us down a narrow passageway much like my own.

Beyond the entrance Jeanne's cave home was quite different from mine. The walls were smooth and gracefully curving the way that a river carves canyons, not covered in detailed relief carvings. The passageway opened into a room so large that it included several thick trunk-like pillars throughout to keep the ceiling from caving in.

The kitchen sat off to the right with a long counter along one wall embedded with a large, deep stainless steel sink, a four burner stove and oven, and wooden cabinets above and below with the same smoothly curved aesthetic as the walls. Another freestanding counter sat parallel and just opposite the first with more cabinets beneath.

The other side of the huge room held three long couches organized in a U shape topped with thick, comfortable looking cushions in a muted sunset color, and several matching chairs here and there. A broad, thick pine coffee table sat between the couches, covered with a Monopoly game, apparently in progress. Brightly painted wooden toys—chunky carved animals, trees, and alphabet blocks—lay strewn about the floor of the living room.

Between the kitchen and the living room stood a

massive pine table with eight matching chairs, all polished to a tawny sheen. The table looked like it had once been quite elegant but now bore the dings and stains common to well-used family furniture. The wall on the far side of the living room sported four doors in a row to one side of a shadowy arched hallway.

"Jeanne, Frank and their two kids live here, along with Noah. Hallie lives with Beto and their little girl, Uma..." Victorio explained quietly into my ear as Jeanne frenetically pulled food out of the refrigerator and serving dishes and plates out of the cupboards. Jeanne's older children, Noah and his sister Hallie, were now in their mid-twenties. Beto had owned the hot springs cabins and campground down the road. Hallie had only been a teenager the last time I saw her.

"Sit down, sit down!" Jeanne commanded cheerfully, gesturing to the dining table. Seeing me eyeing the furnishings she said, "You know Hallie made the tables and all the wooden toys for the children, in her workshop, and all the cupboards and the island in the kitchen. She also made the bed frames, closets and shelves in the bedrooms. She has a real gift for woodworking and she's built a lot of things for the other homes too."

Two small children, Obsidian, or "Sid," sporting a brown spiky hair cut, and Rose, a little older and adorned with bobbing copper curls, materialized from one of the four doors. Scuttling like crabs to Jeanne they clung like burrs to her legs, nearly tripping Jeanne in the folds of her colorful Indian print skirt as she carried a tray holding roasted piñon nuts and teetering mugs of tea to the table.

They stared wide-eyed at me, as if I had just emerged from a spaceship wearing three heads.

Never in their lives had they seen anyone besides the people they had known since they were born.

As the children bravely clambered upon seats on either side of their mother, watching me with less fear and increasing curiosity, we heard the clunk of a door opening from the back of the cave and male voices that sounded like they were coming from the dark hallway. Soon two men, one middle-aged and one much younger, rounded the far wall and clomped in heavy leather boots into the living room. Both wore heavy canvas jeans and shirts, were slung with a crossbow and hunting bag, and reeked of the healthy sweat from a morning of exertion. The younger one had been talking animatedly to the older one when the older one stopped suddenly, staring at me with much the same expression as the toddlers. The younger one, who I recognized as Jeanne's son Noah, looked over and stared for just an instant before his face broke into a wide-toothed smile.

"Oh my god—Lakshmi! I knew you'd make it. I just knew it. God I wish we could've brought you sooner." Noah rushed up to me, arms pulling me up out of my seat and squeezing like his mother had. It was strange to be almost as tall as Noah now, since I had been a scrawny child of nine and he a gangly teenager last time we had seen each other. Holding me for a moment at arm's length he gazed at me as if in wonder at my own transformation.

The man who I had correctly assumed to be Frank, Jeanne's partner and father of her younger children, stood watching, a slight grin on his face. I saw where the curly-headed Rose had gotten her flaming red hair.

When Noah finally released me back into my chair, finding one of his own and reaching for the bowl of nuts, Frank stepped forward, hand extended, "Hi I'm Frank. I'm one of the evil ones who insisted we follow our own rules and see if you could make it through the winter." His tone was wry and tentative, but warm. "I gotta say, everything they said about you," nodding towards Jeanne, Noah and Victorio, "was sure true. I'm really glad you made it. We're gonna need you here."

"Yeah, well...I'm glad I made it too...um, yeah...." as I shook his hand. I couldn't think of how to finish that sentence so I just let it hang. Jeanne shot a pointed look at Frank who promptly took a seat himself and stopped talking.

Over the course of the day word spread of my arrival and the occupants of the other cave houses trickled into Jeanne's large, comfortable living room.

Hallie showed up next, her small girl, Uma, tucked peacefully asleep in a broad sling strapped across her chest. Hallie's eyes shone happily at the sight of me, and she clasped me to her like a long-lost sister, "Ooooh! I'm so glad to *see* you!" My heart swelled a size, bumping up against my ribs.

Jeanne interrupted Hallie, her expression solemn, "She was living in that shed *all winter*, the rodents ate all her food...."

Still holding me close Hallie turned to her mother as her face flushed scarlet, the implication of Jeanne's words sinking in. Turning back to me, eyes flashing brightly, Hallie said, "I was so worried about you! I was glad that Victorio went to check on you, even though he got into trouble for it. If I had known you hadn't left but were starving in that shed I would have gone to get you, no matter what!" I believed her. Already she felt like my best friend.

Hallie's husband Beto arrived a few minutes later.

"Oh my god, if it isn't the Chica Conejo, the Rabbit Girl!" he laughed out loud and tossed his silver-streaked black hair before he too gathered me up, nearly cracking my ribs. "Oh mijita we *worried* about you!" He stepped back, looking me over in astonished delight.

I knew Beto as another neighbor of Sita's, and the proprietor of a hot springs campground on the other side of the village. I found out that now he shared the responsibility for the horses and hunting with Victorio. Beto had known Grandpa Joe since he was a child. Beto's father and Grandpa Joe were friends and had a shared Apache heritage. Although I hadn't known him as well as the others he clearly remembered me fondly. Apparently, the love of a grandmother for a grandchild can spread to others in her life as well.

I was squeezed, kissed and exclaimed over by Kate-the-goat-lady too. She had lost her son, daughter-in-law and their three children all within a few days of each other. I noticed that all these years later she still seemed kind of shell-shocked – laughing a little too loudly – then staring into space at times. Kate was living with Ching Shih, who I was told would be along shortly, and Benjamin, who I would have to see later, when I could go to their home.

Benjamin was quite elderly now, and wasn't sturdy enough to leave their home often.

Grandpa Joe enfolded me in his thin creaky arms for a long time. He felt like firewood that had been curing a little too long. Strong, but brittle and light. My heart surged with happiness that he had survived the virus. If I held any reservations about joining this group up until this point, I knew then, without question, that I would throw my lot in with these people.

I also met those who I had never known. Some had worked for the Forest Service – Frank who had been a law enforcement officer, Yazmin, an anthropologist, Devon, an agriculturist and Gavin a biologist. Others had been camping in the area when the virus came – Ching Shih, a martial artist and detective from Hong Kong, Tochuku, the community's engineering and technical expert, and Olga and Patricio, an artist couple that had adopted the three orphans, whose grandfather had succumbed to the virus while camping with the children.

Enough of them opposed my joining them as soon as they spotted me by my little shed cabin to make that agreement stick. Still, I wasn't too surprised to find that none of them seemed particularly malicious. Like Frank, most expressed sincere happiness that I had, in fact, made it to them. It turned out that Frank was the one who had first noticed me near my shed in early fall. They had no idea that I had already been there a half a year at that point. Others hung back from me, whether from distrust, shyness or guilt I didn't know. It was easy to keep my distance from the new people, while basking in the warmth of my newly reacquainted longtime friends.

The orphans Walt, Zoe and Thomas, seemed wary at first, much like the toddlers, but soon jostled each other, vying for a spot close to me, once we had all moved from the table to the couches. Walt and Zoe, twins, had just turned twelve, and Thomas, the eldest, was fourteen.

"Your gramma made up that song," Grandpa Joe said in his low, gravely voice, turning to me, next to him on a couch, "the one that brought you here. She had read a book about the Australian Aborigines, *Songlines*, it was, about how they used songs as a map, and it gave her the idea. She made your mama learn it, and told her to teach it to you kids, "just in case," though your mama thought she was being a little silly. Your mama didn't know about the cave, see. We couldn't tell anyone. We just wanted to make sure you young ones could make it here, if need be. We knew you could always find Standing Mountain, you know, Cooke's Peak, so she made a song starting near there." Grandpa Joe stared into the air for a moment then said, "I sure miss her." He paused again, looking down. "But I'm sure glad *you're* here." He grinned abruptly, patting my hand, black eyes beaming straight into my own.

My brain buzzed with the questions they all had for me, some insisting I tell them all about my journey, while others said not to rush me, that I was probably overwhelmed and tired. I obliged them as best I could, although the many interruptions with questions caused my narrative to wind around and backtrack a lot. I remained somewhat fuzzy about the exact reason for my escape from the compound. I wasn't ready to talk about Sylvia yet.

Maybe never would be.

Jeanne, Victorio, Hallie and Noah produced a proper feast for the whole group as we talked, the cooks listening from the kitchen to my chaotic narrative. They set out a huge salad, the ingredients of which had been plucked from the garden minutes before. Fresh bread appeared on a plate next to a generous piece of soft herbed goat cheese. A large pot of rabbit stew with onions, young carrots and cabbage also materialized, the scent of which lured the rest of us to the massive table to dine. I tried to remember when I had last eaten so well but couldn't. Probably before the virus.

The sun was sliding behind the high western ridge when people began making their way back to their own homes, though it was still a while before true dark. Jeanne's house was quite full, between her, Frank, Noah and her toddlers, so I spent the night at Victorio and Grandpa Joe's place which had several unused bedrooms, in the next cave upriver from Jeanne's. The walls and ceilings at Grandpa Joe's were covered with elaborate relief carvings, just like Grandma Sita's. Bears, wolves, ponderosas, flowing water and every other form of flora and fauna to be found in the Gila surrounded us, giving the sensation that we were outside even though we weren't.

After Grandpa Joe was tucked happily into bed, snoring nearly loud enough to wake the dozing river, Victorio and I sat silently on the hillside watching the night deepen from pale blue-gray to deep indigo. The temperature plummeted from the gentle daytime warmth and would be near freezing before dawn.

In a low voice Victorio began to hum a familiar tune, then softly added words:

Turn north onto the new road, sunrise to the east
March on between layer cake, fam-ly hills on right
Look out for the rattlesnakes, when the weather's warm

I turned to him in shock, mouth open in mute astonishment. He was singing the fourth stanza of my song.

"How...?"

He shot me a quick sideways grin then kept singing, verse after verse, not looking at me but out at the night-drenched forest before us. I shut my mouth and listened as he sung the rest of the song. With each verse I saw nearly my whole journey there, from the turnoff from the highway, to the final rise before dropping down to the burnt village of Gila Hot Springs.

When he finished Victorio said, "Grandpa Joe helped your Grandma Sita make up that song. One summer when I was staying with him, they took drives to the turnoff from Silver City and figured out the route. Mostly Sita made up the lyrics but together they would try out different phrasing until she was satisfied. It's not very poetic, I think because she wanted it to be clear enough for a child, not so concerned about it being beautiful. I heard them practicing it so many times I learned it too.

"For the first few years After I would look down the road for you every time we went downstream far enough. It wasn't often because we figured that if someone were going to come this way it would probably be by that road. I was just sure you and your mom would come find us, after you had come to bury Sita. I knew you survived so I thought you'd be back. But after a while I figured you all must have died some other way." Victorio looked down at his feet and fell silent.

Mama must have made up the stanzas from Columbus to the turnoff then added the ones Grandma Sita and Grandpa Joe had made. Sita would have assumed we would come from Silver City, on the same highway but from the opposite direction. I didn't know what to say. To think Victorio had been looking for me, for us, all that time. And finally here I was, the only one that made it. A survivor amidst the ghosts.

Sung home.

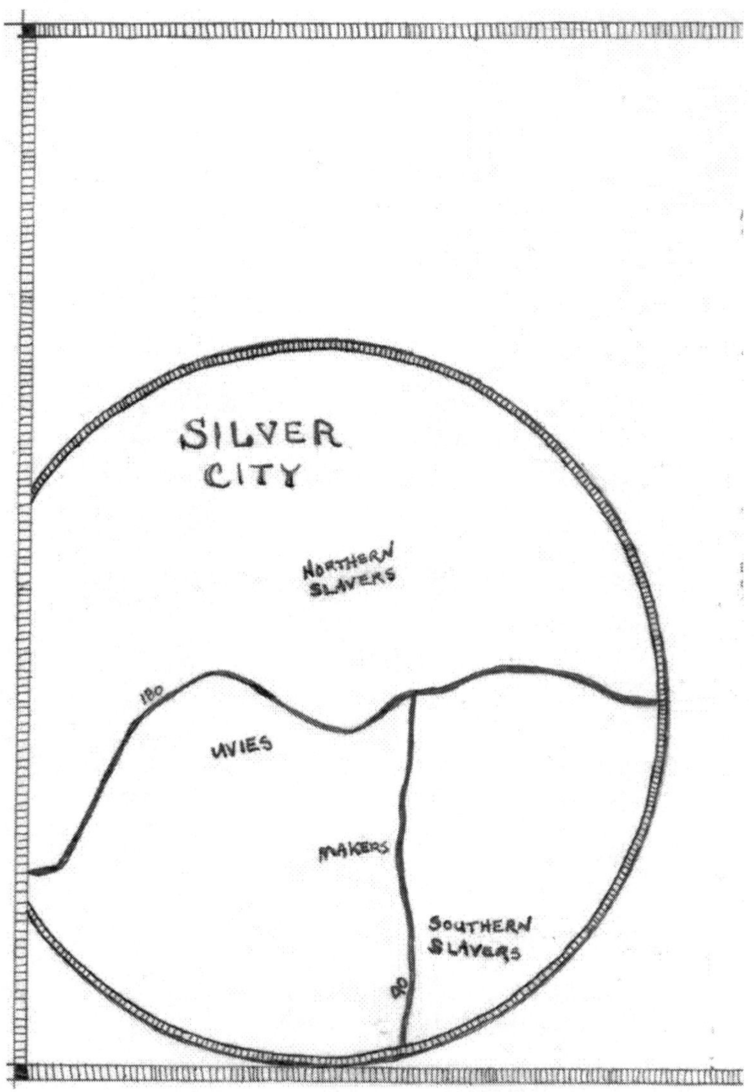
SILVER
CITY
NORTHERN
SLAVERS
180
UVIES
MAKERS
SOUTHERN
SLAVERS
90

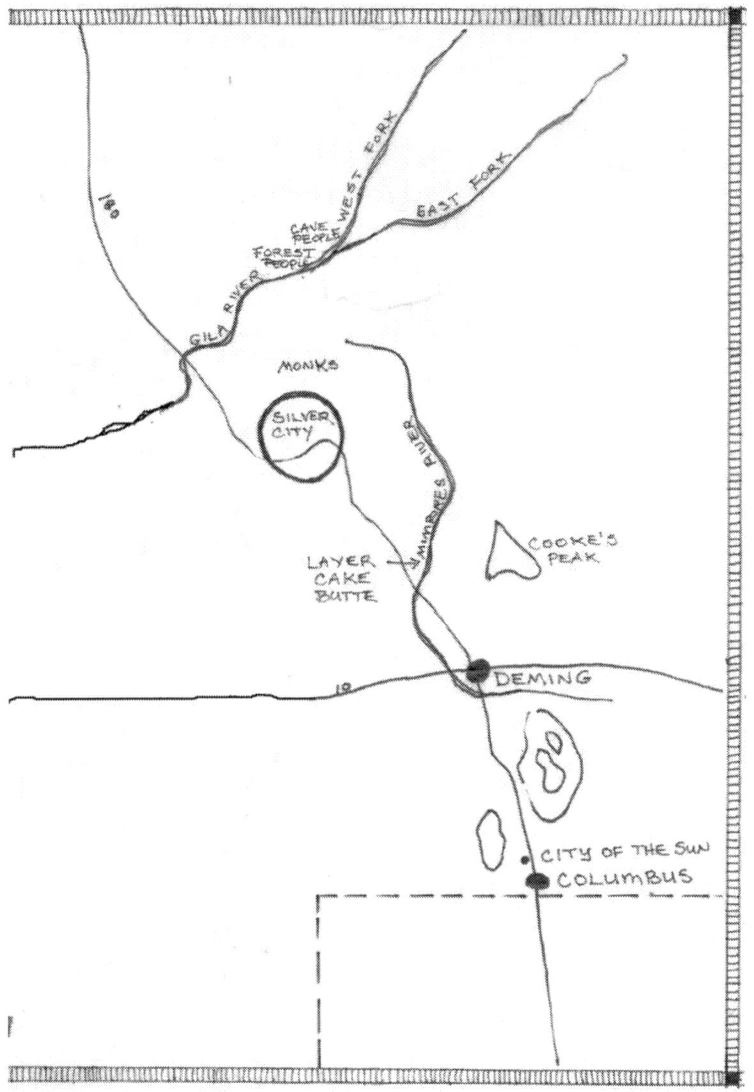
180
WEST FORK
EAST FORK
CAVE PEOPLE
FOREST PEOPLE
GILA RIVER
MONKS
SILVER CITY
MIMBRES RIVER
COOKE'S PEAK
LAYER CAKE BUTTE
DEMING
10
CITY OF THE SUN
COLUMBUS

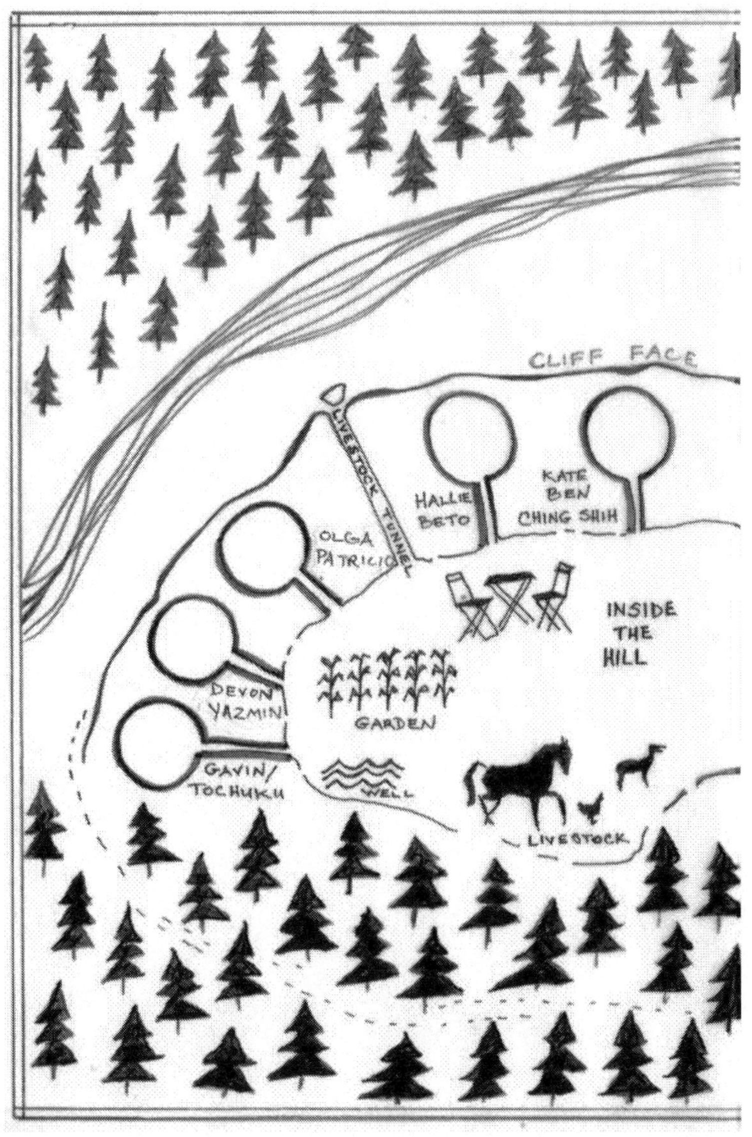
CLIFF FACE
LIVESTOCK TUNNEL
HALLIE
BETO
KATE
BEN
CHING SHIH
OLGA
PATRICIO
INSIDE
THE
HILL
DEVON
YAZMIN
GARDEN
GAVIN/
TOCHUKU
WELL
LIVESTOCK

VICTORIO
JOE
JEANNE/
FRANK
GILA RIVER
LAKSHMI'S
CAVE

12

Weeding is not my favorite pastime, but it's really important if you want a good harvest in the fall. Three weeks after first crossing paths with Victorio, Devon and I crouched in the rows of new zucchini and yellow crook-necked squash, tugging at the invasive little miscellaneous sprouts of plants we did not want to compete with the new squashes. New Anasazi beans climbed the graceful latticework of narrow willow shoots standing between the neatly mounded rows. The mountain sun beat steadily onto our bare arms, legs and faces, darkening my skin to a pecan wood shade and multiplying Devon's already considerable freckle population. I swiped the sweat from my dripping brow, accidentally smearing the dirt from my hands across my face. A fat mosquito perched on my forearm and I slapped haphazardly at it, leaving a blotch of blood along with more mud. The rains had been coming regularly, forming and sustaining the small puddles in which the mosquitoes multiplied.

"Aren't these beautiful!?" Devon asked, rust eyes

gleaming, nodding towards the burgeoning growth. She yanked off her cotton baseball cap and wiped her brow with the sleeve of her threadbare "Let me be perfectly queer" t-shirt, her short salt-and-pepper hair crowning her head like a porcupine's spines. Devon radiated relentless enthusiasm about gardening, and about most other things too, so I enjoyed her company even if I did not particularly care for the work. Devon's presence nearly always improved my own outlook. I wished I possessed her persistently jovial orientation, but short of that I felt grateful that hers rubbed off onto me when in close proximity.

"Yes, they are beautiful..." *Whack!* I popped another blood engorged mosquito on my shoulder.

"Well," Devon sat back with a satisfied sigh, "we've done a good job. Let's get cleaned up. We'll have time to rest before our meeting."

We strode up the rise to the doorway that led into her cave home, Devon still with a spring in her step, me dragging my feet as if they were made of oak boles.

After an exquisitely long shower and a change into clean clothes I felt a lot more human. Devon had disappeared for a nap after her own shower into the bedroom she shared with her wife, Yazmin. I flopped onto the comfy couch in their living room, closing my eyes and drifting off, my sore muscles relaxing into the blissfully soft cushions.

I had felt overwhelmed when I first came to live with the "Cave People"—the term they used for themselves. After being completely alone for so long, over a year, then to be suddenly surrounded by so many other personalities, it was a bit much for me. I would mix up the new people's names, or get confused about who had what skills and knowledge. Everyone showed me a lot of patience, and seemed genuinely glad to have me. Still, sometimes I had to walk away by myself and just sit by the river, or go hunt rabbits or other small game. At first Jeanne hovered over me a lot when I did this, asking over and over if I was okay, but after a while she started believing that I just needed some space sometimes. As I got to know people, bit by bit, I felt more relaxed and less overstimulated by all the chatter and activity.

Each of us were expected to learn skills from each other. It was foolish to rely only on the expertise of one person for certain sources of food, how to maintain our solar electrical systems or for other crucial kinds of knowledge. Not to mention the fact that it took the labor of more than one person to keep up with some jobs. Like a garden big enough to feed us all, for instance. Yazmin shared Devon's enthusiasm for gardening, although she had been an anthropologist for the Forest Service, specializing in pre-colonization social systems. Everyone had specialties and subspecialties that contributed to our tiny community somehow or another.

Noah, Jeanne's son, was the building maven so he worked closely on any new construction, or improving on what had already been done. Gavin had been a school teacher as well as a biologist for the Forest Service, so he was in charge of teaching Olga and Patricio's adopted children, and would do the same for the younger ones when they grew old enough. Tochuku, our resident technological genius, always combined his gardening day with meeting days in order to keep the interruptions of this other work to a minimum. During the summer everyone worked in the garden, gathered wild foods, hunted or prepared the food for storage, in addition to whatever else they did.

Kate, the goat lady, took care of the goats and chickens and Jeanne knew all about local plants for food, medicine and other uses, just as they both had before the virus. Jeanne's cave included an infirmary where she treated the rest of us for everything from sprained ankles to headaches to serious flus.

I was the librarian.

It was my job to locate information needed by the others and to generally familiarize myself with the contents of the library. I loved my job, especially since it gave me an excuse to spend time in the quiet presence of the books, and away from the bustling activity of the Cave People. My mom, and her mother, Grandma Sita, had transmitted their love of books and learning to me by way of their own focused enthusiasm. I felt Sita's presence in her cave strongly and, by extension, my mother's presence too. I knew they would both be proud of me for taking the role of librarian in our little settlement.

We came together as a whole group four times a month, the lunar month, since the Gregorian calendar we had all used before the virus held little use or meaning to us. The moon was nearly always clearly visible in our desert sky. New moon, first quarter, full moon, last quarter. About once a week.

At our meetings we planned the next week's work, figured out who would be learning what skills from whom and generally checked in with each other. In such a small community it would be easy to think that we didn't need such meetings but there's a lot that can be missed in each other's lives if we didn't check in deliberately. The Cave People had eight years in which to develop their ways of sustaining our small hamlet and they were good at it. But there were differences too.

"There are materials we could use to live better, to *do* more," said Tochuku in his deep, rich, Nigerian lilt at our late spring, first quarter, meeting. We had gathered in Jeanne's massive living room, discussing the possibility of a trip to Silver City to scavenge electronic parts and other needed equipment. Tochuku had been in charge of all our technological needs so it was his idea.

"Better? How *much* better? Enough better to risk being caught, or followed back here?" returned Olga, sapphire eyes flashing like winter lightening.

"Our current systems will wear out if we don't replace wiring and other components now and then," said Tochuku simply.

"The problem is, you don't really care what happens to us," said Olga, gesturing with one hand to the rest of us. "You just want to tinker with your electronics."

"This will help all of us," Tochuku's eyes blazed now too. "Why can't you understand that?"

Yazmin rose from her place next to Devon on the couch to her full Amazon-like height and raised her hands, facing the two, "Hold on, hold on" she said, pumping her palms, trying to calm them. "Let's see if we can figure something out." She looked down at the combatants sitting in their chairs, conveying an authoritative effect even as she spoke in soothing tones.

Tochuku sat back in his seat, massaging the side of his cleanly shaved head as if trying to rub away his exasperation. Olga eyed Yazmin warily, waiting for her to continue.

"We can talk about this, okay?" asked Yazmin, looking back and forth between the two.

Chastised, the debaters maintained strained but compliant silence while the rest of us sat listening to the exchange, waiting to add our own thoughts.

"Tochuku, how can you do this without taking too many risks? Without being followed back here? Can you?" asked Yazmin.

"If Frank and Ching Shih come with me, we could travel quickly and quietly. We could be there and back in two weeks or less—I know *exactly* where to look!"

Olga looked dubious.

"What do you think?" Yazmin asked, looking around at the rest of us.

"I'm game. I've traveled most of the route enough times. There really isn't much between here and there. We'll just have to get in and out of town as quickly as possible. That's the risky part," said Frank.

"I'll go. I think we can do it without being seen. If Tochuku knows exactly where we are going, we can keep our time in town to a minimum," agreed Ching Shih.

Gavin glanced at Olga, shrugging apologetically, "I'm sorry Olga, I understand your concerns. I think those are valid. Still, we could use the materials. What we have is bound to deteriorate over time. I could sure use some lab equipment for my research on the local plants and animals. We know the weather has changed here somewhat in the last fifteen years or so but we don't know exactly how much, and how it will affect the available foods, and what we can grow, down the line."

"Think about it. We can't afford to lose anyone. Anyone *else*. We need each other. *All* of us," Beto said heavily, contrary to his usual joking manner. He reached for Hallie's hand as he spoke. Hallie remained silent, studying the floor.

The smaller children, Uma, Sid and Rose, played quietly with their wooden toys on the floor, nearby. The older children, Zoe, Walter and Thomas, sat at the massive dinner table working on the homework that Gavin had given them that afternoon. Even the children sensed the tension in the room and avoided drawing the adults' attention.

"We only need that stuff if we think what we have here isn't enough," threw in Noah. "But it *is* enough. We don't need all that technological stuff. We've got water, heat, food. We only use the electricity for lights and some small equipment now and then, but we could do without it just fine."

As if reluctant to contradict her son, Noah, Jeanne spoke so softly I strained to hear her, "Not if we ever want to communicate with others. We have no idea what's going *on.* We don't know who's out there, where they are, or what they're doing. We learned a lot just from hearing Lakshmi's story. But we really need to know a lot more. If they can even find just a radio, we'd be able to find out *something.*"

"There's so few of us, all it would take is the wrong person, or people, following you back...," said Noah.

"Actually, we need more people. We don't have enough people for the long term. We're just lucky we lasted this long," put in Yazmin.

"What?! Now we're talking about bringing people *back*?" Olga shook her head at Yazmin. "I have *children* to think of!" Patricio nodded his head in agreement with his wife.

"No. I didn't mean..." Yazmin amended quickly, "I mean, not right *now,* but sometime we're *going* to have to think about that. We'll at least have to have friendly relationships with other groups. We don't have to all live together, but we do have to have more people to collaborate with.

"Look, we keep coming back to this discussion." Yazmin continued, "I don't think it's going to go away. I know there are risks, so the question is can we find a way that Tochuku, Frank and Ching Shih can go without being seen? They're right that we don't know what's going on elsewhere, and maybe they can find out. And our energy systems *will* need to be maintained. The stores of electrical and technological equipment could be all scavenged already but if they aren't we need to get to them ourselves soon. Sure, we can live without them, but do we want to?"

"You know, if we know more about what is going on in

the area, we can better protect ourselves. We do need *information*," added Frank, hands lifted at the argument he saw coming. "I know that means taking *risks* too, but we can't protect ourselves from something we don't see coming. Ching Shih and I can escort Tochuku while scoping out what else is going on out there along the way."

Olga pinned Tochuku with her picadillo stare. "Do you promise me that you will not tell anyone about this place, where we live?" She glanced at Frank and Ching Shih, indicating that she included them in her question.

Tochuku shifted uncomfortably in his seat, looking back at her, then nodded. Frank and Ching Shih nodded too.

Ching Shih added, "Of course. I would not risk what we have here."

Yazmin looked around the room, gauging dissent.

Noah shrugged, resigned. Beto, arm around Hallie, said nothing.

Ching Shih and Frank were charged with the community's security so that might have swayed Olga and the other ones with reservations about the expedition, at least enough for it to go forward. Our security team had done a great job for us so far, so there was plenty of reason to trust their judgment. Tochuku was clearly so focused on the supplies he needed to further his work that he genuinely seemed unconcerned about the risk of such a trip. The group may not have trusted our safety to him but they did trust Frank and Ching Shih, so it was a go.

My home, Sita's cave, was far enough away that I usually stayed with Victorio and Grandpa Joe, since they had several spare bedrooms and I knew them best. One room I claimed as my own, bringing a couple of Sita's quilts, clothes and even a few of her paintings. Surrounding myself with these familiar belongings made me feel like she was close, looking over me.

Grandpa Joe had only remembered the existence of the library after I had mentioned it to him, which is why even though they knew about Grandma Sita's cave the group didn't use it. Wise as he was, between advancing age and possible damage to his brain from the virus, Joe's memory just wasn't the same as before.

The others were very happy to learn of the library. Each home had some books since after the virus but all of those had been read by everyone in the eight years that had passed and most were thrilled to have so much new reading material. In addition to its entertainment value, the library would help us to survive, even thrive.

I returned home to the library about once a week, staying a night or two. As lonely as I had been before, and glad to be welcomed into the arms and homes of the Cave People, I also enjoyed some quiet time alone with my books. I carried a list of requests for books from the others on my trips.

Jeanne consumed all the books on herbalism and on ancient low-tech health and wellness systems like acupuncture and Ayurveda. She also studied anatomy and texts on surgery. Our library contained a huge section on building which nearly made Noah swoon when he saw it.

Gavin, our resident biologist, stood staring, shaking his head in wonder at the selection of books on local flora and fauna.

As I stood quietly to the side while he communed with these offerings, he said, awe in his voice, "This is going to make my work so much easier. I won't have to try to remember what's supposed to be out here, it's all *written down."*

He paused to read some more of the titles, then spotting the stack of notebooks I thought he might actually weep with joy. "You have paper? Paper to write on?"

"Yes, and pens too," I said, pulling open the drawer to show him.

"I can take notes," he whispered. "Notes."

And that he did. Gavin used the notebooks and pens to keep detailed records of what he observed in the species of plants and animals in our ecosystem, pursuing this objective with the same kind of zeal Devon showed in the garden. No one knew how things would change, what plants and animals would continue to thrive, which wouldn't, and how we might need to adapt over time. Plus, now Gavin no longer had to compose all his lessons for the older children from memory, since our library contained textbooks from elementary through college level. We needed a good teacher to help the children get up to speed, and Gavin was that teacher. In addition to his love of biological research, he had a passion for passing on knowledge of all kinds to the next generation. His patient ear and thoughtful way of speaking showed that he genuinely cared for each student as individuals too.

The parents of the youngest children—Jeanne, Frank,

Hallie and Beto—all made constant use of the children's section, in addition to anything that appealed to them personally. Every so often one of them would come with me to raid our store of children's books, leaving with a satchel they could barely carry.

The older children, Walter, Zoe and Thomas, were escorted regularly by Patricio and Olga and encouraged to pick a few that appealed to them. Their excitement at the selection was infectious and I felt thrilled to be able to encourage their healthy craving. Children throughout time have always loved a good story, fiction or true to life, as much as anything else in the world.

While she made good use of the books on animal husbandry, Kate loved the fiction section best of all. I could swear that reading about the troubles and triumphs of imaginary characters eased the pain of her own trials. She seemed steadier and more upbeat as she made her way through the selection.

Tochuku wanted to know if there were any books or other information stored in electronic form but I found none. No electronic readers, no DVDs, no audio CDs and certainly no flash drives, one of which could contain almost as much as our whole library of books. I could only assume that it just hadn't occurred to Grandma Sita, since she had never been very big on computers herself. Despite his disappointment at this oversight, Tochuku devoured the science texts like a man starved. While the others only requested one or two books at a time, Tochuku usually read five a week. He also used the notebooks and pens for detailed notes.

My cave was much farther from the others for a reason. The information in the library could not be replaced. If the community was found, it would be especially important to future generations that it be preserved. Everything we did came from knowledge and understanding carried by people and inside of books. Sita and Grandpa Joe had wanted to minimize the risk that the library would be discovered if any of the other caves were found.

Whenever I walked into the library I felt the way I had facing the ice cream section in the grocery store freezer as a little girl. I had a very hard time deciding which ones to pick and which to leave. I wanted to consume them all at the same time. I walked slowly down each aisle, running my hand across the spines of the books, scanning the titles, the smell of paper and leather bindings heavy in the air. Our world had become so small since Before. Books expanded that world immeasurably.

If I had just finished a book I chose a new one, if I was still reading my last book I would consider which one I should take next. Was I in the mood for a swashbuckling pirate story? A mystery? A romance? I went wherever my literary hunger pangs took me. I simultaneously couldn't wait to read all the fiction in it and dreaded coming to the last book. I was a glutton for stories.

The non-fiction section represented to me all that had come before, all that humanity had learned to date, the mistakes we made and the triumphs we had celebrated over the millennia. It seemed immense, to try to understand even a little of every field we had explored: mathematics, biology, geology, architecture, art, social sciences, how to make shoes from plant fibers, which mushrooms were edible and which would kill a person—there literally was no end to what we had learned and done. There was no way one person could understand, much less expand upon, all that knowledge.

But there was more to it than that.

I found only one un-shelved book when I first entered the library, left on the closest table as a message to whomever entered the library first. A history book, describing in great detail the famous library of Alexandria, Egypt. That library, destroyed two millennia ago, after having served as a center of learning for hundreds of years, had stored the accumulated knowledge for thousands of miles around.

During its height royal agents were given ample money and the task of buying and collecting as many scrolls (because that's the form books came in then) as they could, on any topic by any author. Books that came in on ships were confiscated and copied by the library's scribes. The copies were returned to their owners and the library kept the originals.

Scholars from all around were enticed into staying with the promise of being fed and housed, and also given time to pursue their own interests. Their only assigned task was to teach what they knew to students along the way. The library housed anywhere from 40,000 to 400,000 books. They represented the best, most complete knowledge on every subject in that part of the world at the time.

But it came to be in ruins, gradually during some periods of time, and suddenly at others, including destruction by fire during Julius Cesar's civil war in 48 BC. Because of the destruction of the Library of Alexandria, about ninety percent of the knowledge it had housed was lost to later generations. Grandma Sita had left this book to inform the finder of the importance of the library to future generations, and as a warning to keep it safe at all costs.

I learned that it was only very recently that the kinds of libraries I had loved as a child, and were found in most towns and every city in much of the world, had only been common for a hundred years or so before the virus came. We had gained so much in such a short time. It would be terrible to lose it again.

One day, soon after the group agreed that Tochuku, Frank and Ching Shih would take a trip into Silver City, Yazmin accompanied me on my pilgrimage to the library. We rode side by side on our usual mounts, a young roan called Grannie and a pinto called Beans, both named by Beto.

It was late spring, not summer yet, but I felt the evening's condensation evaporate by mid-morning, hinting at the heat to come. The grasses turned from pale avocado green to emerald, their slender leaves reaching hungrily towards the sun and thickening stiffly. A Cooper's hawk swooped lazily on a breeze rising above us as if surveying our short journey through the woods. Tying the horses outside we lugged the slack, empty saddlebags into the cave, to be filled with books as if they were pirate's booty.

"Here's the book, about the library of Alexandria," I said, handing her the hefty volume I had told her about.

"Oh yes, yes! I know this story," she exclaimed. Flipping the pages, she said, "It's easy to take for granted what information we have. You might be too young to remember but the internet made any knowledge available at any time to anyone with a modern phone. But that's all gone now."

She paused, staring at the book in her hand for several long seconds. She looked up at me again, eyes shining, voice low but dense with emotion, "After a brief, magnificent flowering of knowledge all across the world, that brilliance was suddenly extinguished. While this library includes more knowledge than any one of us could hope to digest, what we have here contains only the tiniest fraction of what was available to virtually every one of the eight billion people alive just a few years ago. We are now infants, surrounded by an ocean of ignorance."

Clearly, she had given this a lot of thought, while I was just beginning to grasp the scope of the problem.

"Do you mean that we could sink into a Dark Age again?"

"Yes. In fact, I think it's inevitable to some degree. How bad it gets depends on what we can do to counteract it. It could be much worse than the last Dark Age in Europe since this is happening all over the world at once."

What we did now would affect the trajectory of our descendant's lives in immeasurable ways. Our ability to conserve and spread knowledge accumulated over the millennia would make the difference between my great-grandchildren living lives of ignorance and squalor, or of possibilities fueled by information. We had to do everything we could to restore as much knowledge as possible before weather and the soporific advance of generations made recovery impossible.

"What about cultures that never had books? They had good lives, right?" I asked.

"Yes, that's absolutely true, Lakshmi. It's also true that those cultures all had strong oral traditions. They passed on their knowledge verbally down countless generations. Many so-called "myths and legends" include valuable information."

"Couldn't we just do that then?"

"In a few generations, sure, somewhat. We aren't trained to remember so much. We also don't have the "volumes" of stories and teachings that contain all of what we know. We'd have to create those before we could pass them on," she said. "Much of that sort of knowledge is passed down in a sort of code, condensed in the stories."

"What about the Apaches, Navajos and Pueblo peoples? They have those traditions, right?"

"Yes, but a lot of their knowledge was destroyed, just as surely as the burning of the library of Alexandria, and just as deliberately, by the colonizers from Europe. It happened here in north American, in South America, and also in Central America, where I'm from. We indigenous people still have a lot, but it's not going to be a *substitute* for this knowledge, here," she said, gesturing towards the rows of books. "Besides, their knowledge is specific to their location and culture. We're going to have to decide ourselves what we want to pass on, and how. We are literally going to be constructing new culture, almost from scratch."

Yazmin continued, "Even if our community had access to all the knowledge that had been created, there aren't enough of us to ingest it. The billions of people in the world before the virus came served as storage containers and transmitters of knowledge of all kinds, and not just those who were considered well educated."

Yazmin held my gaze as all that she said sank in.

"You've got an important job, Lakshmi. And not just important to our little group here, now."

As I had once grieved the loss of abundant and varied foods I now grieved the knowledge that no longer had enough people to learn it. We might be able to retain electricity and all it could power—lights, machines, maybe even vehicles, computers and the like. But how would the loss of people who were experts at astrophysics, indigenous forms of agriculture, social systems and mathematics change our collective conception of the world, the universe and ourselves? How could we retain the breadth and depth of understanding, of vision, unless there were people to learn about the countless subjects we had absorbed jointly and who passed on that learning?

On top of that, as I had scanned the non-fiction books, I realized that a lot of them were completely beyond my ability to understand. I was familiar with the Periodic Table of the Elements but I didn't understand the book that described using the various plants or minerals to create those in their pure forms, much less what I might do with those substances. I loved the book on the basics of aviation but we didn't have a book on how to actually build an airplane. As much as I treasured what our small library contained, it was obvious that there were huge gaps too.

Nevertheless, much of what humanity had done, thought, and created was intimated in those books. Our library didn't contain all the information generated by humanity. But it did contain the seeds of that knowledge, enough that we wouldn't have to start completely from scratch as we rebuilt human society. On the one hand we needed more people to learn the information and pass it on, but on the other hand it was risky to let others know where we were, and especially about this library.

Very few people had come across the cave community in the eight years since the virus. That's how limited was the population in the general area, and how remote the caves, deep in the Gila. Most of the Cave People believed that others would inevitably come, however. That's why they had agreed to stay hidden from any new people who came to the area until they had proven that they were not a threat, and that they could care for themselves. It hadn't occurred to them that any of them might actually *know* such a new arrival. They assumed that anyone specifically connected to that community would have made it there soon after the virus had passed. That's why they had debated my own appearance so heatedly. During the first community meeting held after my arrival with Victorio they amended the agreement so that if someone in the group knew the person who had shown up they could advocate for their inclusion in our community—or recommend against it.

13

When I first found out about the Cave People I was stumped about how they had been so invisible to me for a whole year. Even though the first cave past mine was a couple of miles upstream, how did they know I wouldn't come that way and see their tracks? Or hear the goats baaa-ing and the chickens clucking? Notice the *garden* for instance?

And then I saw where the goats, chickens and garden were kept.

The hillside into which their cave entrances were set formed a half-circle around the nearly vertical, rocky slope, forming a large, hidden, fully enclosed oblong bowl on the side opposite the entrances from the river. This hidden bowl held deep springs, both hot and cold, which provided the water to the caves. A well had been built near the center of the bowl long before the virus, sporting a hand pump to draw up cold water, mostly used for the animals and garden.

The goats, chickens and horses were corralled at one end of the bowl, and the garden was closer to the other end, watered via a hose. Each of the caves upriver from mine hosted a long hallway from their living and work spaces through the hillside and into this central bowl. By design, only one tunnel had been built before they had come to live there, to further protect the springs and the bowl from being discovered too soon. The exterior entrances to each cave were much farther apart from the exits into the bowl, like the ends of bicycle spokes. This construct kept the community as inconspicuous as could be from outside the bowl, while making it easy for them to communicate, work and gather, from the inside. After they had come to live there they built a livestock tunnel that led straight through the hillside.

During the period of my unknowing probation, they took turns watching for me just below the cave closest to mine, Jeanne and Frank's, on the river side, just in case I wandered up there. No one said what they would have done if I had come that far and I didn't ask.

"You guys have been here for *eight years* and not gone to town to see what you could find?" I asked Kate the first night after Tochuku, Frank and Ching Shih had departed on their quest to Silver City. Her pale curls formed an airy nest atop her head which bobbed as she kneaded fragrant bread dough in a firm, steady rhythm. While Ching Shih was gone I would stay with Kate and help her with the goats, chickens and Benjamin.

"Oh, yeah, sure we did. It didn't go that well," her voice

quavering as if reluctant to discuss the matter. *Knead, knead, knead...*

I looked at her, raising my eyebrows inquisitively as I chopped a juicy white onion for the stew we were having for dinner. Kate had already tucked Benjamin into bed.

"Well, the group was ambushed on their way back," Kate continued, less tentatively, "They had horses loaded with tools, spools of wire and the like." Kate paused, deep in thought as she broke the dough into half and set the spongy blobs to rest on a wooden cutting board. She looked up at me, eyes shining with sadness. "It was Noah, Beto and Michael, Hallie's boyfriend, who went. Noah and Beto made it away but not without losing the tools and all. The thieves killed Michael in the fray."

I stared at Kate. No one had mentioned that Hallie had lost someone *after* the virus. Not even Hallie.

Kate continued quietly as she plucked a head of garlic from a bowl, popping off several cloves to mince, "So everyone forgot about such forays until just lately. We just concentrated on making our little hamlet as good as possible.... Oh, yes, and Uma isn't Beto's child, not technically. Michael and Hallie didn't even know she was pregnant when he left."

So that explained why they were debating the trip so much. Having come even farther by myself I had been having a hard time understanding why it was such a big deal, but now I knew. None of the members of this tiny community were expendable, not practically or emotionally. Every risk was a big one, when it included the potential loss of three of our own.

"What else don't I know? What else has happened since you've been here?"

Kate looked down at her hands holding the knife poised against the garlic. Sighing deeply, she resumed both chopping and speaking.

"Well, let's see...Olga lost a baby. She went into labor nearly full term but it was stillborn, dead. A little boy. I helped with her delivery but there was nothing to be done. It's a good thing she had the other children to care for or I think she might never have recovered. She's a natural at mothering that's for sure. Fierce as a mama bear, and tender as an ewe."

We took turns folding piles of colorful chopped vegetables and herbs into the stew in silence, while Kate tried to remember more. Setting down her wooden stirring spoon she wandered around lighting candles as the dark settled outside our small windows. I picked up our mugs of mint tea, placing them at either end of the coffee table where Kate joined me while the pot simmered fragrantly on the stove.

"Benjamin was still real sharp for a long time after the virus. He was a huge help bringing people together, working together. We were all so scared and traumatized. Somehow he knew how to help us sort out our differences, and figure out how to live together without anyone trying to dominate the rest of us. It was a hard time. I doubt we'd get along as well as we do now without all he did at the beginning. But he's changed a lot in the last couple of years. Maybe had some small strokes. He just seems to live in another world now, spaced out all day, having to be reminded to eat and helped into bed."

I had known Benjamin as a friend of Grandma Sita's. Back then he had been a natural leader in the community, a dynamic force. He often came up with ideas about things that could be done to make life in the village better, from coordinating rides to town, or organizing a work party to fix someone's roof or whatever. Instead of the outgoing fellow I remembered, I found a quiet man who stared into space most of the time, as if deeply engrossed in a riveting movie. He usually only spoke when spoken to face-to-face and when the speaker used simple, clear sentences.

"How did Tochuku and Ching Shih end up here? I mean, from *Nigeria* and *Hong Kong*?" I was having a hard time imagining it.

"Tochuku had come here to go to school at WNMU, where your mama taught, then he transferred over to Las Cruces to get a Ph.D. He had won some national awards even before then so some of us had already heard of him, through the papers. It was rumored that Sandia and Los Alamos labs were competing for him before he started his PhD program. He was that good. He came camping with four friends from school, to show them the Gila. They came out of the forest just as the virus was exploding in the village and the campgrounds. He was the only one of his group who survived. When he realized that the virus was everywhere on Earth he figured the chances of him making it home to Abuja were pretty slim.

"Benjamin was the one who checked the campgrounds and rounded up Tochuku, Ching Shih and the three kids whose grandpa had died. Tochuku joined us but kept to himself mostly, at first, constantly immersed in his work developing and maintaining our solar energy and water systems and other tinkering. He wasn't unpleasant, he just doesn't have as much interest in people as in his work. He and Gavin moved in together in the farthest cave upstream. Gavin could get along with anyone but I think Tochuku liked the idea of living with Gavin since he's also a scientist, a biologist. They speak the same language, in a way.

"Ching Shih came as a *tourist...*," she emphasized the word "tourist" and raised her eyebrows at me, chiding me for not considering that possibility myself, since the area had always hosted visitors from all over the world, "...camping in the same campground as Tochuku and his friends. I guess you know she was a detective on the police force and a hot-shot competitor in the martial arts world there in Hong Kong."

"So what's the bigger plan? For the community? For the future?" I asked.

"Well, that's been a sore point. Some feel that we should stay as isolated as possible, others think we should try to find others. Some want to expand our technology, others don't."

"It feels so good here. Safe. Comfortable. Just the way it is. You know?" I said.

"Yes. It sure is. Still, what's going to happen as the kids, children, get older? Not a lot of choices for mates if they stay here. And after another generation or so there would only be cousins to marry. Or they'd have to leave here to find someone."

Good point.

"So maybe we don't have to find others right away but some day..." my thoughts trailed off.

We sipped our tea in silence, considering.

Then Kate said, "There's a chance that someone out there is rounding up captives, as slaves. Some of us are afraid we'll be attacked, maybe taken the way you were. We gotta find out who's out there and what they're doing, so we know if we need to protect ourselves."

I could see the sense in that.

A few days later I went to Grandpa Joe's and Victorio's. Kate had given me the day and night off so I could sleep in my bed at their place. I found Joe sitting at the dark oak table in their kitchen, sipping some tea and reading a book he had gotten from the library, *The Story of 'B'*. Joe looked up from his book, laying it face down on the table. His eyes lit up and his mouth twitched into the slight smile that meant he was very happy. He usually wore a poker face, even when he was feeling pretty pleased.

"Victorio's out hunting with Beto...want some tea? There's still plenty in the pot."

Taking a chair, I nodded yes to the tea. "It was you I was hoping to see actually."

He turned his face from the mug he was filling, one eyebrow lifted questioningly.

"I'm wondering how the Apaches dealt with the people coming into their territory, I mean, like right here."

Both eyebrows lifted.

"Well, we didn't exactly win that one did we?" he answered wryly, shaking his head as he sat back down on his chair, handing me my tea.

"No, well, I mean I guess not...But why not? What did they do wrong?"

Joe sat for a moment, considering.

"You know Lakshmi, I'm pretty sure the only thing we did wrong was not have as many people or guns."

He paused again.

"You see, there were so many coming and so many more that would keep coming. Compared to that there were only a few of us. And they didn't want to live with us. They wanted to live *without* us. They called us "savages" and thought we had no right to exist. Just like they thought the wolves and bears and coyotes and mountain lions didn't have a right to exist."

"But what *happened*?" I had heard enough from mama and daddy to know the Apaches were here first, and that they were treated badly, killed and put on reservations, but the rest was fuzzy.

Joe sighed deeply.

"First the Spanish came and took our people as slaves, way down south to Mexico. They were always a thorn in our side, though we did trade with them some. Later the Americans came here for the silver and copper. We didn't like that because we believed it was wrong to dig into the earth so much. They told their government we were interfering with their mining so the government sent soldiers to run us off and kill us. Geronimo resisted them here, like the Victorio that our Victorio is named after. Geronimo was born here, up the Middle Fork of the Gila River, and Victorio just to the east. But even Geronimo gave in at the end, and the leader Victorio, killed. Most of us were sent off to reservations, some to prison. Some hid in the mountains in Mexico."

"What if people come here?"

"Well, that could happen, though we *are* pretty far from any big town. It is a good place to live for sure. We're protected somewhat by the caves and the bowl. But it means we can't stray too far either."

We sat in silence for a few minutes, thinking.

"What's your book about?" I asked, lifting my chin towards the book on the table.

"Oh, I guess it's about how we got into this mess. Or, you know, it was a mess before the virus came. I suppose the virus kind of settled the matter a bit. Got rid of the problem, or most of the ones causing it."

"What do you mean?"

"Well we pretty much knew that something bad was going to happen, push things over the edge. Everything was polluted, the animals were going extinct all over the world, there were too many people everywhere and more being born. We were causing the world to heat up with our cars and other machines. The hurricanes and tornadoes were getting real bad. And the wildfires were whipped up out of control. The icecaps were melting...."

He stared into his tea mug, as if seeing it all in the steam that arose. I had learned that when Grandpa Joe stopped talking that he was often letting his next sentences collect in his mind before speaking them, so I said nothing.

"We don't know what caused the virus. Could've been

any number of things, maybe an ancient virus come back to life after the thawing of the glaciers, or something mutated. Or maybe even something man-made. But now we have less than a billion people, at least that's what they figured before the media went down. Here, this area, about one hundred miles around, we probably have about three thousand, or at least we did right after the virus. Who knows how many killed each other in the panic afterwards, or of their own stupidity? Most people couldn't even grow a little corn and the grocery stores were used up in a few days. I just hope whoever made it this long keeps to themselves. Away from us. And then, we have to be sure we don't repeat the mistakes of the past. We're going to have to rebuild. We've gotta make sure we do it right."

Just then Victorio arrived, sweaty and dust covered. His game bag bulged with rabbits and he held a long string of fish in one hand. His eyes met mine and he broke into a broad grin.

"Hey hey! Looks who's here...I thought maybe you had forgotten about us here while you're off having fun with Kate and the goats."

"Forget *you* maybe, but never Grandpa Joe!"

He grimaced in mock pain, hand to his heart, as if stung there. "Very funny Lak," turning to Joe he added, "I'm going to put the rabbits in the cool room for now and fry up these fish for lunch. After I get cleaned up."

Victorio set the fish in the sink and disappeared down a dark hallway with the rabbits. I got up and set to work scaling and filleting the fish, putting the remains in the compost bucket by the sink. Just as I pulled the large cast iron skillet from its hook on the wall Victorio re-emerged from the hallway, wearing clean jeans, no shirt and rubbing his long, loose hair with a towel. Draping the towel over a chair, he sidled up next to me at the counter, pulling salt, pepper and sunflower seed oil from the cupboard above. He smelled fresh and clean. Something about his nearness made me uneasy so I ceded the cooking to him and returned to my seat beside Joe. Victorio took pride in his cooking ability so it was better to give him his space anyway.

"I'll jerk the rabbit meat and take it to the storeroom at Jeanne and Frank's," said Victorio. Joe nodded in acknowledgment.

Each cave had some unique feature to contribute to the whole community, and Jeanne and Frank's place sported an enormous pantry deep in the center of the hill for dried, canned, pickled things and food otherwise suitable for longer term storage. We kept what we needed for the short term in our own kitchens.

When the fish was nearly done Victorio pulled a waxed fabric wrapper of cooked onions, squash and pinon nuts out of the refrigerator and set them around the edges of the fish to heat. Joe read his book while I set the table.

After I had shoveled enough of Victorio's delicious fare into my mouth, I slowed my eating in favor of posing questions. I had a lot of questions for everyone.

"Do you think it was a good idea that Tochuku and the others left to find more materials?"

When in Joe's presence Victorio nearly always waited for him to respond first unless addressed directly.

"Well Lakshmi, us Apaches lived just fine without the solar electricity or radios and all that for thousands of years before the White Eyes showed up. Sure, it's nice to be able to turn a knob on the stove and cook food, but it's not that hard to cook using a campfire, or woodstove, and use candles for light. There's a big difference between a want and a need." Their kitchen featured an old-fashioned wood cook stove right next to the electric one Victorio had just used.

"So I don't really care about that," he paused for a couple of beats, "but it's also true that there are others around so it would be good to know who is where, and what they're up to. We don't want to be taken by surprise." Grandpa Joe dug back into his plate.

Victorio said, "After they get back from looking for electronic supplies, Beto and I are thinking about scouting out the area, in all directions. See what we can see."

"Yeah, you gave us some good information about what you saw on your way here. Sounded like there are some folks around, but they're just keeping to themselves. Except those guys from the compound you said were going to Silver City," said Joe.

The thought of riding out to search the area made my stomach clench a little. Now that I was here, I was scared to leave. I didn't know if I would ever stop being afraid of being taken back to Darian's, certainly not before the regular nightmares I had about him stopped.

Victorio said, "We've been settled in for a long time now. It took us awhile to get over the shock of what happened, to figure out how to work together. You know, like a real community. I think that your coming here made some of us think more about what's going on outside. Also, the fact that some wouldn't let us bring you in right away, and now they see how wrong that was, how scared they were for no reason, well, it's made some of us think we shouldn't be so passive, so fearful. We should know what's going on and think about our future."

After lunch Victorio and I prepared the rabbit meat for drying, working at the long table in the "cool room," set deep in the hill with no windows. Above us blazed two bright lights hung from the ceiling so we could see what we were doing. A good thing, since Victorio kept his skinning and butchering knives razor sharp. We worked together like this often enough that we had settled into an efficient routine. Victorio skinned, I deboned, then we both sliced the meat into thin strips, salting and spicing it for drying.

As had become typical, Joe went to bed early and Victorio and I stayed up together. I was glad to have his company and his friendship even though I still felt some distance from him. I understood that Victorio had tried to see me against the group's wishes, which was a risk to his own safety, but it still left a raw feeling under my skin when I thought of how close I came to starving to death, while he sat up here, well fed.

We were sitting on the couch, a stack of books next to me on the end table. Victorio picked up some strands of yucca fibers from a pile on the coffee table to twist into thin cordage, twine, for everyday use.

"Are you reading anything good? That you could read

to me?" Victorio asked.

"You like being read to?"

"Yeah," he said, looking at the floor for a second, "my mom used to read to me. All kinds of stories. I like to read too, I mean, I like to read to *myself*, but it's nice to be read to by someone else sometimes."

I laughed, following his lead to ignore the pain in his voice when speaking about his mother. "Well, of course my dear, you are one of our most *accomplished* readers," I said, in a mock officious tone.

"Yes," I continued in my normal voice, "I've been reading this story about a girl in ancient Russia, who finds she has a magical connection to the 'old powers.' I think you might like it."

"Would you mind? I mean, making cordage isn't really that interesting by itself..." he said with a grin.

"Sure. I used to read to my brother, Seth, and mama and daddy read to us all the time too. I liked it both ways."

So I began.

"It's called, *The Bear and the Nightingale...*"

An hour later my voice began to crack. I finished the chapter I was on and closed the book. Victorio looked up in alarm, "You can't stop now! It was getting so good...."

I laughed, happy that he was enjoying it so much. "I bet that's what you said to your mom when she was tired of reading too."

He smiled, "Yeah, I guess I did."

I leaned back into the couch, my arm brushing his. He looked into my face, as if searching for something.

I stood up.

"I guess I'll get to bed then. Good night!"

I turned towards my room, crossing the distance in five steps, leaving him staring at my back as I disappeared behind the closed door.

14

The day I returned from my stay with Victorio and Joe, Kate and I were making dinner while Benjamin sat at the table, dozing off and on. Occasionally he looked around, bewildered, as if not sure where he was. During one of his more alert moments, he announced, "They found the others, with the big round tents…."

"Which others? And who found them?" Kate asked.

Benjamin scowled, furrowing his brow. "You *know.* Those kind of tents. Like the Chinese use. No wait, not Chinese…you know…."

Kate looked at me and I shrugged.

"Did you have a dream during your nap Benjamin?" I asked.

He turned, frowning at me, eyes clear and bright. "No. I told you. They found those people. With the Mongolian tents…."

"Oh, okay. I'm sorry I misunderstood you Benjamin. It's alright…," I said.

Kate and I exchanged another glance, silently agreeing to let the matter drop. Ben stared intently into space for a few minutes before dozing off again.

The days passed quickly with all the work to be done at Kate's—milking the goats, making cheese, cooking, caring for Benjamin, cleaning and other household chores. In the early evenings, before sunset, the rest of the group visited each other inside the hill to trade stories of the day and generally catch up. The tension grew amongst us the longer Tochuku, Frank and Ching Shih were gone.

One evening, Kate and I had just tucked Benjamin into his bed when he suddenly started talking, after having been silent for a good half an hour. Lying on his back staring at the ceiling as if watching some kind of show, his mouth stretched into a huge, toothy smile, eyes beaming in happiness.

"They're back. They're back! Almost. Almost! So happy. Good kids. They're good kids, those ones. Strong. Smart! Now we can *talk*! Now we'll *know*!" He shut his eyes and his breath deepened towards sleep.

Kate and I kissed him goodnight before leaving him to his dreams, however oblivious he was to our affections.

It hadn't been quite two weeks yet, about the amount of time we thought it should take the explorers to make the trip there and back. No one said it out loud but we were all scared they wouldn't come home. Or that someone would follow them and tell others where we were, or only one or two of them would make it back, like last time. Noah became much more irritable and argumentative. Hallie and

Olga were extra attentive to their children and Beto was unusually quiet. We all avoided going outside the hill unless absolutely necessary.

The day after Benjamin's latest outburst, near dinner time on the thirteenth day since the three had left, they were spotted by Gavin from his and Tochuku's cave farthest upstream. While the riders took their horses through the tunnel built to transfer them from the outside of the hill to the inside of the bowl, Gavin dashed inside of the hill and rang the large metal bell that was used to call everyone together quickly.

Many of us were already filtering into the bowl for dinner. Kate had been the first into the yard, pushing Benjamin in his wheelchair bumpily over the grass. Devon brought a huge salad she had made of colorful vegetables fresh from her garden. Noah emerged with a pot of some kind of hot stew, and Patricio and Olga arrived carrying jugs of cool herb tea, trailed by Zoe, Walter and Thomas. I placed a platter of goat cheese and sacaton bread with the other food on a picnic table near the garden. "Are they back?" Noah asked Gavin, "All of them?"

"Yes, yes! They're all back," said Gavin.

The anxious few who had arrived first relaxed visibly.

Benjamin exclaimed, "Ha ha! Good kids! Such good kids!"

Jeanne sprinted out her door to a tired but happy looking Frank, nearly knocking him over before kissing him long and hard in front of everyone, apparently oblivious to the cheers, clapping and catcalls from adults and giggles from the children. Frank scooped both Sid and Rose into his arms before making his way to sit at a table, smiling so much it looked like his face might split in two.

Ching Shih joined us in her usual reserved manner after dropping her pack at home, receiving our hugs and kisses on the cheek with a shy grin. Tochuku was the last to arrive, looking tired but more content than I had ever seen him. Whatever else had or had not happened I was just glad to see that they had all come back, and no one showed any sign of injury.

After the laughter, hugs and back slapping died down, some sitting and some standing, we all turned our attention to the returned trio, waiting to hear their story.

"Well," began Tochuku in his warm honey lilt, "we had a good trip...." Tochuku had never been the story-telling type, and Ching Shih wore a similarly taciturn demeanor. Turning to Frank, Tochuku asked, "Frank, could you please tell it?" Frank laughed with the rest of us and began the story.

"We did just fine for the first couple of days, sticking to the lower trails so as not to be too visible. We saw some old camps but not any people. Then Ching '*Sharp Eyes*' Shih *(laughter)* spotted what looked like a yurt on a hillside across the valley." Frank was the only one inclined to tease Ching Shih, but she didn't seem to mind.

"She took Tochuku on ahead a bit while I snuck across the little valley, around the downwind side, and up the hill to scope things out. Turns out there was a whole cluster of yurts and tipis by the one we first saw, set around a broad meadow, and protected on the north side by a curving hillside. I counted an even dozen dwellings. Men, women, kids. All ages it looked like. Plus a couple of dogs. There was a tanning rack set up, a big fire pit in the center of the cluster—stuff like that. A little village. I marked the spot on our map so we could be sure to steer clear of it on our way back. And for future reference of course."

"Daddy what's a yurt?" asked Rose, arms around Frank's neck.

"It's like a big round tent. The Mongolian people, in Asia, used them a lot."

Kate and I, standing side by side, exchanged a look.

"Daddy, who were those people?" asked Rose.

"We don't know honey. Just people living. Like us...."

"Did they look like they had been there awhile? Or did the camp seem sort of new?" asked Beto, tugging his sparse black chin hairs, the way he did when he was excited, or nervous.

"Looked like they had been there at least a couple of years. Pretty well settled in. And, oh yeah, I did spot an area on the other side of the hill where it looked like a spring might be, lots of growth there. And a big garden plot nearby. Seemed like they were doing okay."

"Can we go meet those people mama?" young Walter asked his adoptive mother, Olga, who shooshed him.

Frank continued, "We sort of paralleled highway 15 but stayed way west of it so we wouldn't run into anyone there. Kind of rough riding. Then we crossed Cherry Creek and Bear Creek, so we knew we were getting close. We got a good look at Pinos Altos from the ridge before dropping down into that canyon that goes west of it. Definitely people living there still. Saw smoke from fires, plenty of houses still standing. So we cut a wide swath around that, being a lot more careful. We ended up on LS Mesa...." Frank paused to take a drink from his mug of tea.

Warming to the story enough to overcome his inhibition Tochuku added, "Then Frank had the idea to visit the monks at the Benedictine Monastery! On the road from LS Mesa into Silver City. Ching Shih argued with him but he said he had visited there before the virus and thought they would be a good source of information if they were still there. Then they decided," nodding to Ching Shih and Frank, "that just Frank would go, that Ching Shih would stay with me and the horses and Frank would go in by himself." He finished resentfully, "Sometimes they treated me like a child."

Ching Shih responded, "Tochuku, our job was to *protect* you! Protect. You. Get it?" She sat back in her seat arms folded, determinedly making her face impassive again.

"I know, but where I come from a man isn't-—how do you say it here?—*babysat*, by a woman while the other man goes to danger."

"Then maybe you should show up for martial arts practice more often," Ching Shih said shortly.

Raising his eyebrows at them momentarily, Frank picked up the thread, "In any case, I did go to the monastery," seeing Jeanne's hand rise to her mouth and eyes widen, "being *very careful* of course to scope out the place before making myself visible. I just saw a few monks and some other people outside, doing normal chores like cutting firewood, tending goats and working in the garden. So I walked up and knocked on the front door!"

Gasps and astonished laughter broke out in the group, with exclamations of "Oh my god!" and "Noooooo!" along with head shakings.

Frank laughed, eyes sparkling.

Olga, Hallie and Noah, who had completely opposed the trip to begin with, were not enjoying this part of the story as much as the others.

"You promised you wouldn't allow yourself to be seen," Olga's crystal blue eyes glinted.

Noah glowered.

Taken aback, Frank flushed suddenly, "I said we wouldn't allow anyone to *follow us back*. We never told any of them, not one, where we had come from. And we're certain they didn't follow us on the return trip. I circled back around to check that myself."

"They made it back fine," Beto pointed out, abandoning his pre-trip skepticism, then prodded Frank to continue saying, "C'mon! Get back to the story!"

Frank continued, "Wouldn't you know it, my old friend, Brother Matthew opened the door. We had gone to high school together, when we were both partiers...."

"What's a partier daddy?" asked Rose. More laughter.

"Nothing honey, nothing...I went and got the other two and we spent a night there. We got a *lot* of good information there, I tell you. Smartest thing we did," Frank added nodding emphatically.

Tochuku raised an eyebrow at Frank, who grinned and looked down for a second, then looked up again.

"Well, I mean, *almost* the smartest thing...."

"What? What was the smartest thing?" asked Beto.

All three of the travelers broke into wide grins.

"We'll get to that," said Tochuku.

"Anyway," continued Frank, "Brother Matthew told us that right after the virus hit there was a lot of panic in town. The stores were looted of course. There was a lot of people who had mental breakdowns, and in a place with so many guns that had some predictable results. On top of all the people killed by the virus many were shot by people who were scared they weren't going to survive." Frank's voice softened as he stared into the air as if seeing it all in front of him. "A lot of killings happened in the grocery stores, which were stripped really fast. Neighbors who didn't trust each other slaughtered one another. People broke into other people's homes, sometimes shooting, sometimes getting shot. Most of the unbalanced people with guns killed each other or others killed them in self-defense. And, not surprisingly I guess, there were a lot of suicides. It got pretty ugly. Again." Frank's voice trailed off momentarily, "More mass graves."

I felt glad that mama and I had left as soon after Seth and Daddy died as we did. People in the solar community had thought ahead more, so weren't quite as crazy.

"The Monks had been growing a lot of their own food before the virus, and they lived simply anyway," Ching Shih picked up the thread of the story, "so they were in a better position than others right afterwards, though they said that they also lost most of their people to the virus. Matthew said that people came there from town, some to find a safe place, others because they believed that God had brought the virus and they wanted to learn to live lives that would please God from then on. They gained enough people to keep caring for their gardens and goats.

"And, we call the people who live there 'Monks' but they aren't all monks. It's just what we started calling the people at the monastery."

"We rested there a couple of days, and they fed us very well. We decided to leave the horses with the Monks since they made us a lot more visible. Stealth would matter from that point on. The Monks told us the best ways to go into town, and where to avoid," Ching Shih glanced at Olga and Noah, "It's more likely we would have been seen if they hadn't advised us.... They said there are a couple of warlords with compounds, 'Slavers' they call them, like the one Lakshmi came from, with slaves held captive and forced to work. One on the north side of town, and one south."

Ching Shih paused thoughtfully before adding, "The monastery was very beautiful. It reminded me of the Buddhist monasteries a little bit. Simple, built of stone and brick, very peaceful. I noticed a statue of Buddha in one part of the yard, among a flower garden. I asked Matthew about it and he said that it wasn't only Catholics that had come there, but other Christian denominations and people from other religions and spiritual traditions of all kinds. He said he wanted them all to feel welcome, so now it is a place for people from all kinds of backgrounds. Their library has religious texts from many religions."

Frank spoke again, "That's when it became a little sketchy. We walked slowly through the forest, away from the road, checking for signs of people. We had to backtrack and find another way several times because we kept coming to places that looked like people lived in them.

"All we knew up to that point is that Tochuku had some idea where he might find some electronic gear. Stuff for the solar systems, maybe computers, stuff like that.

"The Monks had told us how to get to the university, which did have people living there. The Monks call them 'Uvies.' They said it was pretty well defended. I had thought many times since before we even left that anything of value must have long since been found by others. I honestly didn't think we had much of a chance of coming back with anything we could use. But he seemed so sure, and I thought it would be good to see what was going on anyway, since it's the nearest populated area.

"Anyway, lucky for us, the place that Tochuku wanted to go to was an old maintenance shed at the far northwest corner of the University property, away from the dorms and bigger halls."

At this point in Frank's tale our normally aloof genius, Tochuku, smiled like the Cheshire cat. Ching Shih had a bemused look on her face, shaking her head slightly. Everyone else looked at Frank in silent, rapt, attention.

"We snuck over there in the dead of night," Frank continued, "after holing up for the day in an abandoned house on the north edge of town. Tochuku takes us to this gray cinder block building not much bigger than a double garage. He *pulls a key out of his pants*, sticks it in the doorknob, and turns. Then he uses the key on the dead bolt. And it turns too."

Frank paused to look around at our astonished faces. Tochuku looked like a kid who had gone around to the same houses twice at Halloween and had scored the mother lode of all candy stashes in the process. I had never seen him grin so broadly, white teeth sparkling in the sunlight.

Frank resumed, "We go into the building and it looks just like any other maintenance shed you've ever seen in your life. Weed eaters, shovels, rakes, clippers, garbage bags – stuff like that. But there's one more thing. There is a big wooden panel in the cement floor at the far end of the shed, with a handle on it. Tochuku lifts this panel, and what do you know. There's a wooden ladder leading down beneath this stupid shed.

"Tochuku, you gotta tell this part...," said Frank.

Looking ready to burst, Tochuku said, "Yes, okay. Yes. Well...you know I was going to school in Las Cruces right?" We all nodded.

"Well, before that I went to Western New Mexico University, in Silver City. In fact, I had just moved to Cruces, to start my Ph. D work. I had come back to go camping with my friends, yes, but I had also planned to go to the shed to get the rest of my things to take to Cruces. But I never got the chance of course.

"I found out about this place under the shed because I had gone there to ask the maintenance man to borrow a shovel one day and I saw a guy coming out of that hole. I asked what that was for and he told me that it was where they stored some hardware and that there was a workbench down there as well, but they didn't use it much.

"See, I had been having a hard time because I wanted to do some things that required special, cutting edge equipment, but things got stolen a lot in the dorms. So, I asked the maintenance guys if I could use that place to store some things and to work there. And they said yes.

"I had been learning to use a couple of 3D printers, had some solar projects I was working on, a new compact wind generator, and I had bought a HAM radio like I had as a child. And a brand-new computer. A really good one. With good engineering programs and other design programs installed."

Turning to me Tochuku continued, "And something for our librarian."

"Huh?" I said, baffled. What could he possibly be talking about? What does a librarian need besides books, except for maybe pens, ink and paper to make more?

"I have two hand-held scanners that I bought on a whim. It's the newest technology. You just press the device against the center of the front of a book and it scans and saves every page. They came with readers too. I have two sets, one for you and one for me to keep, maybe to replicate if I can."

The implications of what he was saying sank in bit by bit. He had a computer to design things. He had 3D printers to make things. He had solar equipment, and a wind generator that could be replicated by the 3D printers. And a way to expand my library, if I could find books to scan. I felt thunderstruck by the possibilities

"What's a HAM radio?" Hallie asked.

"It's a kind of radio that you can use communicate with

people anywhere in the world if done right, and they can communicate with you," said Gavin in an awed tone, also processing the possibilities implied by Tochuku's new equipment.

"You mean...," I began, then stopped.

"Yes," said Gavin, "it means we can communicate with others. All over the world possibly. We can find out what has happened elsewhere, not just nearby. At least places where others have HAM radios."

An animated silence settled upon us all as the potentials percolated through our astonished brains. We could increase our electrical output through improved solar and by adding wind generated electricity. The 3D printer could make things that we need, or even just want. And we could find out what was happening in the rest of the world with the HAM radio. In one short, strategic, trip into town Tochuku had increased our community's long-term viability dramatically.

Later that evening after Kate and I had put Benjamin to bed, Kate asked, "Kind of interesting isn't it? What Benjamin said about the Mongolian tents, the yurts?"

"Yeah. Interesting for sure. Has Benjamin ever been known to have intuitions like that?"

"Not that I've ever heard."

15

The next day we all gathered again, taking most of the day off our usual work to discuss the prospects that our new capabilities might afford us. There was a lot of excitement about what we could do with more electricity, Tochuku's engineering programs, the 3D printers and the HAM radio. I was the only one excited about the book scanner.

On top of all of this, the Monks had told them about another group, the Makers, towards the south end of town, who had a lot of technology.

"We could trade with them, information for information, technology for technology," said Tochuku.

"The Monks said that it would be hard, because the Slavers were constantly hunting for new slaves," said Frank. "Although, they did say they didn't go out as much at night. Maybe we could sneak our way over to them. It'd be risky, but, yeah, it could be worth it."

We were all outside, having just enjoyed a dinner of

fresh venison fajitas, garden greens, mesquite flat bread and raspberries that had been picked that morning by Devon.

"What about introducing ourselves to the yurt and tipi people, before we try another trip into town? They're close by, and must not be too aggressive or we would have seen them before now," said Yazmin.

Shaking his head at the ground Noah said, "You know, we have a good situation here, just the way it is. We've lived here for eight years and been just fine without anyone else, and no one else has caused us any trouble. The only person we even worried about was Lakshmi," tilting his head my direction. "I'm glad the trip worked out well but, geez, that doesn't mean we have to stop taking safety in to consideration at *all*!"

"It's just a matter of time before others come," sighed Frank, then chiding, added, "And what are you going to do Noah, stay celibate the rest of your life? Don't you want a family of your own? How's that going to happen if we don't communicate with others?"

Noah scowled but held his tongue.

Speaking with all the authority of her Ph. D in anthropology, Yazmin said, "Isolated groups of our size cannot survive. It's that simple. We *will* die out if we don't join up with others. It's just a matter of when. We don't have to live *with* them but we do have to have friendly relationships with others. Either they come here to meet us or we go there. We can let other's actions determine if, when and how that happens or we can decide ourselves, and make a plan that minimizes the dangers."

No one refuted this.

"What do you propose we do?" asked Gavin, "Just march into their camp and say 'hey, you all want to be friends?'"

Grandpa Joe shook his head. "That'd be a great way to get hurt, or captured."

"No, no, no!" said Yazmin, waving her arms in the air and stalking into the middle of the group.

"We're not going to march in there like we're a bunch of white guys coming from Europe, acting like we own the place." Yazmin flashed a quick sardonic grin, enjoying stirring the pot, then added in a mock serious tone, "No offense of course," nodding to the white guys in the group.

Frank rolled his eyes in feigned annoyance and said sarcastically, "Oh, none taken, of *course*."

Victorio repressed a laugh and Beto shook his head, smirking.

"We need to come up with something more creative, clever, more *safe*." said Yazmin. She scanned the group. "Who can come up with something that won't scare any of them, and make a case why we should be friends?"

The whole group was silent for about a minute when I had an idea.

"What if we left them a note?"

"A *note*?!" said Gavin, shaking his head, face crinkling in comic disbelief.

Some laughed outright, some grinned like they thought I was joking while others were clearly considering the idea.

"Wait, wait, yes, I see...." Devon seemed to be getting the gist. "We write a letter explaining who we are, but not where we live of course. Maybe we give a day and a place to meet, not at their camp and not here either, somewhere in between—kind of like an old-fashioned parlay."

More thoughtful silence, then Victorio added, "Yeah, we could just ask them to send a few people of theirs to talk to a few people of ours. We could have a few others hang back, out of sight, just in case things get sketchy."

I ducked back into Joe and Victorio's place for my notebook and pen while the others fleshed out the idea.

When I came back, they were talking about what should go into the note, and I wrote it all down. I summarized, "We'll tell them how many people we have, and general ages. We'll tell them that we would like to be friends and allies. We would like to trade with them, help them if they need extra help, and get help from them too. We'd also like to socialize once in a while. We will *not* tell them about the caves, the solar, the radio etc."

I looked around at the group, "That about right?" Nods and assenting murmurs all around. "Okay, I'll write this up and show you the final version tomorrow."

I read the following to the group the next evening:

"Dear Neighbors,
Some of us were traveling earlier in the summer and noticed your camp. We are a small group of seventeen adults and eight children. We have been able to live fairly well since the virus but we believe that we cannot survive as a community for more than a generation unless we enter into a cooperative relationship with

others. We also think that we can be of benefit to your group too, for the same reasons. You also appear to have too few people to sustain yourselves for very long. We know that you have no reason to trust us and that you might think that we are slavers looking for an easy way to bring more captives to a compound. We have seen such places and know that they are to be feared. To show that we are trustworthy, we would like you to send a few people of your choosing to meet with just three of our people. We will go to the large meadow about five miles downstream from your camp on the day of the next full moon. It would be a huge loss to our community if we were to lose three adults, so we put our lives in your hands in the hope that we can build a better life for us all."

We decided not to send others to hide in the forest in case the parlay group was ambushed. If these other people were spotted after we had said we would only send three people, then they would reasonably assume it was a trap and the whole plan would backfire. If we wanted to create a trusting relationship with these people, then we had to be trustworthy ourselves. Even if it meant assuming more risk for ourselves.

Frank and Ching Shih would travel to the tent dweller's location and leave a note where it would easily be found. Frank would hang back some distance while Ching Shih would be the one to place the note. Ching Shih was as stealthy as any of our hunters, plus she had the added advantage of being able to defend herself better than anyone else, including Frank, who still consistently lost to her when sparring. Yazmin also pointed out that if she were caught Ching Shih would, ironically, register as less of a threat than any man, and so her captors would be less likely to kill or otherwise harm her.

Then we would wait until a few days before the full moon, which would still be two weeks away when Frank and Ching Shih returned from leaving the message. Ching Shih, Victorio and Noah would serve as our representatives in the parlay. Noah insisted on volunteering, saying that if we were determined to endanger the whole group with these overtures to others then he would at least like to have a part in making sure it went well.

Frank and Ching Shih made the trip to leave the note without incident.

"We had noticed that they came to the spring a lot to haul water so I built a tall cairn right next to it late in the night. I put the letter in between two of the rocks, sticking out near the top. I don't think there's any way they could miss it," explained Ching Shih.

There was much discussion during the next two weeks, in and out of our regular meetings, of what our relationship with the Forest People, as we had begun to call them, might be like. We seemed to have the advantage in terms of our ability to produce and store food without a doubt. What did they have to offer us?

"I could show them how to make cob cottages if they wanted to make permanent homes," said Noah.

"What about sharing our solar equipment, or let them use the wood-working studio?" asked Hallie.

"Bad idea!" said Frank, "we can't let them know about all that we have."

"You mean we're going to be friends with them, and share food and skills, and maybe *people*, but we're not going to tell them about the things that might be the most use to them?" Hallie shook her head, mouth pursed.

"I don't mean that we'll *never* tell them that stuff...," said Frank.

"How will we know what to tell them, and when?" asked Hallie.

I had become more anxious as they talked about what we would share, an inkling of danger tickling the back of my mind. As the inking grew to a full-blown realization I burst out, "The library! We can't ever tell them about the library!"

Everyone's heads swiveled my direction as one. I almost never expressed a strong opinion when important decisions were being made, since I was so new to the group and knew so little about the topics discussed.

"Look...I...you know," I stammered, "the library is really important. If anything were to happen to that, it would be like going back to the stone age in just a couple of generations. Information has to be passed down to the kids, and their kids. Or it will be like starting from scratch. It's the one thing that's truly irreplaceable, our written knowledge." The group murmured, considering.

"She's right," said Yazmin. Others nodded, comprehending. "None of us has known a time when people have not been educated, and learned to read and write. None of us come from a generation when written works were not everywhere."

Grandpa Joe stepped in, "Yes. I think she's right too. We Apaches lived just fine without the written word, but our children heard stories from the moment they were born containing all our knowledge. We had good memories for all the details, and how the stories fit together. But we don't have those skills now. It would be good to learn them again but even I don't know many of the old stories. Our culture was damaged when we were forced into the boarding schools, and forbidden to practice our traditions. We have to protect the little knowledge we have very carefully. We can decide what to share in stages, as we get to know them. And to trust them. First, we don't tell them where we live, or how. But we should bring them food, to show them good will. Maybe we meet just once a month, bring more of us to meet them. Not too many at once. That's enough to plan for now. But the library. Maybe we don't ever need to let anyone know about that. We are its guardians now."

We sat in silence considering.

Then Beto broke the solemn mood by proclaiming, "I just hope they have a nice young woman for Noah. Someone to take the edge off of his grouchiness!" A wave of laughter spread briefly through the group. Noah looked sideways at Beto for a moment, as if considering his response, but said nothing.

As had become usual, I took notes for the meeting, for posterity. For those future generations.

I had been reading accounts of the earliest settlements of our country, first in our region, in the American southwest, and then on the east coast. Those people had come from other countries with their leadership structures and plans in place before they set sail from Europe, even if they didn't always hold up. We were just a smattering of survivors trying to cobble together a way of life from the remnants of our once massive and complex society. Despite that difference, it was interesting to see how our forebears had handled the task of survival, and of settling down to raise families. It seemed to me that future generations, if there *were* future generations, would want to know what we talked about, how decisions were made, what we did, and how we did it. They would want to know about our failures and our successes. I decided to keep a journal of not only our meetings but the day-to-day goings on in our little settlement.

That line of thinking led me to the history section in our library. Once a week I hauled several volumes back to Victorio's—Greek, American, Chinese and Egyptian history—every kind of history from every part of the world. I wanted to understand why Grandpa Joe and others believed that all of humanity had been heading towards disaster, and find out how we had come to that place. What had we done wrong? What was going to prevent us from making the same mistakes as they made? With most of the human population wiped out how could we start over and do better this time?

I had read aloud to Victorio a story called *A Canticle for Leibowitz,* where civilization collapsed because of its mistakes, then rebuilt itself, then made the same mistakes, collapsing again. The story left us both feeling like that could easily happen to us too, and I wanted to make sure it didn't.

"Right now, we're just trying to survive," said Victorio.

"Yeah, I know, but we have to think ahead too," I said.

Victorio held my gaze for a moment, considering. "Yes. Yes, we do."

We sat together on the couch, me leaning against one overstuffed arm, my legs draped across his lap, Victorio squeezing my tired feet pleasantly as I read to him. We had become more comfortable together but I didn't know what that meant, or what I wanted to happen between us. I had become close to some of the others, Hallie, Kate and Jeanne especially, but I felt most truly at home with Victorio. With him I felt most myself.

16

The morning came of our emissaries' departure to visit the Forest People. The cloudless sky seemed to go on forever and the mid-summer's sun, brilliant and warm, quickly evaporated the cool dew from the now dense grasses. Noah, Ching Shih and Victorio mounted their horses, saddle bags full of provisions for their trip, and somewhat more than that to offer as a gesture of good will – mesquite flour, venison jerky, Kate's finest goat cheese, and fresh vegetables and dried herbs from Devon's garden. We had made the decision not to give them anything that would indicate that we had stores of food from before the virus.

I stood next to Victorio on his horse feeling inexplicably awkward as he double-checked his bags and took the reins. He turned is hazel eyes on me for a long moment and reached down. I took his hand, acutely aware of its strength and warmth. My tongue stuck at the back of my throat but I managed to croak, "Be careful. Come back...."

They had been gone three days when I took some books on cheese-making and wool processing to Kate. She had been thinking about using the goats for wool as well as milk but was not sure how to proceed. I had just set them down on the kitchen table when she emerged from the pantry with a worried frown on her usually placid face. She gave me a hug and I looked into her face, hoping I wouldn't have to guess at what was on her mind.

I knew Kate still sometimes had terrible nightmares about her daughter, son-in-law and her three granddaughter's deaths. She had been the one person in the household to survive. She had tended each one of them while they slid deeper into the maw of death. One by one she had buried them, day after day, until each and every one was gone.

When Jeanne had finished burying her own three youngest children and husband, and was sure that Hallie and Noah would not succumb to the virus, she found Kate sitting in her kitchen staring unseeing at the opposite wall. She appeared to not have eaten or drank anything for at least a couple of days, her mouth so dry it hurt to open it for the water Jeanne insistently offered her. Jeanne had nursed Kate back to life, even while she and her two surviving children reeled with their own shock.

Kate was alive and functioning just fine now, but she was never quite the same. She avoided the children in our community and they learned never to look to her for affection or help. If I didn't know her history I would think she hated children but I remembered how affectionate she had been with her grandchildren, and how tender she still was with her goats. Now I figured she avoided children because she couldn't stand to love them and lose them.

"It's Benjamin...," Kate began, "he did it again...."

I looked at her, wondering what she could be talking about.

She tried again, "This morning...this morning at breakfast he said, 'there are too many of them. There shouldn't be so many!' I asked him who was there too many of and he said, 'Those Mongolian people! Those tipi people!' After that he wouldn't say anything more."

We looked at each other for a long moment.

"I don't know what we could do. If something happened, it's already happened. It's too far away to stop it," I said. Alarm bells now ringing in my head I added, "Look, maybe we should tell the others."

We rang the gong, the literal alarm bell, inside the hill and the others came. Kate and I explained about how Benjamin had seemed to know about the tipi and yurt dwellers when Frank, Ching Shih and Tochuku went on their trip.

"But how could he know what was happening? That doesn't make any sense," said Frank.

Yazmin turned towards him, hands on her hips, "How does a computer work Frank? The internet? A cell phone?"

Frank looked confused. "I—I don't know. How would I know?"

"But you used a computer, surfed the net, called people on a cell phone, right?" Yazmin pressed.

"Of course. Everybody did," he replied.

"Well, okay then. We don't have to know *how* Benjamin knows these things but it seems like he *does.* He was too accurate, both in what he reported and the timing, for it to be a coincidence. We don't really have to know how Ben knows things, we just have to decide if we need to *do* something about it," said Yazmin.

"Okay, okay. But still, if Benjamin saw something, he didn't say anything was wrong exactly, just that there were too many people. What does that mean? If there were more people than expected that doesn't really mean they were *doing* anything to our folks," Frank shook his head, "they really didn't look like a war-making bunch when I saw them."

"Benjamin always had the Sight," said Joe. "He just didn't let too many people know because they'd either make too big a deal about it, or act like he was crazy, stupid, or some kind of snake oil salesman. I have strong intuition too. And *I* know that Victorio is fine. I feel it in my bones and flesh."

If something went very wrong on the excursion we wouldn't know until it was days too late to help them. Between this fact, the uncertainty of what Benjamin actually saw, Joe's assertion that they were fine, and the fact that we had agreed that we would wait a full week before assuming the worst, we decided to just sit tight.

Sitting tight or not, I buzzed with anxiety like a hummingbird on an electrical wire. I startled at every snap of a twig or rustling in the brush when outside. I listened hopefully for the sound of horse hooves on the hard-packed dirt trail. I tossed fitfully in my bed at night, sometimes bolting upright, awoken by dreams of Daddy, Seth and Mama lying dead and stiff, and of a yawning, cavernous grave waiting to swallow whole all that I loved in the world.

"The Forest People know that we know where their camp is, and they don't know where *we* are. They can't be too foolish if they've made it this long. I don't think they'd risk our retaliation," said Joe, as we sat eating dinner the evening of the sixth day after they left, along with Hallie, Beto and little Uma, who we had invited to eat with us.

"Yeah, I see that Joe. I'll just feel better when they're back," sighed Hallie.

"It'll mean a big change, to be involved with them. What if they're some kind of nutty religious group with a crazy leader?" asked Beto, half-jokingly, as he held Uma on his lap, offering her a forkful of steamed carrots. Uma opened her rosy mouth like a baby bird, then chewed contentedly.

Joe sighed. "We can't predict. We'll just have to hear what they have to say when they get back. If we don't like what we hear then we'll just let 'em be." We might have to stay hidden more carefully for a bit, in case they come lookin' for us. But they're the ones most exposed, not us."

I just sat in silence, shoving my delicious meal around my plate as it turned cold. I felt like I was so far away, and yet, still way too close to this perilous world.

It was early evening on the eighth day and my nerves rang like clamorous gongs. Frank, Beto and Yazmin would leave in the morning to find out what had happened to our little expedition, so I was pre-emptively worried about them too. It would be a disaster to lose three strong adults. It was unthinkable that we could lose six. I was certain that the worst of my fears had come to pass, that Victorio, Noah and Ching Shih were dead, or even worse, traded by our would-be friends to others as slaves. I thought grimly that it was a good thing I hadn't gotten *too* close to Victorio, or this would be even worse.

Joe and I ate dinner in pensive silence. After I washed the dishes, I paced outside for a time, then sat on mine and Victorio's favorite rock outcropping. The western sky glowed a molten orange above the sun that had just vanished behind the mountain, leaving the whole valley in pale shadows, punctuated by the towering, spectral, ponderosas.

At first I thought that the faint rhythmic beating I heard was that of my own beleaguered heart. Then I realized that the sound echoed down the canyon from upstream. The thudding soon grew louder and coalesced into the sound of horse hooves on the trail. Emerging from the shadows like the ghosts I had expected them to be, Noah and Victorio rounded the curve of the hill, side by side, sauntering beside their respective horses. My chest convulsed, flash-freezing my breath. Then just as suddenly I could breathe fully again, if gasping. Boundless relief, then fury, then laughter rushed through me like successive gusts before a storm.

I ran to the cave door, yanked it open and yelled inside to Joe, who by then may have been sound asleep in his bed for all I knew, "They're back! They're BACK!"

I spun away from the door and ran back towards the trail. Victorio was waving goodbye to Noah, who continued his journey to his own home. Ching Shih had already stopped at hers with Kate and Benjamin further up the canyon. Victorio turned to see me running towards him and his face lit like the mid-summer sun. I swear it actually glowed. I threw my arms around him and he pulled me close with his free hand.

Half laughing, half scolding I hollered into his jacketed chest, "How could you let me worry like that?!"

He threw the lead rope around a branch and drew me in more tightly with both arms, lightly kissing the top of my head.

Later that night, after Victorio had eaten and showered and Joe had gone to bed, Victorio and I sank into our usual spots on the couch for a little reading. We had been reading *Outlander*. We were at the part where Claire had agreed to marry Jamie.

"You miss me?" Victorio interrupted suddenly, his voice low, hopeful uncertainty in his eyes.

"Yes," I said, a little grudgingly.

A tiny grin snuck into one corner of his mouth. "Well, you *did* seem happy to see me...."

"Yeah...," I sighed, "I didn't want to. I don't want to...*like* you that much."

"Do you? Do you like me...*that* much?"

Droplets threatened to leap from their eyelid precipices onto my cheeks. I felt so childish.

Victorio wrapped his arms around me. "It's okay, it's okay...."

I pressed my face into his chest and we sank into the thick soft corner of the couch. Soon we were asleep, the couch blanket draped over us, curled together like littermates.

The next morning, we held a celebratory breakfast that also served as a community meeting. I knew a little bit about what had happened from talking to Victorio the night before, and surely those that lived with Ching Shih and Noah did too. But we all needed to hear the whole story from the start, together. Clearly it had been a successful expedition, and that was largely why they had taken as long as they did to return.

To the amusement of all, Noah, one of those who had vehemently opposed the idea of exposing ourselves to the other group, was the most enthusiastic of our three ambassadors. Even Olga and Patricio dropped their parental fears and smiled at his exuberance.

I picked up my pen and started writing in my notebook as Noah began speaking while he paced back in forth in front of the group.

"Well you already know that we're pretty happy with the way it came out, but at first it seemed like a *disaster*. We got to the meadow where we were supposed to meet them, the evening before the full moon, and saw no sign of them. The next morning we were cooking breakfast when Ching Shih jumps up from the log she was sitting on like she'd been stung by a bee. Me and Victorio looked at her then realized it wasn't a bee because she was looking all around, into the trees. They had us surrounded...."

Victorio said, "We all backed up towards the fire, facing the trees. I had a fork in my hand, Noah had nothing and, well, Ching Shih had *her hands,* the best weapon we had between us at that moment...."

"Then the people in the trees walked out, into the meadow. There were about twenty of them, mostly young men," continued Ching Shih, "They had bows with arrows, one had an atlatl, others had large sticks."

"One stepped forward, a middle-aged woman," Noah continued, "she said, 'don't be scared, we're not here to hurt you,' and I said, 'that's kind of hard to believe!'" Laughter all around the table. "Well, it turned out they were just being cautious, because they knew we knew where they were and were scared for *their* families. Which makes sense."

"They had scoured the forest just before dawn to make sure there wasn't anyone else with us, but they still didn't know whether we were armed and what we were going to do if only a couple people showed up. So we did the right thing by not bringing others with us. We'd have had a full-on *battle* on our hands instead of a friendly discussion," said Victorio.

"The woman, Barbara, held out her hand to shake each of ours, very formally and with great dignity. She apologized for scaring us and asked us our names. Then, at a nod of her head, the others put down their weapons and came into the camp site. They each told us their names, and shook our hands," said Ching Shih.

Noah continued, "After we had told them a bit of our story, that some of our group knew each other before the virus, and some we met in the aftermath, they told us how they came together. Turns out they had been living in the villages of Gila and Cliff when the virus came.

"After the die-off had finally stopped they got together to figure out what to do next. They decided they would all be safer if they lived near each other, in Gila proper, since Cliff was right on the highway. There was plenty of water and they already had farms with crops that would need to be harvested soon. Some of them also had large stocks of dried goods in cellars, since they also figured something catastrophic was going to come down sooner than later.

"They did okay for a while—through the fall, winter and next spring. They figured that people in Silver City were living on the food stored in the grocery stores and houses, and probably harvested what they could from the gardens and fruit trees there.

"Problem was, the food in Silver was used up eventually, no matter how hard people there tried to grow enough that summer they just couldn't. There were lots of people in Silver that knew about the farms in the village of Gila. Some knew that they'd starve to death unless they could grow more food, and lots of them had guns. The folks in Gila had guns too, but there were more Silver City-ans. The Gila folks had already gotten people re-settled together in homes, most people sharing with others that weren't family members since so many families had just one or two survivors, if any.

"Barbara said that the invaders had given them a chance to leave peacefully, and the ones willing to leave packed up horse carts full of tents, clothing and other supplies. They were allowed to bring some food with them but not much. After they left, some turned back to do battle with the invaders. They don't know what happened to them."

Noah fell silent staring into space as if captivated by the vision of it all.

Ching Shih picked up the story, "They first went to Turkey Creek hot springs to camp. It was far off the road and of course had water. They stayed there for two years, hunting and gathering. Some died of the flu each year and a couple babies were born. Then some of them worried that the others, from Gila, would come there too eventually. Plus, it was too rocky to garden and they wanted to grow their own food as well as hunting and gathering. They hiked for part of one summer looking for the right place. Finally, they found the place they are now, near the west fork of the Gila River. They say they are doing pretty well there and want to build more permanent homes."

Noah continued, "THAT is where I come in! I checked out the soil there and it's the perfect mix of sand and clay for adobe or cob building, like a lot of places here. One day I dug a big basin into the center of an arroyo, hauled some buckets of water from the spring, threw in some cut grass and started building them their first cob hut. Pretty soon everyone wanted to help, including the kids, and next thing you know we're in full production making cob loaves and stacking them into walls.

"Normally we'd build a stem wall from rock first but for this first one, for demonstration purposes, I used a kind of flat stone slab, about as big as a living room, as the base. We had to dig a deep trench around the rock so water wouldn't accumulate at the base of the wall. It was all I could do to keep up with instructing them all on how to make, place and trim the loaves, so that it was built right."

"Okay, we get the idea about the building Noah, you don't have to tell us all about how to build a cob house," said Hallie in a teasing tone.

Noah made a rude gesture towards his sister before finishing his story.

"That's why we took so long to come back. I just couldn't leave them until I knew they had the hang of it. One guy there," Noah blushed and hesitated at this point, then resumed, "one guy, Juan Carlos, worked for a construction company building adobe houses. He knows a lot about building, though he never used cob before. He's taken over as the 'site foreman'."

Victorio whispered into my ear, "It wasn't just the *building* that made Noah want to stay."

It turned out that Barbara was the most respected older person in the group, a natural leader, and mother to a couple of the younger adults. She and some of the other de facto leaders spoke at length with Victorio and the others about how the two groups might help each other. Their group was about three times larger than ours.

Ching Shih said, "They were bothered by the fact we wouldn't tell them where we lived, but we told them that we had promised all of you we would not, as a condition of our visit, but maybe we could another time. They seemed to understand our fear but didn't like that it was unbalanced this way that we could come to them but not them to us. We agreed to meet again in a few weeks, and that some different people would come."

Turning to Kate she added, "One of the things they want are some goats."

That night, after Joe had gone to bed unusually early, Victorio and I settled onto the couch again with our current book. But the book remained unopened that night. Something had changed between us during his absence, visiting the Forest People.

We held each other silently on the couch for a long time before I said quietly into his neck, "Do you want to try kissing?"

"Y-yes...," he said uncertainly.

"Oh! I mean, uh, oh, if you don't *want* to...," I stammered, sitting abruptly upright.

"No. Yes, I mean, yes, I *really do* want to kiss you!" he said as he sat up too, now looking as alarmed as I probably did. "I-I just, you know, I mean...I mean," his eyes widened helplessly for a couple of beats before he finally blurted out, "I've never kissed anyone before! I mean not a girl—a woman you know, like *that*...."

"Oh!" I said, then again, "Oh!"

We sat for a few long moments in silence.

I turned to him and said, "Well. Me neither. There wasn't anyone my age, except Robert, and he was too much like a brother...."

We sat some more. I realized that he had literally not one person he could have had a first kiss with. Everyone was either much too old or children. Not until I came along.

"It's not like either of us exactly had a chance to date or anything," I said.

"Yeah," he said.

"Not like we could go to *prom* together...."

"No."

"So maybe we can learn together," I said.

Taking my hands in his, woodsmoke gaze searching my face, he said, "Yes."

After that, Victorio and I practiced kissing each night, then fell asleep on the couch together, not wanting to part but not wanting to take it further either. Joe had taken to retiring to his room soon after dinner, somewhat pointedly I thought. We took our time venturing further into this unknown territory. Bit by bit, we explored each other, tentatively, curiously, happily.

"Are you and Victorio...?" asked Hallie one day, raising

her eyebrows suggestively as she plucked several lettuces from the garden for dinner.

"No!" I said, a little too fast. "I mean, not exactly...."

She grinned as brightly as the clear, sun washed southwestern sky above us. "Okay, I see... well, whatever it is you're doing, I think its sweet. You seem really happy these days."

"Yeah," I smiled back at her. "Yeah, I guess I *am* happy...." An orientation to pure survival had been such a strong, necessary habit for so long, I felt surprised to realize I was really and truly happy—content—for the first time since I could remember. Something about my increased intimacy with Victorio had a deeply soothing effect on me.

17

Noah, Kate, Frank, one male goat and two females, ventured off for another visit to the Forest People. Now that the first group had gone and returned successfully, none of us were as worried as before. We set about our usual daily tasks and before we knew it they were back.

I was happy to see that Kate's eyes were brighter than usual, and she was more talkative upon their return. I had never seen her so bubbly before, at least not since before the virus.

"I met a man there, who keeps bees for the Forest People. He was real interested in the goats because he used to have some when he was growing up. He had already built a tidy little corral for the ones we brought, since Frank had told them he'd ask me for some. I showed him all about how to care for them and I'll probably go back some other time to check in. He also promised to teach us how to build bee hives and show me how to care for them, next time I come. By next fall we could have our own supply of honey instead of having to risk our necks raiding the hives in the forest."

Noah and Frank had helped with more cob building, completing the roof on the hut started during the first visit. They all tried to get to know the people there, especially their de facto head woman, Barbara.

Frank said, "She said that the group had become restless, wanting to either move on or to settle there for good. Together they chose the latter, but hadn't decided on how they would construct their permanent homes. Noah teaching them how to build with cob came just at the right time. It's easier and faster than cutting trees for post and beam, or frame construction, or making adobe bricks from scratch. She also said that they wanted to visit our home too, which seemed reasonable. I agreed to bring a few of them back with us on our next visit."

Frank had been given permission to speak on our behalf before they left so no one was surprised by this development. We had agreed to abandon our protective concealment forever, if only to a select few for now.

Not only that, but Kate and Frank returned without the goats and *without* Noah. He had stayed on to help with the building, as a guest in Juan-Carlos' yurt, news which was received with grins and raised eyebrows. It appeared that Noah would not remain celibate after all. This was turning out to be a romantic summer in our little corner of the Gila.

Mine and Victorio's quiet romance continued to develop until one night, after we had been kissing and sliding over each other for a while, he took me by the hand

and led me into the quiet coolness of his bedroom. We were like children learning to swim by being thrown into a deep eddy in the river, thrilled and scared and clumsy all at the same time.

Of course, I could have looked at the books on sexuality in the library, or we could have looked at them together, but I didn't want to. I figured that sex must be as natural and instinctive as eating and sleeping and I wanted to uncover its secrets bit by bit with this man, together. Like learning to sing a song with someone else we bumbled a lot at first. Gradually though, we learned to sense into each other, anticipating the other's yearnings, harmonizing touch, movement, tempo and pitch more easily with each encounter.

Soon Victorio began accompanying me on my stays at the library cave and to my surprise I didn't mind trading a little of my treasured solitude for more time with him. Private time. I'm sure it was a relief to Joe too, not having to tip-toe around us while we were gone.

Summer solstice had long since passed and while the days were still hot and the nights stayed warm, fall loomed large on the horizon. Crops matured and were harvested in turn. All the available adults worked in long shifts picking, cleaning, slicing, canning and drying garden vegetables as well as hunted meats and gathered nuts and berries. I remembered all too well my own fervent efforts the summer before, working non-stop in my little cabin to prepare enough food for winter.

I had been slicing a mountain of zucchinis for drying for what seemed like hours when I became suddenly aware of

Victorio standing on one side of me and Hallie on the other, also slicing zucchinis. It was as if their selves extended beyond the boundaries of their skin and washed right into and through me. Grandpa Joe perched on a tall stool on the opposite side of the counter facing down his own zucchini hoard, grumbled that he didn't really even like zucchini much. Hallie laughed beside him at his grumpiness as she hurried to arrange the zucchini slices onto drying screens, trying to keep up with our slicing. My head swam for a moment, as if buffeted by a sudden gust of wind. For the first time since I had come to live with these people I felt how truly a part of them I was. We were preparing for winter *together*. I belonged. I felt a deep settling inside me, as if some gnats had been buzzing in my veins for years, and had only now gone quiet. Silently I thanked the powers that be, whatever or whoever they were, for that.

Devon, Yazmin and Ching Shih made the next trip to the Forest People, only two weeks after the last group returned. With fall looming on the horizon we had only so much time to establish a more solid relationship with our new allies. The first snow fall would make it much harder and dangerous to travel that far. After that it was unlikely we would see our new friends before spring.

Devon was torn between taking the trip and staying to oversee the remaining harvest but we convinced her that we could make do without her for a week or so. She deserved a break since she was the hardest worker of all when it came to the garden. We saved a large portion of the seeds from our harvest for next year's planting and Devon carefully wrapped samplings in colorful swatches of cloth, as if they were precious jewels, as a gift for the Forest People.

"I'm hoping they'll feel like returning the favor," she said, eyes gleaming at the vision of more varieties to plant come spring.

That night as we just were getting up off of the couch from our evening reading, Victorio asked, "How about if you and I go next time. To see the Forest People?"

My stomach tightened at the thought. "I don't know...."

"I'll be with you," he said softly.

"I know...it's just that...well, I'm scared. I know it doesn't make sense since there isn't hardly anyone for a long way away as far as we know, but, well, what if the slavers pick right then to come this far, looking for new workers?"

"I'll be with you," he repeated, "and so would Frank." Either Frank or Ching Shih went on every trip there so far, to keep the others safe.

"I'll think about it."

And I did think about it. I realized that if I didn't take the chance of leaving our little nest that it would get harder to do as time went on. I hoped to have a long life and I didn't want to think of myself as someone who was afraid of something as simple as traveling a few miles away, for the rest of my life. I would go with Victorio and Frank on the next visit.

Yazmin, Devon, Ching Shih and Noah returned with stories of seed trading, more building and some martial arts demonstrations by Ching Shih. One of the Forest People was especially skilled at flint knapping and the three women had engaged in some lessons, with varied results, which each displayed for our admiration or pity, depending.

They also returned with three visitors—the leader, Barbara, a tall muscular son of hers, Daniel, and a young midwife, Sarah. All of them stayed at our place, at Joe's, since we had the most unused bedrooms.

At first our visitors stared around our cave homes as if they had stumbled into a fairy land. Not surprisingly they liked the hot running water the best, showering or taking long soaks every day. Victorio, Joe and I either rose extra early or stayed up a little late in order to get our own baths. During their stay we all met for dinners inside the hill and the three seemed to enjoy our banter. We pressed our new friends for stories of their lives in the forest, which they obliged readily, and which I wrote down. They had plenty of questions for us as well.

Our guests spent their days visiting with each household and learning about our way of living. Sarah and Jeanne talked a lot about herbs, healing and midwifery. Sarah volunteered to teach midwifery to anyone who wanted to learn, an offer which Olga, Jeanne and Kate enthusiastically accepted. Daniel exhibited a strong affinity for plants and spoke at length with Devon, Gavin and Jeanne. Gavin took him on short field trips to introduce him to more plants and their useful properties. Daniel also pointed out some that we didn't know how to use, so the education was mutual. Barbara frequently gravitated towards Grandpa Joe, plying him for traditional Apache knowledge about living in this area—how to predict the weather, coexist with predators and how to build a sturdy wikiup, among other things.

In the evenings, our guests sang for us. They knew a lot of different kinds of music but somehow Frank convinced them to do a long round of Irish ballads one of the nights. Several of us accompanied them by rhythmically pounding on the tables with our hands. Another night they sang folk and country western songs.

The day after that, Hallie came to me surreptitiously. Her face was like a lamp that had been lit from within, shining with pure inspiration.

"Do you have any books on how to make instruments?"

"It seems like I might have seen something like that in the music section."

"You know, we've never really made music here. Noah had played guitar before, and I played the flute, and I'm pretty sure others played other instruments too," she shook her head in confusion, "I don't know how we could've completely lost that. How could we have gone so long without music?"

I didn't have an answer to that question, but I could look for books that might help us to bring music back into our lives. And sure enough, I found a couple. One on making guitars and violins, another on making wind instruments. It would be a start. Hallie was a master woodworker. If anyone could bring music to our little hamlet, it was she.

Noah had returned but to our surprise it was not for long. The night before Victorio, Frank and I were to escort our guests back home, Noah called for our attention.

"Good evening everyone," he said, standing at the head of the table where he had eaten. "I have something to tell you." Murmurs and furrowed brows traveled through the group. "I have decided to live with the Forest People."

Astonished sounds emanated from around the tables. Jeanne stared stricken and Hallie looked at her lap.

"I...you know I love you all," Noah's voice grew rough, "I know you know I met someone...but that's not the main reason I'm moving. The main reason I'm leaving is that I see that this community is starting to head a direction I don't really believe in. A direction I don't want to go. I believe in living with less technology and I know you're working on developing more."

Tochuku said quietly, looking down at the ground, "Fire is technology my friend. So are bows and arrows."

"I know that Tochuku. But the occasional forest fire never caused our entire planet to heat up. We didn't cause thousands of entire species to go extinct by using bows and arrows."

"Yes," nodded Tochuku, "you have a point. So maybe it's not technology exactly, but what kinds of technology and how we use it."

Noah continued, with a nod to Tochuku, "Maybe. It's just that we can't always *calculate* the potential effects of our newer technologies. That's what happened. The smartest people around at the time created petroleum-based vehicles which in just a few decades directly or indirectly poisoned our air, water and soil, and caused a frenzy of resource extraction of every kind. Not because the scientists who developed all those new gadgets planned it that way, but because it didn't even occur to them that would happen, or that it would become a problem big enough to threaten our survival."

"Look, it's not that I don't understand why you want radios, solar electricity, and stuff made from 3-D printers, it's just that I believe that our world was on a bad track before the virus, with pollution, climate change, and extinctions which almost included us. And that had everything to do with the technology that required that we mine, log, destroy habitat and the rest. Thanks to some reading I've done," he looked away from me, as if afraid he'd slip and give away my secret to our guests, "and things that Yazmin has told us, I know that people who live more simply, and don't try to accumulate a lot stuff, don't do as much harm to the world, to other people, animals, plants, soil, air, water.

"Look, I don't want to argue about all this. It just comes down to the fact that the Forest People live the way I want to live. I promise to come visit. And of course, I want you to keep visiting there." Noah looked down at the ground, chest heaving as if struggling for breath. "I don't want to lose *you...*," his voice cracked, "I just want to live in a way I really believe in." Pause. "That's all." Noah sat down, staring blindly at the remaining food on his plate.

Silence sat atop the dinner party like an invisible boulder, pressing us into the ground.

Frank turned towards Barbara. "I guess then that this has

been approved by the Forest People?"

Barbara stood. "Yes, Juan Carlos brought the idea to our regular meeting and after much discussion it was agreed unanimously that Noah would be welcome to live with us." Looking at Jeanne she continued, "He's a good man, and he has skills that would benefit us quite a lot. We don't want you to feel that we are stealing him from you because I'm sure you value him as well. But we are happy to have him. I hope that this does not create bad feelings from you towards us. We are glad to have you as our neighbors." Barbara took her seat.

Grandpa Joe rose, chin up, clearing his throat before addressing Noah, "Each person must live in a way that fits with their deepest beliefs or those beliefs turn to poison in their soul and in their flesh. Life without integrity will ruin one. I am not happy to see you leave, but I would feel less happy to see you stay, knowing how you feel. That is all." Joe sat down.

Beto stood next, eyes sparkling with mischief, "So our going to meet the Forest People wasn't such a bad idea after all, eh?"

"I was wrong before and I'll probably be wrong again someday," Noah said, one corner of his mouth lifting.

Jeanne stayed seated but gazed at Noah with red-rimmed eyes. Seeing this, Noah swept from his seat and over to her in one quick motion, wrapping his arms around her. She wept silently into his neck for a few long moments as he rubbed her back and murmured reassurances into her hair. Next, Noah went to Hallie, who stood to hug him long and hard.

One by one, each of us Cave People stood and walked to Noah, forming a line, hugging him. Some stayed silent, and some spoke quietly into his ear. Some shed tears and some stayed dry eyed, but we all held sorrow in our hearts.

18

Frank, Victorio, Noah and I set out early the next morning with our three guests. Frank and Noah took the lead, since they knew the route to the Forest People's home. Our visitors rode behind them, and Victorio and I brought up the rear. It had been nearly a year since I had ventured so far from our neighborhood, on my hunting trip before I came home to my rodent-ravaged pantry.

The night time chill lifted as soon as the sun cleared the eastern horizon, the late summer rays quickening our blood as we sauntered through the fragrant ponderosas, broad, dense junipers, and flat palmed cedars. The surrounding mountains thrust into the iridescent turquoise sky and the air smelled of the lazy river algae, pine needles and the rich soil steaming from a night of rain. Fat jays squabbled over bunches of plump juniper berries while hawks circled above. Two squirrels raced up a Douglas fir, scolding us as we passed. Farther along we encountered tiny purple and yellow wildflowers perched atop delicate green stems amidst their minute leaves, scattered in festive swathes across a broad hillside.

As the sun rode high in the sky we came upon a thick stand of yuccas sheltered against a steep north-facing slope and stopped to fill canvas bags with their delicately flavored, cream colored blossoms. Later, Victorio and I paused at a deep eddy in the river to spear several Gila Trout. The river bank wore a thick carpet of purslane so we pulled up several handfuls of that, rinsing it in the river before stashing it with the yucca blossoms. When we stopped for lunch Barbara came upon a cluster of wild oregano, some of which she draped in small bundles across her saddle to dry. My chest swelled happily as we penetrated more deeply into this riotous, bubbling cauldron of life that was our mountainous home. This home that fed, housed and protected us, so superbly, so richly.

Around the campfire the first night, Frank sat close to Noah and they spoke in low, somber tones while we all ate a delectable stew of fresh fish, yucca blossoms, wild oregano and purslane. After dinner Noah and Frank ceased their serious exchange while Barbara, Daniel and Sarah entertained us by singing some folk songs brimming with rich harmonies and heart-rending lyrics.

"I came from a very musical family," said Barbara, face flushed with her happy exertions when they had finished. "I have tried to keep the songs alive by teaching them to our group. It would be a shame to lose all our songs."

"That's the thing, isn't it?" asked Frank. "How do we hang on to as much of what we had as possible?"

"Maybe we shouldn't hang onto *everything*," said Noah seriously, then turning to smile at Barbara he added, "just the good things, like folk songs!" Serious again he continued, "I mean, is metal, for instance, good or bad? What does it cost the land, the water, to mine it? Is it really worth it?"

"There are so few of us left, humans, and so much in our landfills, we wouldn't need to mine new metal, just dig it out of our dumps, and scavenge it from all the dead cars and empty homes," said Victorio.

"But how long would that last? If we re-build a way of life that requires metal, and our population expands again, we'll be right back to where we left off. Mining more and polluting more and destroying more habitat," said Noah.

"For centuries people used metal that was easy to get to, and that didn't cause so much harm. Few people, a little digging here and there, limited use. The earth heals easily from that," said Frank.

Sarah chimed in, "Some of our group are of Amish descent. Their parents and grandparents never did get into technology much, though they did use a minimal amount of metal."

"Some of our group too!" laughed Victorio. "No, really though, the Apache side of my family was living just like we are right now, right here, camping, just a few generations ago. We also used metal that we found on the surface. We had a strict prohibition against mining it though. We were taught not to 'grub in the earth.' We don't think it's such a big deal to go back to living that way."

"But you aren't going back that way, are you?"

countered Noah.

Victorio flushed. "You know that Grandpa Joe isn't as healthy as he used to be, since the virus. He spent his whole life here in the Gila riding horses but he hardly ever gets on a horse any more. He's just not strong enough. He sleeps a lot and gets tired fast. He built that cave with his own hands, right here in our traditional homeland, just in case something happened. Which it did. I'm not taking him anywhere."

"Well what about after...?" started Noah.

"After he *dies* you mean? I don't know. I think our life in the caves is pretty low tech. I don't think a few solar panels makes that much difference," said Victorio.

"Yeah, it's just that now we have a chance to start over, without too many people, using too many resources." Noah's tone softened and I detected a slight pleading, "We don't have cattle destroying the soil, and we *do* have wolves back. The mines aren't draining our water table, or poisoning what's left. That's a good thing. I'm afraid we're going to make the same mistakes that got us into the situation we were in. We could create a great world, for humans and for everything else. But we can't do that if we live the way we were living."

"Yes," said Sarah, "That's been a big question in our village. How can we move forward without recreating the problems of the past? There's a lot of debate about that, but we all agree that things weren't good before, and that we can do better."

"I think you're right. We can't live the way we did before. But we also don't all have to live the same way," I said.

"Yeah, okay, I know...," said Noah, letting the matter drop.

Other than a brief encounter with a mother bear and her two cubs, which we handled diplomatically by quietly changing our direction until we had safely passed, and a sharp stone that had lodged in Barbara's horse's hoof, which Victorio skillfully removed, our trek proceeded without incident. Victorio and I made our bed out of earshot of the others each of the two nights out.

We arrived around midday on our third day of travel, crossing a short steep valley and up the other side to a broad meadow protected by a tall, curved hill that hunched inwards on the other three sides. The spacious circle of tipis and yurts sat near the hillside, the corral and stable for the horses to the west and the goat enclosure to the east. Their late summer garden bloomed gaily on the near side of their home site, along with a large corn patch, near the spring.

The backs of several gardeners huddled amongst the greenery indicated that their harvest was proceeding as rapidly as our own. Long, stout tables stood next to the plot topped with knives laid out neatly at one end and drying screens woven of thin cordage stacked next to those. As we walked past the garden I spotted a shallow flint knapping pit a dozen yards away, set about with low stump stools and occupied by three youngsters and an older man, all who had been focusing intently on the stone in their hands until they heard us coming and looked up in interest.

Barbara whistled shrilly and a stir ensued inside the circle of shelters as a score of people—large, small, old, young, quick and slow—gathered to watch our arrival. One man in particular, broad shouldered and raven-haired, strode forward to meet us. All but one of us may as well have been invisible to him because, once located, his eyes never left Noah's face. Noah dismounted as soon as their eyes met, tugging his horse impatiently so as to join his lover as soon as possible. The two embraced each other and kissed passionately and long as everyone laughed and cheered. Noah's horse stamped and huffed as the rest of us passed.

As I rode by I overheard Juan-Carlos whisper to Noah, "I was so afraid you wouldn't come back...."

Yazmin was right. We had to make friends with other groups. And we needed each other for more than food and technology. We needed each other for love.

Sarah welcomed Victorio and I into the tipi she shared with her sister Nell, a younger, shier, version of herself, while Frank was invited to stay at Barbara's and her husband's yurt. After tending to the horses and unloading our belongings, Victorio and I rested on our guest bed in Sarah's tipi, Sarah discreetly tugging her sister out the door.

A couple of hours later, Victorio and I emerged well rested from our womb-like lodgings to wander around the camp. The camp bustled with activity. Everyone was involved in work or play of all sorts. One man was butchering a deer while a woman strung the fresh hide onto a tanning frame, a few people washed freshly picked root vegetables, while another carried a basket brimming with raspberries from a nearby stand. Some children were kicking a ball, playing a game that might have been soccer. The inhabitants of this little village seemed happy, or at least content.

As we wandered around many of them either stared openly at me and Victorio or glanced surreptitiously as we walked by. I couldn't help but stare at everyone myself. It was so strange to see so many people I had never met, after all the years in Darian's compound and my time with the Cavers. Now I knew why the others who had traveled here were so happy and animated when they returned home. To see so many new faces and experience a whole other way of living from ours felt invigorating.

Soon we crossed paths with Frank, looking relaxed and well rested. He joined us on our rounds, introducing us to many of the people we encountered. I had so many questions for them. Where did they get the clay that one woman carefully coiled into what looked like would become a broad bowl? In addition to the clothing we all wore Before and expertly tanned leather, many of the people wore a comfortable looking cloth I couldn't identify. What was it made out of? Did they grow it or collect it? Where did they find the obsidian and chert that the knappers used to form arrowheads, axes and knives? I wondered, if I only had time to learn a little about one of the two, should I pick clay or stone?

Noah was nowhere in sight.

That evening we gathered around the large fire pit in the center of the circle of tent-homes. Rough-hewn tables held a buffet of fresh corn, salads of wild and garden greens, rabbit fajitas in hand ground corn tortillas, an herbed sacaton grain dish that reminded me a little of rice, mesquite mush and a salsa made from tomatoes, green chiles, garlic, cilantro and onions. Everything was served on hand-carved wooden or ceramic platters or bowls. I ate my meal with a hand-made wooden fork, sturdy but surprisingly fine and smooth too. A lot of care and skill had gone into making that fork.

As had happened when I first arrived at the Cave People's home I was also peppered with questions non-stop. They were especially curious about and disturbed by my description of Darian's compound and wide-eyed at my tale of escape from there. I left out the part about how the Caver's had left me nearly to die. I didn't want them to have a bad impression of them—of us. And, of course, I never spoke about Sylvia.

It felt strange and exciting to sleep in Sarah's and young Nell's tipi after so many months of sleeping in caves. The wind buffeted rhythmically against our conical shelter, punctuated by a gentle pattering rain that came and went through the night. Coyotes yipped and unknown critters skittered furtively in the nearby grasses. I had forgotten how much more insulated, protected, we were in our caves. Our garden, goats and horses were sheltered from predators by the circular concave butte. It had been easy to get used to such safety and luxury, although I enjoyed the closeness of the elements that night.

I also had become accustomed to sleeping next to Victorio. After lying face to face with him while my thoughts settled, I squirmed around with my back against his chest, legs tucked up along the inside curve of his, feeling his steady breath in my ear as I drifted off. He had fallen soundly asleep the instant he lay down his head.

The next day, our one full day in the Forest People's camp, I chose to study clay and Victorio went to the knapping pit hoping to at least learn the basics of making a stone knife. We had plenty of regular, metal knives at home but one day we might need to make new ones. Frank spent a lot of the day conferring with Barbara, her husband, and others who appeared to make up some kind of council.

After another feast that evening, we were treated to a whole chorus of singers, singing everything from old-timey bluegrass, to jazz, rock-n-roll, and gospel hymns. Three guitars, a harmonica and hand drums provided accompaniment. A clearing near the central fire provided space for dancers of all ages, several of whom danced for every song played, no matter the tempo or rhythm. I had never noticed the lack of music in our own community before the Forest People came to visit us but now it seemed impossible that we could survive without it.

I thought about what Barbara had said about wanting to preserve the songs. Some paper and pens would go a long way towards doing exactly that. Maybe the library should be storing musical knowledge as well as books. Instruments could be constructed but songs had to be sung regularly by each generation to be remembered, or they would be lost. Even the little that this group had retained, just a few years after the virus, was too much for a few people to maintain over generations. Unless it were written down.

The next morning came too soon.

As we loaded our horses Frank told us, "They aren't going to send any more of their people back with us this time."

"Even though the first frost is probably at least several weeks away, we still need everyone to prepare for winter. We never know how cold, wet or long it's going to be," explained Barbara, "but we'll look forward to more visits back and forth once spring comes."

Noah saw us off too, Juan-Carlos at his side.

"I'm going to miss you all," he said, eyes glistening. One by one we hugged him one last time.

"You're still family," Frank assured him, "Nothing is going to change that. You can come back any time, and," addressing Juan-Carlos, "you're always welcome too. For as long as you want."

"Keep an eye on Hallie and Mom, okay?" Noah asked me.

"Of course. They'll be okay. I promise."

Victorio hugged him hard and said, "I'm gonna miss you, big brother. But I'm happy that you're happy." Victorio turned to shake hands with Juan-Carlos saying with a smile, "Thanks for *making* my friend so happy. Or at least less grumpy!"

"We'll come see you in the spring," said Juan-Carlos. "I'm looking forward to meeting the rest of you, especially Noah's family."

As we rode home Frank told us that he and Barbara and the rest of their council had spoken at length about our long-term relationship with them.

"Their council of leaders suggested an exchange of teachers, since both our communities need as many skills and as much information as we can get in order to improve our chances of survival in the long run."

"How would we do that?" I asked.

"Well, we talked about trading people for a month or so at a time. Jeanne could teach them about herbs and other healing methods. Sarah would come and instruct Jeanne, Olga and Kate on midwifery."

Warming to the idea, Victorio added, "Devon could share some of her gardening techniques. Ching Shih could teach martial arts. I would sure like to get more tutoring on stone knapping myself."

My mind was afire with the possibilities.

"I would love it if the man who was teaching me how to work with clay, Claude, would come and help us identify suitable clay in the river bed, near us. I'd also like to learn about how to fire pots properly and use different decoration techniques." It occurred to me that this new relationship with the Forest People could improve our lives in much the same way as the library. More knowledge, more skills.

"And yet we're going to hold out on them. We have a huge advantage that they don't," I said, referring to our library, the paper, the ink, and the printing press.

Frank cocked his head in amusement at me as we rode side by side. "Lakshmi, you're the one who was so fired up about keep the library a secret! Which is it then? Share and share alike? Or protect the library from others at all costs?"

Confusion buzzed inside my head like bees caught in a jar. Which was the right answer?

19

We arrived home at dinnertime three days later to find that another trip, this one into Silver City, was being hotly debated, even before we could formally address the proposal at the next official community meeting the following day.

"This will probably be the last chance to take a trip like this until after the winter, and I want to have as much as possible to move my work forward during the winter," said Tochuku, leaning forward over his half-eaten dinner. Victorio, Frank and I dug in ravenously, having pushed past lunch in order to make it home before dark. I had whacked a lot of rabbits on their sweet heads for meals along the way but we didn't want to stop to hunt or cook the last day of travel. Some sat back watchfully while others stared at their plates, nibbling.

"We already lost one person because of these trips," said Hallie, mouth tight, eyes bright with pain from the fresh departure of her brother to live with the Forest People.

"I can't believe we're even having this conversation again," added Olga shaking her head defeatedly.

"I understand your fears, but look at what we've gained from these trips. We're now working well with a whole other community. We're already trading goods and information, skills. And the last trip to Silver gave us a lot more viability in the long run. We can't have our decisions based on one disastrous trip," Yazmin declared.

Olga said, "I agree that it's been good to get to know the Forest People. I really do see that. But going into Silver is much more risky. We know they have Slavers there."

"Some of us don't mind taking that risk," responded Tochuku.

"But a risk that any one of us takes will affect the rest of us if it goes wrong. We can't afford for anyone to be captured or killed. Or for the wrong person to follow you back," countered Olga.

The room fell quiet for a few long moments, considering the truth of her statement.

Beto broke the silence, asking, "How would you even get to the Makers? The Monks said the Slavers patrol the whole area a lot. How would you make it from the Monks to the Makers without being caught?" Beto sounded more curious than defiant.

Frank set down his fork, still chewing, "I know how we could do it...."

Everyone turned to look at him. He hadn't weighed in pro or con but apparently took the question seriously.

Frank continued, "We could circle way to the west, before even getting near Silver, then make our way south so that we come into Silver from the southwest, then angle east towards the Maker compound. There's no one at all living in that direction from Silver according to the Monks and from our own observations. The Slavers are probably used to people coming directly from the south, along highway 90, or from the north, from Pinos Altos or the monastery." Nodding to Ching Shih and Tochuku he added, "We scoped things out pretty well on our first trip, and I know my way around Silver perfectly, having grown up there. I think we could do it."

"Frank, I remember you said something about the 'Uvies.' The people living at the university. Didn't the Monks say they were into trading, not hostile?" I asked. My exhilarating, if brief, time with the Forest People caused my earlier fears to drift farther into the background of my thoughts and feelings. I found myself much more attuned to the rich opportunities to be had in our relationships with other groups.

"Yeah, that's true. What are you thinking?"

"I'd sure like to try out my book scanner. They have a whole university library there, assuming it's still intact. Tochuku said each scanner could hold dozens of books. Then they could be downloaded onto one of his hard drives, so we could get more. It could basically quadruple our library easily."

"I would bring my scanner too, of course. And, yes, a hard drive, so we could download them right there, and scan more," added Tochuku, jumping on another angle from which to sell the trip.

"Yeah," Frank said, "We could ask the Monks about how to go about approaching the Uvies."

"It's already September. We could literally have our first snowstorm in another couple of weeks," said Hallie.

"All the more reason to go soon," said Tochuku, sensibly enough.

"I would go if you will," said Ching Shih, lifting her chin at Frank, speaking for the first time on the matter.

"If Lakshmi's going, I'm going," said Victorio, putting his arm around me with a humorous flourish.

"I don't need you to protect me!" I said, turning to him in mock offense.

"Protect *you*!?" he returned, "I just don't want to miss out on a trip before the long winter. I'll probably need you to protect *me,* Rabbit Girl!" using my childhood nickname.

Our joking appeared to break the spell of the impasse. Now that several of us, including our hot shot security team, had agreed to go, the rest let the matter drop, or at least discontinued its debate. Several people glowered discontentedly—mostly Hallie, Olga and Patricio. Jeanne looked worried, whether for Frank's safety or Hallie's distress I had no way of knowing. Beto seemed to keep a studied neutrality opinion-wise, while being warmly attentive to Hallie.

Nodding his head to me and Victorio, Frank continued with the practical matters, "We've gotta rest up for a few days no matter what. We could be ready to go in a week for sure. The weather has been a little warm for this time of year. I doubt it'll snow any time soon."

After indulging in an early bedtime and a leisurely rousing from bed the next morning, Victorio and I worked doubly hard in getting in the last of the harvest with the others before we left again. The riches of the season were ours for the taking, but we still had to gather them from the forest, glean them from the garden and cut and dry it all too. The shelves of all the pantries had been filled nearly to bursting, not to mention the still significant original stores of flour, grains and beans. We certainly weren't going to go hungry this winter, but we never knew what the next year would bring. We couldn't take any of our current abundance for granted. I felt acutely the luxury we claimed for ourselves by taking these trips at this time of year, and hoped to make up for it some by working extra hard before we left again.

Before the week was out Frank, Victorio, Ching Shih, Tochuku and I were packed and ready to head off. The trip would take us at least two weeks, and three was much more likely. Jeanne eyed the sky somberly as she hugged us all in turns, whispering wifely exhortations for caution in Frank's ear before he swung himself onto his horse. Grandpa Joe squeezed me extra-long, an odd look of resignation on his face that caused my guts to tighten and raised the hair on my arms. He did the same with Victorio, except instead of avoiding Victorio's eyes as he had mine, the two kinsmen beheld each other's gaze silently for several unwavering seconds during which I saw a whole conversation pass between them, ending with what seemed to be a slight nod of agreement from Victorio.

Grandpa Joe had spoken neither for or against this trip but, apparently, he had some inkling about it he wasn't sharing, at least not explicitly.

My moment of foreboding soon passed as we made our way through the early fall forest, settling in to the rhythmic plodding of the horses. The deciduous trees had begun to turn colorful in earnest and their leaves would carpet the forest floor soon after our return from Silver. Squawking flocks of Sandhill cranes and various geese and ducks sung their own way to their winter homes, flowing in ribbon-like V formations far above us in the cloudless, turquoise sky. Fall was the time to travel if you really needed to get somewhere before spring. Winter was not.

We followed the West Fork at first, its flow much tamer now that the late summer rains had passed. As usual we hunted, fished and gathered as the opportunity arose. We wanted to save most of the provisions we brought from home for trade. We had brought one extra horse just to carry two large paniers loaded with Kate's cheese, jerked meats, dried wild berries and other foods that we thought the town dwellers might especially appreciate. We veered southward before we passed near the Forest People's home, respecting their wishes to be free of visitors while they finished their preparations for winter.

A few days into our trip we sat around the evening's campfire, a crescent moon lighting the sky, already brilliant with a sparkling treasure trove of stars. Victorio and I sat cross legged on our sleeping mat, leaned comfortably against each other drowsily watching the flames. Frank, Ching Shih and Tochuku had arranged themselves in similarly comfortable manner.

"Tochuku, how did you end up getting into computers and other technology?" I asked. I had been living with the Cavers for months now, and had gotten to know most of the others pretty well, but I knew hardly a thing about him. He was so immersed in his own work that the rest of us saw little of him except at meals, meetings and working in the garden.

He looked at me, thinking a moment before speaking.

"I was living with my family in a small village in the rural area outside of Abuja. We had a one-room school that I attended and I loved learning. My parents were very strict about me and my sisters attending school, but I didn't need to be pushed. I *always* preferred school work to working in the fields any day."

Ching Shih grinned while Frank, Victorio and I hooted with laughter at this revelation. Tochuku always combined his gardening day with meeting days so as to keep his focus on his technical work as much as possible. Every single time he worked in the garden or kitchen he said, "You know, this is really not the best use of my abilities." And every single time someone reminded him that everyone had to help provide food, which was more essential to our survival than electricity, and whatever else he was up to. It had become a standing joke among us, and I suspected that Tochuku kept making that statement just to keep the joke going.

"One day, when I was ten years old," he continued, "we arrived at school to find that our teacher had boxes stacked up next to her desk. A computer company had donated a new kind of computer for us to try. I know now that we were part of some research they were doing, but at the time we were all just excited to be getting laptops. Except they did not come with instructions at all. Either our teacher didn't know how to use them either or she had been instructed not to tell us. There were about fifteen of us in the school and we each got one. The school had electricity so we had a way to keep them charged, although we did not have electricity at home. Our teacher said, 'You are smart children. I know you can figure out how to work them.' And she just watched us as we opened our boxes, figured out how to plug in the power cords, opened the lids and started pushing buttons. Pretty soon we were playing the games that had been installed on the computers, at first ignoring the word processing programs, the calculators and the like. I was hooked!"

"I remember reading about how they did that, just handing kids computers who had never had one, just to see if they had designed the computer intuitively enough for the kids to figure them out. A huge success as I recall," said Frank.

"I heard about it too, in Hong Kong," said Ching Shih. "There was talk at some of the tech companies there of doing something similar in east Asian rural areas too. I remember being amazed that children who didn't even have electricity in their homes could just figure out computers like that."

"Yes, we had reporters show up and interview all our families. It was funny, to see all these foreign strangers coming to see us, acting like we had done something extraordinary. But really, we were just children doing what children will do if they are allowed. We were exploring something interesting. Playing. Playing is very important to learning you know."

"So from then on you just thought, 'I'm going into computers when I grow up?'" asked Victorio.

"No, it wasn't quite that simple," Tochuku grinned wryly, "we didn't know it but our computers were monitored. The first child to successfully learn how to use every program on the computer would be chosen for instruction at a special school in Abuja. I was that child. Not only was I sent to that school, but my family was given a small house to live in on campus while I went. My sisters were able to attend the school too, since they didn't want to separate family members. And they had done well with their computers too.

"I began to see possibilities I hadn't imagined before. There was a student at my school who invented a portable solar water pump for use in springs or wells, and another who invented a portable UV wand to disinfect water. The two spoke all over the country about how to use these together. They improved people's access to potable water dramatically. When I left they were touring other African countries. I wanted to be like them, inventing something that would really help people."

Until then I had seen Tochuku as someone who was mostly withdrawn from the group, as someone who resented being stuck with us and hid from us amongst his technological projects. I had never thought about him as someone's son and brother. He had been a brilliant little boy in a one-room school house, who happened to be exposed to a rare learning experience, and people who would feed his talents.

The fire crackled and sparks flew into the air, as if going home to the stars, while Tochuku stared into the flames a few moments before continuing.

"When I was sixteen I was caught hacking into the Nigerian government's computer, just for fun, not for any bad reason. The government didn't put me in jail, probably because the computer company had a lot of money. Maybe they paid someone off. Or donated to some big cause. But the school principle said it would be best if I left the country. Because of my actions I would always be under watch there. We had already taken college entrance exams and my mentors there wanted me to go to MIT. But my mother was already upset because I would be leaving all the way to the US. I had an older cousin in Silver City. My parents agreed that I could go to the US if I lived with my cousin and went to Western, so he could keep an eye on me. My teachers were not happy about this, because it was not as good of a school, but then they arranged for me to take classes at New Mexico Tech, in Socorro, too, to supplement my learning. My sisters and parents had planned a trip to see me after I moved to Las Cruces. They were going to come for Christmas, but then the virus came."

"I'm sorry you got stranded so far from your family," I offered.

"Thank you. You lost your family too though, right? It has been a sad journey for us all," he responded.

The next day dawned clear and bright and after our usual brief, simple breakfast we were on our way again. Victorio and I each had a bundle of Rabbit Sticks tucked into a bag so we could practice throwing them. It had been Victorio's idea.

"Can you teach me how to throw Rabbit Sticks better?" he had asked that morning.

"It's not that hard. It just takes practice," I said.

"Yes. It is hard. You just happen to be really good at something very hard. You have a gift. So help me out. Don't be stingy."

As we rode along I talked to him about how to hold his elbow at the right angle to use as a guide for aiming and flick his wrist with just the right amount of POP to get the sufficient velocity to kill a rabbit. We whacked stumps, rocks and towards the end of the day, Victorio actually managed to hit a rabbit.

"You did it!" I exclaimed. "That was great Victorio," then in mock seriousness I intoned, "You are now a graduate of Lakshmi's School of Rabbit Stick Throwers." I handed him my last Rabbit Stick with a formal bow after he had tucked the still warm rabbit into his game bag.

20

Brother Matthew welcomed us like family when we arrived at the monastery, enveloping each one of us in his bearlike embrace as we dismounted. Stable hands attended to our horses while Matthew led us to the dining hall and asked someone in the kitchen to fix up a couple of rooms for us.

"Your plan is a good one, but it's still risky," Matthew was addressing Frank as we all shoveled a hearty hot stew into our mouths. The cooks had been delighted by our gifts of goat cheese, mesquite flour and other goods, and made sure we had the best of what they had to offer for our dinner. The smell of something sweet wafted in from the kitchen and soon a plate of cookies arrived in front of us as well. A quiet, smiling man carried a large teapot and filled our heavy clay mugs with a tangy concoction.

"Tell us what else we can do to make it safer then," said Frank.

Matthew ran a hand through his thick black hair, mouth

pursed in thought.

"Well the Slavers don't scout as much at night. Maybe if you left here in the morning, then made your way west and south, then hung out well outside of town until say midnight or so, you'd stand a better chance. The tricky part will be dealing with whoever is guarding the Maker compound. You'll need to get this letter into their hands before they bonk you on the heads," Matthew handed Frank a letter of introduction, embossed with an old-fashioned waxed seal imprinted with an image of the monastery. He also gave us another copy of the letter for the Uvies, who we intended to see on the return trip.

"Any suggestions on how to do that?"

Shaking his head ruefully Matthew said, "I don't know really. I guess as soon as you spot them yell, 'we're friends of Matthew's!' If they spot you first they might have you trussed up before you can say anything. They aren't particularly violent, in fact they don't like using force at all, but they've had to toughen up over the years because they've had so many of their people taken by the Slavers. So, they probably won't hurt you, not much anyway. Just cooperate as best you can and hand them the letter as quickly as possible."

It seemed simple enough.

We spent the night, the next day, and one more night to rest up and further strategize, with the help of Matthew and others who had made forays into town. The Slavers had never attempted to attack the monastery but were certainly feared by its inhabitants.

The night before we left, just after dinner, a young man named Tyrone gave us a clearer picture of what we were up against.

"Anyone caught by the Slavers almost never makes it out. The few that have, told us that the men captured are generally worked to death. A healthy man is more of a threat to them. If a man fights too much they killed him right off, sometimes torturing him first. One guy had a finger a day chopped off while chained to a table, then each toe. He finally died when they cut off the second of his arms. The younger women are used for sex and as household servants, the older women work in the fields and manage the livestock. And what *they* mean by 'woman' is often girls as young as eleven."

My stomach turned at these revelations. Suddenly Sylvia was there rotating above me on a rope strung from the rafters like a newly felled deer, her rainbow dress torn and blood smeared over her exposed thighs. Her mother, Emma, had been sitting in the kitchen, waiting for her to come back from the main house but had fallen asleep, face cradled in her crossed arms.

Technically, Lem, Jeff, Darian and the others hadn't actually killed Sylvia. They had just brutalized her so badly that she could not bear living any longer. Not even for her mother, asleep on a nearby table. Maybe she hadn't even seen Emma. Sylvia had easily found a rope and taken her own life as fast as she could. Her mother awoke to find her like that. She blamed herself entirely for her daughter's death, not seeing that even if Sylvia had not killed herself, in a way Darian and his men had already stolen her life from her. It was their doing, not Emma's, and in a way not even Sylvia's.

"I need to go outside for a bit," I said, extricating myself from behind the dining room table.

Victorio stared at me for a moment then said, "Okay, I'll be going to our room pretty soon."

But a minute later he was outside with me, while I vomited vigorously against a scrubby juniper as I clung to its limbs. He held my hair back with one hand and steadied the rest of me with the other. I vomited another couple of times, wiping the foul spit from my mouth with my sleeve, Victorio's solid form offering shelter from this internal storm. When it was clear that my stomach had finished revolting against me he held me gently against his chest.

Then the crying started, just as violent and uncontrollable at the vomiting. My whole body, mind and soul shook and moaned like a hurricane, tearing me nearly to pieces. How would I ever be whole again?

"They killed her. They killed her they killed her they killed her...." I groaned into Victorio's chest, sobs wracking my lungs and throat. He led me carefully over to a nearby bench and sat me onto it without loosening his grip on me.

"How could they do that? How could they do such a thing to Sylvia!? She was such a sweet person. She was my best friend. I loved her and they killed her. She didn't kill herself, *they* killed her."

Faces appeared in some of the windows of the monastery and a few minutes later Matthew was beside us asking Victorio, "Is there anything I can do? Is she going to be alright?" I felt Victorio nod and heard nothing more from Matthew. A minute later Frank, Ching Shih and Tochuku sat down silently on another nearby bench. As my ranting and sobs transformed into hiccups I saw that Ching Shih looked even more stunned by my outburst than Frank and Tochuku, as they caught the gist of what I was saying.

I had told Victorio that Sylvia had killed herself after being gang raped but hadn't told him anything more than that. Sitting with my friends, my family now, around me, the whole story just flooded out like water through a burst dam. About my mom dying of a simple bladder infection, how Emma took me in, about the beautiful rainbow dress Sylvia made. And Darian asking for her to come serve them that night. All of it.

Ching Shih, the most stoic person I had ever met in my life, had tears streaming down her face and dripping off her chin. I had never heard much about Ching Shih's life before her arrival here but now I wondered.

By the end of my story I had half lain myself across Victorio's lap, snuffling and blowing my nose into a handkerchief someone had handed me, talking more slowly and quietly as I neared the end of my tale, while Victorio stroked my hair.

"We're with you now Lakshmi," said Frank in a soft, soothing tone, "We're not going to let anything like that happen to you. You can stay here while the rest of us go. We'll pick you up on our way home. It'll be fine."

I sat bolt upright. "What? What are you talking about?"

Frank looked flummoxed, "I, well, I just thought, I mean...I know that Tyrone was just talking about how they treat the women and girls there...well, I just thought that made you think of what happened to your friend, and you were scared something like that might happen to you."

"No. No way. There's no way I'm staying here. They've stolen enough from me, they're not going to steal the whole rest of my life from me. That's not happening," my voice rising I said, "you are *not* going to leave me here. If we run into the Slavers I'll fight them with you."

I saw a slight smile curve the corner of Ching Shih's mouth as she wiped away her tears. She understood.

Frank and Tochuku sat staring at me like I was some kind of rabid animal they had just come upon.

Victorio didn't even skip a beat, "Well, I guess we'll head out in the morning, eh?"

As we all walked to the door Ching Shih stepped up and put an arm around me, eyes shining. She whispered into my ear, "We're in this together little sister." I had never heard her express that kind of affection, or solidarity, to anyone before.

That night I slept like a newborn baby, completely spent, completely trusting, if only because I lacked any energy with which to envision my enemies any longer. The emotional labor of my torrential rebirth had worn me out. Victorio slept as if slaughtered by his enemies, as usual, not stirring a muscle from the time he passed out until the morning sun spilled gleaming through the blinds in our east-facing windows.

We had packed as much as we could the day before, so we went very quickly from a dead sleep to each holding a napkin filled with a "to go" breakfast of scrambled eggs with cheese, wrapped in dense sliced bread, kindly prepared by our hosts. The horses clomped into the chill of the early fall morning, while we still rubbed the sleep from our eyes.

Frank led up our band, taking us down out of the hills on which the monastery sat, then south, then west, then south again. It was late afternoon when we came to an area to the southwest of town where we would wait until it was late enough at night to risk the two-mile trek into the heart of the southern side of town. In the meantime, we took turns napping, eating and keeping watch, hidden in a dense stand of oak and mahogany.

"Hey there Lakshmi, time to get goin'." Frank was lightly jostling my shoulder while whispering into my ear.

Night had deepened and a nearly full moon was already high in the sky. Some light would be helpful along the way, but a full moon might shed too much light. A full moon in a place with no electric lights was a powerful thing. I could see my surroundings so well that I had no trouble identifying the species of trees in our little forest, even from many yards off. We would be easily visible too. Still, it would be better than traveling in the daylight.

Victorio had packed my bag for me and was attaching it to my Pinto, Beans, while I wrapped my blanket around my shoulders, shawl style, and slung myself up onto her. The night had already turned frigid, in contrast to the pleasant daytime warmth.

Frank took the lead as we wended our way through the deteriorating streets as quietly as possible. Silver City looked much like Deming had, nearly a year and half ago, some sections completely destroyed, as if bombed, and some areas relatively whole. The horses found it easier going through the areas with less debris, so I was glad when our route wound through a fairly intact neighborhood. Victorio had moved up to ride next to Frank, Tochuku rode several paces behind them, and me and Ching Shih brought up the rear. All of us swiveled our heads—right, left, forward, look behind, right, left, and so on, vigilant for the slightest sign of trouble. Even Tochuku maintained a high level of alertness, despite his notorious tendency to wander into mental abstraction.

A sudden rushing sound emanated from a street to the north and we all halted tensely. Yowls and frenetic barking broke out as one pack of feral dogs encountered another. Frank turned to us and tilted his head in the opposite direction from the dogs, indicating that we needed to get out of there before they came our way. The Monks had warned us about the dogs saying that in a pack they wouldn't hesitate to attack a horse. We turned south at the next intersection, the snarling and barking diminishing.

The tall building that Matthew had described loomed just a few blocks away, indicating the center of the Maker's compound. I saw Frank slip his hand inside his jacket pocket to find the letter of introduction.

Victorio and Frank rounded the corner ahead just as Beans reared suddenly. I barely kept my seat as she kept stepping oddly backwards as if trying to avoid something. As I swung off her back while holding the reins tightly, I saw the problem—her foot was hurt. Speaking soothingly into her ear I finally convinced her to let me look at it. At first I couldn't see anything, but then the moon glinted on something clear and shiny, stuck just along the edge of her shoe. Glass. Ching Shih had dismounted as well and helped me hold her foot so we could pull the glass free. Tochuku turned back towards us to see what the fuss was about.

Just then an uproarious shouting erupted a couple of blocks east, exactly where Frank and Victorio disappeared. Horses neighed in alarm as the human tumult grew more frantic. Without a thought I shoved my horse's reins into Ching Shih's free hand and sprinted down the street, staying as close as I could to the buildings I passed for any cover they might give me. I rounded the corner and could finally see the source of the sounds when someone tackled me to the ground.

"For Christ's sake be quiet!" Frank hissed into my ear as he clamped one hand over my mouth. He had tied his horse to the same bit of fence that hid us from full view of the brouhaha ahead. Eyes popping out of my head I jerked my mouth free of his hand.

"Where's Victorio?" I whispered fiercely.

"There," said Frank, nodding in the direction of the crowd.

"Let me up!" I hissed.

"I'll let get up slowly, but you can't go darting down the street after him or they'll just get you too." Frank growled.

"Okay, okay, I'll be quiet but we gotta go see at least, right?"

"Yes, we do but you've got to promise you'll stay out of sight. It won't do him any good if you're captured."

"Got it, got it! Now get off me."

Frank eased his grip very gradually, watching my face closely.

Once his weight was off me I rose slowly to demonstrate my reliability.

"Let's go down this alley. We'll leave the horse here," said Frank.

Using our best hunter's stealth we made our way down the alley that led to the street where the altercation was in progress.

Peeking around the edge of a house we saw four people on horses and two people on foot being pulled behind them, bound by long ropes. A squirming, crying child was held by one of the riders. The two mounted people who did not have other people attached to their horses confronted one another directly. Victorio was of course one of them. Suddenly three more horses and riders rounded a corner to the east. I hoped like crazy that they were people who would be on Victorio's side in this standoff, or at least not against him, but they weren't. The new arrivals quickly surrounded Victorio, one of them cracking him on the head with a club. As Victorio's body fell forward onto his horse one of the riders dismounted and pulled him off.

My heart thundered like a thousand stampeding bison as Frank wrapped his arms around me like a vise, one hand clamping again onto my mouth. I watched helplessly as two men draped Victorio's limp body over his horse and tied him securely to it with thick ropes. One of them turned towards me and Frank, the full moon lighting up his features and frame nearly as clearly as the noon-day sun.

A man I recognized.

It was Lem. My throat opened in a scream, despite the

hand over my mouth, but fortunately the sound stayed mostly in my throat, and the bit that escaped was drowned out by the sounds of the horses and yelling men.

Soon, the entire party departed, heading north with their two original captives trotting behind the horses they were tied to in order to keep from being dragged. Frank eased his grip on me, allowing me out of the confines of his arms.

"Back there," I said, nodding in the direction of Tochuku and Ching Shih.

"Let's go try to find them. Hopefully there aren't any other Slavers around now."

After retrieving Frank's horse, we found our two remaining traveling companions and the three horses tucked into a little fenced yard behind a house, just steps away from where I had left them.

Frank shot Ching Shih a chastising look and she responded, "She bolted like lightening. I wasn't going to leave *him* alone," tilting her head at Tochuku.

After we had filled them in on events we debated what to do next.

"We have to go after him," I insisted.

"Not yet. We can't go now. They'll expect us," countered Frank.

"You're the one that let him get caught," I shot angrily.

"No, I wasn't. He went ahead of me while I took a piss. I told him to wait. They got him at the intersection. They didn't see me but of course they won't assume he was traveling alone."

"We have to get him," I repeated, my voice rising. "That

was Lem. The guy I told you about. One of Darian's gang. He was tying Victorio to the horse."

My three companions gaped at me, comprehension dawning.

Suddenly Ching Shih and Frank were at either side of me each holding onto one arm each, firmly.

Ching Shih spoke to me in a low voice, "Listen little sister, we have to be careful. On my honor we're not going to abandon Victorio. But if we want to be successful, we have to be mindful, right?"

I nodded mutely.

"I think we should continue on to the Maker's place. They may be able to help us. In fact, those were probably two Maker people they had. They may want our help too," said Frank.

"That's a good plan," concurred Ching Shih, "but they're going to be pretty wound up right now if some of their people just got taken."

"Well I guess we're just going to have to be extra careful," said Frank, "and for crying out loud would everybody *stick together*?"

Tochuku appeared stunned by the whole thing, eyes wide, glancing about fearfully, clearly in no mood to debate anything.

We all remounted, Frank taking the lead as we made our way along our originally planned route, Frank extending his letter in front of him like a flag of surrender.

21

As we neared the compound with the multi-storied building in the center we saw many people outside the buildings but inside the fence, milling about. It sounded like some were arguing, some crying.

We were only a block away when suddenly a masculine voice behind us said, "Stop or I'll shoot! Put your hands up!" We didn't have to be told twice. I wished very hard that the voice belonged to a Maker and not a Slaver.

Hands raised I turned my head very slowly to get a look at our captor. My hands flopped downward and my jaw dropped nearly to my knees.

"Robert!? I didn't recognize your voice. It's deeper."

Robert stared at me as if I were a phantom.

"L-l-lakshmi?" his voice dropped several decibels as he lowered his crossbow. "Is that really you? I...I thought you were dead."

Turning my horse, the others did the same, probably having sensed that it was safe. The others dropped their hands.

"Why did you think I was dead?" I asked. My head felt like a floating balloon. Crossing paths with one old enemy and one old friend, minutes apart. That's how small our world had become.

"Well, because Darian said you were. Said they killed you and buried you in the desert."

"God Robert. I'm so sorry. I escaped. They didn't catch me."

"Uh, you guys...," said Frank pointedly.

Suddenly vigilant and looking around anxiously, Robert told us, "Keep moving. I doubt the Slavers will be back tonight but we can't be too sure. Let's get inside!"

Robert led us to the well-guarded gate as the people milling about the yard inside the fence stared at us suspiciously. A woman with short, unnaturally scarlet hair and dressed in a flowing, floor length desert camouflage dress and heavy boots marched up to us authoritatively.

"Who the hell are these people?" she demanded of Robert.

"Friends, at least one of them...," said Robert defensively.

The woman scowled at us, looking us over for several long seconds before visibly relaxing.

"Well I know you're not Slavers because two of you are women. And you don't dress like them. Not enough leather."

Frank handed her the letter, "This is from Matthew, at the monastery. We've been friends since we were kids...."

"Why didn't you say so?" Her face lit up as she read.

"Wow. You mean you came all the way from there? Risking the Slavers and everything to get to us? What on earth for?" Looking us over again she added, "It doesn't look like you're starvin' or anything.... Hey Robert, could you please get their horses to the stable so they can be taken care of?" Turning back to us she added, "We don't keep many horses since we don't really go very far, but we do have a few, and there's plenty of room in the stable for yours. Oh, yeah, and my name is Mystery."

We each introduced ourselves as we removed our packs from the saddles. Robert led our horses away.

"I'll come find you soon," Robert assured me.

Mystery led us into the tallest building, the one we could see coming into town.

I couldn't stop myself from thinking about Victorio and what he must be going through as Mystery led us through the lower floors of the building, so I didn't hear much of her brief comments about the areas we passed through. Still, I couldn't help but notice some things through the doorways we passed.

One room smelled of growing things, radiating warm moisture, with marvelous scents wafting out. I caught a glimpse of greenery that seemed to extend for a very long way into the room, and up as well. Another room looked like a clay studio, and still another contained hulking pieces of metal machinery that I couldn't identify.

Many people milled about in the open areas, and passed us in the broad hallway through which we traveled. Finally, we came to a wide brick lined stairway that took us steeply upwards and out of the building we had walked through. The air was drier and somewhat stale. After we had ascended a full story the stairs topped out into another large, carpeted, hallway, this one dotted with doorways every few feet, much like hotels used to have.

After walking down that hallway for about a half a block it opened into an enormous room littered with comfortable chairs and couches, a huge television screen in one corner with seating arranged for easy viewing. In another corner opposite the screen was a pool table, a foosball table and a ping pong table. A few people were watching the TV, playing an old Star Trek film, and a couple were playing pool. We passed all these then turned down another hall like the one we had first gone through. Mystery stopped at one door, knocked, and hearing no response from within, swept into it. We followed her in.

"This room is connected to the next room," she said, gesturing to the closed door in one wall. "Between the two rooms you have four beds. The bathrooms don't work so you bathe and pee down the hall, just a few doors down. It says 'bathroom' so you won't get confused," she added wryly. "Drop your stuff so we can go talk. Clearly you folks came here for a reason. Robert said you lost someone in your party to the Slavers raid just now. We did too."

While there were a surprising number of people awake and busy so late at night, we were able to find a quiet corner to sit and talk in the big common room. As we settled in Robert found us, bringing a large tray of food and drink for us all. While Frank, Ching Shih and Tochuku told Mystery the story of our trip there, our reasons, and the misadventure we had, Robert and I settled into a couch a few yards away. The knot in my stomach sat in constant vigilance in worry about Victorio.

Robert shook his head in disbelief as we sat close together on the couch, him holding my hands in his.

"All this time, I thought they had killed you. I've cried so much for you. We even had a secret memorial service for you, late at night. How did you get away? Who are those people you're with?"

I gave him the highly abridged tale of my journey and my life with the Cave People, leaving out our location and the fact we lived in caves. Now Robert shook his head in wonder.

"God I'm so happy you made it. But what about...."

I cut him off, "I'll tell you more details later but you've got to tell me what happened at the compound! How did you escape?"

Robert launched into his own tale, which turned out to be every bit as strange as my own.

"Oh man, things got really weird after you left. When it became clear you were gone, Emma got out of her bed finally, acting a little zombie-like but otherwise doing all the stuff she normally did. She cooked, cleaned the kitchen, fed everyone like usual, but she almost never talked and looked like she was a million miles away. I took your place in the kitchen, working with her.

"During the days they looked for you that's how she was. I'm pretty sure Darian hadn't ever realized that she was so checked out, just lying in her bed, all that time, because they were gone so much of the time after...the thing with Sylvia.

"Anyway, when they came back the last day, Darian saying they had found you north of Deming, and that they had killed you and buried you, things got even weirder with Emma. She started making a point of being the one to take food to the big house, or serving Darian herself if he ever came in the kitchen to eat.

"The rest of us were reeling. Some were so scared they could hardly work or think straight. Me and some of the others talked at night about how messed up it all was, that we didn't want to stay there and be slaves anymore, no matter what. It seemed like maybe they wouldn't have killed you if you hadn't gone alone, that you would have stood a chance anyway. So some of us started stashing bags with provisions and sneaking knives from the kitchen and the like. Emma sort of provided cover for us by being so nice to Darian, even though we never talked about it with her.

"In the meantime, Darian sent Lem and Jeff away. It wasn't too ugly because they were so outnumbered by the others, who were still totally loyal to Darian. He said to them, 'you can either leave peacefully or we can kill you. You choose.' So they left.

"About six of us had packed enough for a week or two and were just putting the fine points on our escape plan when Emma did something that none of us saw coming, least of all Darian.

"Darian sat there in the kitchen late one night, eating after a scouting trip. The other gang members were already in the big house, asleep. Emma was there serving him like usual, like it was no big deal, while I finished the sweeping. Emma had handed Darian a bowl of her chile stew, which he loved, and he was hungry so he ate it up. But before he got halfway through it his face just landed in his bowl and he sat there like that.

"I was freaked out. Did he just fall asleep all of a sudden? Would he drown in his soup? I just didn't know but I ran over to him and lifted his face out of the stew. He wasn't drowning in it. He was dead. Really dead. Just like that.

"I looked up at Emma and she stood there, a long kitchen knife in her hand, her eyes gleaming and very creepy smile on her face. She marched over, with more energy that I'd seen her use in years, grabbed him by the hair while shoving me aside and set her knife against his neck as if to saw his head off. I stopped her because I really couldn't see the point in trying to make him more dead than he already was, and the mess would have been a really big problem. She didn't fight me, just stepped back with that smile on her face.

"I realized we had better get out of there, and fast. And so did she. Emma had known about our plan after all. She said, 'you young people get the hell out of here. I'll hold them off. They won't get you. I'm already dead and have no use for living anymore. I'll die happy if I know that the rest of you are free.'

"I didn't argue with her, just laid Darian down on the bench he was on, then went to wake the others. We also woke the ones who hadn't wanted to escape, telling them quickly what had happened and that it might go badly for them if they stayed. Most of them were still too paralyzed with fear to do anything but we had to get going so we did. There were ten of us that ended up leaving, and having only eight horses we had to double up some.

"I went into the kitchen just before going, and found Emma there with a bunch of large buckets that were filled with rags soaked in oil. She often saved oil for soap making so it took me a second to realize the rags were a new addition. We hugged a long time. And really, I have never seen her look so happy in all the years I knew her. Then she pulled one of the larger rags out of the oil and rubbed it all over herself, her clothes and everything. My skin crawled but a couple of the others had come in, pulling me away, to the horses. Maybe I should have taken her with us, made her go. But she looked so happy. So clear.

"As we finished loading up outside I saw Emma setting clumps of rags at the base of the main house, where all of Darian's men slept. She splashed the remaining oil against the walls. Then she went back inside the kitchen and came out with a big lit torch and walked serenely around the perimeter of the house, lighting each oily bundle. As I rode with the others I kept glancing back. The last thing I saw was the house starting to seriously flame, and Emma sitting on a bench right outside it, like she was sitting down to watch a movie in a theater. Then she lit herself on fire, going up in flames like the torch she held."

I stared at him numbly, trying to take it all in. Within a week of my leaving, Darian and his men, and Emma, were dead.

"But, if they all died, then why didn't you just stay there?" I asked.

"You know, we talked about it but we just couldn't go back. The others who were left, they could start over. I just knew I could never be at peace there ever again. I had to get out of there. And the others with me felt the same. We rode northwest to stay clear of Deming, then west to Silver City, staying a long way from the highway but paralleling it.

"Just before we made it to town, we ran into a small group of Slavers. We scuffled a little and they got one horse with a man and his young daughter on it, and another woman, but the rest of us got away. We had no idea what to expect in Silver City, but just dumb luck took us right up to here, to the Makers. We stayed out of sight, peeking around a corner to see if they seemed dangerous or not. It didn't look like a slaving place, all clean and neat and fruit and pecan trees growing in giant planters outside. The people tending the planters looked happy. So we risked it. I went alone at first, just walked up to the fence and asked if they would help us. And they did."

Frank walked up to us at that point.

"We've got a plan."

22

"What, what are we going to do? I can leave right now!" It had been all I could do to keep from bolting after Victorio as it was. If it hadn't been for my reunion with Robert I would have been begging to go before we even set down our belongings.

Frank held his hands up in anticipation of my assault. "No, no, no Lakshmi. We've got a good plan, one that might actually work, but we're going to have to play it cool if we're going to stand a chance. And we're going to have to rest up for the night before we do anything. Everyone needs to be sharp if we're going to get Victorio and the Maker people out. The Slavers are used to people trying to break other people out. We can't go off half-cocked."

Robert and I returned to the other group to hear the plan.

"This is going to take more courage from you," said Ching Shih, nodding her head my direction, "than from the rest of us."

I nodded, a tingling sensation rolling across my skin.

The combination of pre-dawn light and the full moon lit up the Northern Slaver's compound enough for me to perceive the layout and orient myself, while still providing enough darkness and shadow for cover.

The tall chain link entrance gates faced the deteriorating street. A dusty field on the other side of the street served as a parking lot of sorts for about a half dozen supply wagons for the Slavers. A bit of pinon and juniper forest formed a deep U shape around the lot.

Coming from around one of the wagons, I took a deep breath then ran straight towards the closed and locked gates at top speed, finally allowing the pent-up fear and rage over Victorio's kidnapping free reign. I had spent the short night tossing and turning, trying to think clearly, trying to remain rational. All that was gone now. The Slavers weren't going to kill another person I loved.

"Victorio!!Vic-tor-io! Let him out you troglodytes! Let him go!" I screamed through the gate like a deranged lunatic, loud enough to wake everyone inside, Slavers and prisoners alike.

"You brain-dead brutes, you let me in there right now! I'm taking Victorio and you can't stop me!"

I climbed a couple of feet up the fence, rattling it ferociously with the weight of my entire body.

Pounding on the gates caused that entire side of the fence to jangle clamorously. The razor wire topping the fence bobbed and swayed.

"Lakshmi, don't come in! Don't' come in!" I heard

Victorio yell, somewhere inside the gates. I couldn't see him but he sounded close enough that I should be able to get to him pretty quickly. His voice sounded rough but if he could yell then he definitely wasn't dead or seriously maimed. My heart jumped with happiness.

In moments two guards were at the gate, unlocking it as fast as they could.

"You want your man little girl?" sneered a greasy man of indeterminate age, as he turned the key. I spat in his face. He wiped it away and glared at me before continuing.

"Stay out Lakshmi! Please don't come in! Run!" yelled Victorio hoarsely.

"Hey girl, I've got a special present for you, for you and your man," said the other, leering at me and grabbing his crotch.

"Just let me in you slimy cockroach spawn!" It took every bit of will power I had to stay there, the two of them inches away, but I did. Timing was everything and I needed to get this just right.

Soon there was a whole swarm of Slavers beside the guards, all taunting me and laughing, making vulgar gestures and speculating with one another about who would get me first. I was shaking with fear but they couldn't see it because I was rattling the fence so hard. I worried my legs would give out.

The thick chain was being unwrapped from either side of the gate.

"Get back!" the greasy guard snarled at the others, "I can't get the gate open if you're pushing against it." They inched back, just enough to allow the necessary play in the chain to finish unwinding it.

"You're going to let me in you overgrown worms, and I'm going to get Victorio out!" I bellowed, while they continued their jeering insults.

I felt the doors of the gate release and start to open.

I jumped free of the fence and ran as fast as I could towards the wagons on the dusty lot, a good twenty Slavers on my heels. I could smell the stench of Greasy Guard's breath behind me. For a moment I was sure I had misjudged the timing and that I would soon be pulverized by the Slaver's boots, or worse. I darted around one wagon and between two others, the Slavers splitting around all the wagons, some going between to follow me, and others running around the outside of the cluster to head me off when I emerged.

Just then silent groups of Makers stood up inside the wagon beds, not noticed at first by the Slavers because of the poor light and their focus on me, at ground level. Armed with long blowguns of narrow-gauge PVC pipe they blew tiny darts into my pursuers. When hit, each Slaver jerked a bit then continued running towards me, then fell to the ground as if in slow motion. Several had made it past the wagons and the blow dart brigade but more Makers with blow guns popped up from behind trees claiming the rest of them. I flew by Frank, on the ground, who also wielded a blowgun.

"Get them into these two wagons!" yelled one Maker guy and others fell instantly to the work of loading the fallen Slavers, while some kept a lookout.

I hadn't slowed down at all but tore in a circle, back

around to the gates, now standing open. I bolted in as fast as I could straight through them.

"Victorio!"

"Here! I'm here! Lakshmi you shouldn't be here!"

I ran straight down the entry corridor and paused at the first intersection, not sure which to take.

"Victorio! Where are you?" I called. I knew he couldn't be far since I had heard him from outside the gate.

"Here! Here!" I turned and ran in the direction of his voice.

I found him in a large grey cinder block room with several hallways coming off it in the other three cardinal directions, south, west and north. There, in the middle of the room was Victorio. Locked into an old-fashioned stock, like something out of the Middle ages. His head and hands emerged from holes and the top piece was secured with a heavy chain and lock. I ran up to Victorio, who looked the worse for wear, bruised all over but at least with no missing body parts that I could see.

I crouched down next to him, kissing his swollen lips.

"Ow!" he said.

"Oh god I'm sorry!"

"Honey I'm so glad to see you but if you don't get me out of this thing, we're both going to be dead pretty soon. Or worse."

I popped up and looked around in the semi-darkness for anything I could use to break the lock. In a corner I spotted some old tool handles, apparently awaiting repairs, or to be disposed of. As I walked over to them, I heard a familiar voice, and not Victorio's.

Lem.

My intestines turned to water for an instant as I turned to face him, emerging from the southern corridor. He stopped momentarily at the entrance to the big room, as surprised to see me as I was to see him. Glancing around he saw no one else but me, and Victorio, still secure in his stock. He relaxed and swaggered our direction. He was still on the opposite side of the big room, but closing the distance.

Keeping my eyes on him I bent my knees just enough so I could reach back for the sturdy axe handle I had spotted, wishing fervently that the axe itself was still attached.

"Well, well! Look who's here! My old friend who got me and Jeff kicked out of Darian's!" crowed Lem.

I stood my ground, axe handle in hand, trying to think of what to do.

"I wonder if you'd be as sweet and tender as that friend of yours? The one in the pretty dress?"

I fought down the bile that rose in my throat.

"Naw. She was a nice girl. You're just cold and hard and tough. But you know, even the worse piece I ever had was still pretty damned good! So, you know...," Lem shrugged and leered.

"Stay away from her!" yelled Victorio, straining to see Lem from his clamped position.

"Or what Tonto? What the hell are you going to *do* about it if I don't?"

"Yeah, stay away from me," I said raising the axe handle, reflexively sensing the weight and length.

"What are you going to do sweet cheeks? Hit me with a *stick*?" Lem guffawed.

So I did.

As I had hundreds of times since I was named Rabbit Girl, I raised the axe handle, took a sharp bead on my target, and released.

No prey had ever meant so much to me, no matter how hungry I had been. I hit him for Sylvia, for Emma, for Naomi who died while trying to escape the compound all those years before, and for Sammy, who Darian and his men had tortured to death, long before I dared to escape.

The axe handle connected with a loud thunk just above one ear and Lem dropped like a sack of rocks off a very high cliff. Blood trickled from his temple as his eyes rolled up towards the ceiling, wide with disbelief.

Just then, Jeff appeared from the same hallway Lem had.

It took a second for Jeff to comprehend what he was seeing. He kneeled down at his brother's side, checking for a pulse. Jeff rose slowly, eyes widening with a tsunami of hated gathering behind them.

"You bitch! You killed him!" Jeff stalked straight for me and I stood helplessly, my brain completely devoid of any notion at all of what to do next. I tensed, hands now empty, bracing for his assault.

A woman's hand appeared at the side of Jeff's neck. He started to turn to face her but before he could complete his turn she squeezed his neck in a way that didn't look particularly lethal, but he dropped like a sack of carrots to the floor nevertheless. Ching Shih stood before me.

"You took care of the first one," she said, looking pleased with both of us.

Just then four more Slavers rounded the corner of the west hallway, barreling down upon us like a fury of hyenas.

"Take this," said Ching Shih, shoving a bolt cutter into my hands. "Get him out of there."

She turned to meet the onslaught like a hurricane of swirling arms and legs, cracking one jaw, rupturing a kidney, snapping a spine and apparently sterilizing one of them for life, all in the time it took for me to dash to Victorio.

As our latest assailants settled into unconsciousness or were rendered incapable of movement by excruciating pain, I snapped the links of the chain until it fell away from the lock holding Victorio. I lifted the heavy stock and grabbed him, draping one of his arms over my shoulder as he tried to stand and largely failed.

"You DID save me Rabbit Girl!" said Victorio, a dynamic duo of pain and joy dancing across his face.

More steps running towards us down the north hallway, from the area where slaves were held.

I set Victorio onto the floor, where he struggled to lift himself despite the cramping of his legs. As Ching Shih and I braced ourselves for another fight, several Makers emerged from the mouth of the north hallway, leading their friends who had been taken with Victorio, along with several other captives.

"Are there more slaves to get out?" I asked.

"Yes," answered one Maker, "but Slavers are coming behind us. We gotta get out of here!"

"This way!" I gestured towards the open gates.

We all sprang like jackrabbits across the street and into the forest, Ching Shih and I half-dragging, half-carrying Victorio. Slowing down a bit as Victorio gained his feet, we cautiously wound our way eastward through an abandoned neighborhood, then south to the Maker's place. Such a large group would be easily visible to anyone in the area and those of us who weren't injured looked around constantly in every direction. As risky as it was, none of the Slavers came after us. The loss of so many of their own must have made them wary, at least for the time being.

It was still early in the day when we arrived at the Maker complex, the massive solar array atop their buildings shining like a beacon. Victorio and I went to their infirmary, along with the two Makers who had been abducted with him. Like Victorio the other man had been beaten. The man's daughter, a girl of about eight, wasn't physically harmed but stared wide eyed and was trembling, still so petrified she wasn't even able to cry. She clung to her father so hard that he had a hard time taking off his shirt so the medic could look him over. A kindly woman, who turned out to be a psychologist, took the pair aside to a quiet part of the infirmary and spoke softly to them while the father held his daughter on his lap.

As a medic cleaned up Victorio and treated his scrapes I watched the little family out of the corner of my eye. After a few minutes the girl's trembling subsided and she started crying, which the psychologist seemed to take as a good sign. Before long the girl's crying waned and she fell asleep in her father's lap. Then the father wept as the psychologist spoke quietly some more to him, as if giving him instructions.

Victorio was pretty shaky too, and once his physical wounds had been sufficiently attended to, the psychologist came over to us, speaking to Victorio.

"My name is Nola. You've just been in a potentially traumatizing situation. I recommend that you drink lots of water, eat some food, take a long bath and then sleep as much as you can for the rest of the day and the night. Allow your body to tremble or shake without trying to stop it. This is your body's way of releasing the trauma, not something to be alarmed about, even though it can seem weird or scary."

To me she added, "The same pretty much goes for you, even though you didn't get beat up. Don't share what happened, or ask him to, for a few days at least. When you are both eating and sleeping somewhat normally you can talk about it. This is a good time to be quiet together, be of physical comfort without talking too much."

"I killed a guy. Who was going to hurt me and Victorio," I blurted out.

Her eyes widened. "Oh! In that case, everything I said to him definitely applies equally to you too."

That would be easy enough. I felt completely spent. I had killed Lem. I figured I should feel happy about that, and I was certainly relieved. People like that just shouldn't get to be around others, and death was one way to make sure of that. But I felt more sick than joyous, and I didn't know why. Ching Shih said that she probably hadn't killed

Jeff, just knocked him out. I didn't know how I felt about that. I sure never wanted to see him again, that's for sure.

"I'm usually in the room next door to the infirmary," Nola said, "you can come find me there if you have anything especially alarming come up." She gave us both a sympathetic look and left.

We met Robert in the hallway as we were walking towards our room. He had come bearing food on a large tray, along with a pot of what smelled like lavender and mint tea. The three of us continued to our room and found Frank and Ching Shih already there, talking about the operation.

"Nola, the psychologist, said that Victorio and Lakshmi shouldn't be talking about what happened," Robert informed them. Frank and Ching Shih looked at each other and rose from their chairs. I had been sleeping in the same room with Ching Shih while Frank and Victorio had shared the other.

"The room on the other side of this one is free too, if you two don't want to share a room," said Robert.

"Yeah," nodded Frank, "that'd be good. Thanks. Rest well everyone."

Ching Shih departed through the little doorway connecting our rooms, and Robert left us with our meal.

Victorio looked a lot better than he had, but still wobbly. The bruises all over him gave him the look of someone who had been dead and buried for a few days but his strong appetite alleviated my concerns.

It was easy for us to keep our promise to Nola that we wouldn't talk about what happened yet, because neither of us particularly wanted to. Victorio collapsed on the bed after our meal and I went to soak in the tub. The image of Lem and Jeff, vicious and taunting, kept resurfacing in my mind, clattering against my nerves. My body started to tremble and, as instructed, I let it, even though it disturbed me. As the trembling subsided tears of relief poured down my cheeks. The image of the brothers, dead on the floor, evaporated and my mind and breathing quieted. I dried myself quickly and slid into the bed next to Victorio, drifting easily to sleep.

23

I awoke as the sun was setting to see Victorio sitting on the couch eating from the tray that Robert had set on the coffee table. Wrapping a blanket around myself, I joined him. He fed me little bites of some delicious cracker type thing that I couldn't identify, except for the rosemary and garlic in them. Kissing me gently with his still bruised lips, Victorio then went to take his own bath. I crawled back into bed and sank into a dreamless oblivion.

The next day we found Robert in the common room, which was like a giant living room. He showed us where the dining hall was located so we could return our tray and dishes and get breakfast. Then he filled us in on the activities of our traveling companions.

"Frank and Ching Shih are planning with Mystery and the others. Tochuku has been in thick with the other techies since you first came. Hardly seen him at all. Would you like me to show you around?" Robert gestured broadly, apparently indicating the entire complex.

I certainly had been intrigued. I wondered what was in all the strange rooms. How did they live in such a small area and still support so many people? They had to have at least two hundred citizens in their little neighborhood.

We descended the steps from the housing block down to the maze-like building where nearly everything the Makers used was either grown or constructed.

"What was that room where things were growing?" I asked.

"Ahhhh...the greenhouse! Yes, that's actually my favorite place," said Robert, as he led us to the room where I had spotted greenery when we first arrived.

Large double doors opened into the multistoried central building that we had seen as we made our way into town. It wasn't so much a building as one humongous room, holding more plants that I could ever have imagined in an area that size, square-footage wise anyway. Cubic feet were another matter. Not only were there long, densely packed rows of wooden planters on the floor brimming with a huge variety of grasses, but small white round containers of plants, strung together with a thin white plastic strips that rose up in columns all the way to the ceiling several stories above us. The entire volume of the room, dozens of yards long, wide and vertically, held plants, some native ones that I recognized, and many others I didn't.

A number of people moved amongst the planters, on the floor and at all levels above, picking what was ready to eat, trimming away dead leaves and placing young plants into empty containers. One man was singing a cheerful song about birds and bees, and a few of the others joined in for the chorus when it came around.

"We grow using hydroponics mostly, though the ones on the floor and outside are grown in soil. You probably couldn't see from where you came in the building but all around the perimeter of the residential area and the east side of this complex we have a whole orchard with fruit and nut trees. They dug up the cement sidewalks all around to plant the trees," explained Robert.

At a glance there seemed to be an unimaginable variety of plants there. In one column rose marjoram plants, the next cilantro and the next thyme. Beyond that were pinto bean plants that wound themselves around the plastic strips, climbing towards the ceiling. The broad wooden planters below these, placed on the floor, grew amaranth, brilliant maroon heads swaying in the gentle breeze generated by the mist and air that moved through the whole room. Devon would swoon if she could see this.

Between the rows sat tall extendable ladders so that all the plants could be accessed for planting and harvesting. Horizontal scaffolding had been built every 12 feet up or so, providing another perch for tending the plants. This giant garden spread out and upwards.

"Here's our algae farm," Robert pointed to a series of enclosed tubes, like cylindrical aquariums that also rose upwards.

"Algae?" Victorio asked. "What do you want with algae?"

"People all over the world have used it for food. Very high protein and full of minerals and vitamins. And they hope to use it for fuel too."

"Sounds gross!" I said.

Robert laughed, "Its actually okay once you get used to it. They dry it in thin crunchy slabs, and flavor it with herbs and salt. You can powder it and drink it in water too."

"And down this way," Robert continued, leading us down one long row of greenery and around a corner, "are our aquaponics tanks."

I stared in gaping wonder at giant metal open-air tanks in which flitted and swirled a huge population of fish. Tilapia. A sturdy latticework of plastic strips was suspended across the surface of the water, and on top of those sat long, narrow planters, each with lettuce, spinach, kale or other leafy green vegetables growing in them. The roots of these plants grew out of the bottom of their planters and straight into the fish tank water.

"The plants use the nutrients provided by the fish poop, which also helps to keep the tanks clean," explained Robert. "The Mayans, Aztecs, and Chinese did this, ages ago."

"Is this your only source of meat then?" asked Victorio.

"Yeah, pretty much. We grow plenty of legumes and nuts so we really don't need meat. Some people here don't even eat the fish, but a lot of us like it."

The next part of our tour took us through a series of metal warehouses that completely surrounded the greenhouse building. The entire complex, not including the residential building to the north, took up two full blocks.

We moved into a hallway that connected the greenhouse to the warehouses. The long hall was dotted periodically with doorways.

The first few of the rooms we explored held a variety of 3D printers for making pretty much anything one could imagine—clothing, tables, chairs, game pieces and boards, dining utensils, pots and pans.

"We never worry about not having enough. Anything we're not using can just be put in a hopper and reprocessed and put through a printer again. We have virtually no waste," explained Robert. "We could use more raw materials, but the Slavers make it hard to get out and scavenge the houses and the dumps."

One room held large tables with sewing machines, and looms of various sizes. The walls in this room were lined with plastic utility shelves containing bolts of fabric, colorful bunches of yarn, knitting and crochet needles, and other implements of fabric arts and crafts. Two people sat side by side, spinning some kind of fluffy fiber into yarn on old-fashioned spinning wheels. A man was sewing while a woman pedaled a stationary bicycle next to him, while the two chatted.

"The bicycle generates electricity for the sewing machine," Robert explain. I then noticed the wires and gadgets connecting them both.

Another room contained a giant kitchen and pantry, where all the food was processed for storage and prepared for meals. There was a wood working room that reminded me of Hallie's shop except much bigger. A clay studio, complete with foot powered potter's wheels. A glass blowing studio. An old-fashioned blacksmith's forge.

"The people who started this place actually set up most of this before the virus hit. They knew that the systems that people were dependent upon weren't going to last, though I guess they had a lot of different theories about why. A monster virus wasn't anywhere near the top of the list."

I had a hard time taking in the scope of everything we were seeing, and judging from Victorio's face, wide eyed and slightly slack-jawed, he was experiencing something similar.

"I know it's a lot to absorb at first," said Robert, "but you get used to it after a while." He continued, "still, you know, I've never really been able to get used to living in town, basically in a prison, since it's so dangerous to leave. I miss the sky and the air, working outdoors."

"The Slavers are a pretty big problem, eh?" said Victorio.

"Yeah, but we also have a chemistry lab, and our chemists, the ones who came up with the sedative for the blow guns we used the other night on the Slavers, have some ideas."

"Sedative? I thought it was poison! You mean they weren't killed? What happened to them?" I asked. As much as I hated the Slavers, I felt a little relieved. Mass killing, however justified, wasn't something I was ever going to feel great about.

"Well...," Robert hesitated, "Actually, they've all been taken to drug rehab."

"Drug rehab?" asked Victorio, shaking his head in puzzlement, "you mean, to get them off drugs? I didn't think there were enough drugs left to be a problem."

"No. Not to get them off drugs. They use drugs to help them. I don't know that much about it. I should take you to Nola. She can explain it better than I can."

This place seemed more wonderful, and baffling, by the moment. Soon we were back near the infirmary, at Nola's office.

"Oh my god no, of course we didn't *kill* them," Nola exclaimed. "Well, I can't say we've *never* killed anyone, the Slavers, but only in self-defense, when there was no other practical alternative. No, no, what we do here, or attempt to do, with varying levels of success, is rehabilitate them. People aren't born being hateful and violent. They're made that way. And while some have been hard-wired for violence from such a young age that there's not much we can do, most of them we can help to heal. At least, we've had some success with the few Slaver's we've captured over the years. Now we have a big group, I think eighteen of them, that were brought in from the raid yesterday. We've never tried it at once with so many, but we're optimistic."

"What do you do?" Victorio asked. I leaned forward on the table at which we sat, completely perplexed. What on earth was she talking about?

"Well, first we take them to the Secure Room, several rooms actually, inside another, completely surrounding room, inside another completely surrounding room. All locked," Nola explained.

"A prison, you mean," I said, raising my eyebrows. I didn't know how much I was going to trust someone who spoke that way about what was basically imprisonment, having been a prisoner myself for so long. Not that I felt sorry for the Slavers, since I had accepted the idea that they had been killed. But I figure we should call things what they are and not kid ourselves.

Nola sighed, pursing her lips before continuing, "Yes, I suppose that's one way to think of it. We don't think of it as punishment, but keeping that person from hurting any of the rest of us. The Inner Sanctum is a large room, with several cubicles for privacy. They are all equipped with comfortable beds, tables, chairs, closets, an assortment of clothing, toilets and showers. In addition to good food, we also bring them other things they might want, craft supplies, paper, etc. We leave books about the nature of trauma, violence, its causes and cures, for the ones that seem to know how to read. We talk to them every day through a window with two-way speakers, encouraging them to relax and to talk if they want. The person often still resists but their defenses weaken and they often have a kind of breakdown emotionally. Anger, crying, peace. If they stay peaceful for a few days or so, they are allowed into the next ring outward where they can interact more naturally with the others who are at a similar stage in their process. Once we see they get along with those people for a while, then we see how they do out here with the rest of us."

"It sounds like you're kind of deprogramming them, like they used to with people who had joined cults or something, right?" ask Victorio.

"Kind of. Really, we're all programmed in a sense. We all hold beliefs and attitudes in life. These beliefs determine how we see things around us and those perceptions determine our actions. So we are actually deprogramming them, then RE-programming them in a way that fits well with our way of life, the culture that we have deliberately cultivated here," Nola continued.

"But what's the 'drug rehab' about?" I asked.

"That's for the people who are more resistant, who don't seem to be pulling out of their violent tendencies during the process I just described. Some people just need more help. The idea for our drug rehab process has its origins in some experiments done decades ago, using psychedelic drugs to help people heal from addiction and a variety of mental illnesses. They actually made some good progress before some folks decided to distribute these substances willy-nilly and pretty soon they were made illegal.

"Anyway, it's a very carefully conceived protocol. We start by putting them in one of the rooms and seeing what they do in there, through one-way glass. Once they have stopped raging we send in one of our specially trained rehab people. They have a small needle on a ring they wear, filled with a strong sedative, just in case. They bring the person a drink they like, laced with some LSD-25, or DMT or MDMA, depending on the person, and sit down to talk with the them. When they start to come on to the drug, the therapist talks them through their experience, and holds a place of compassion and non-judgment for them. It's pretty amazing what can happen."

"You drug them?" I was shocked and horrified.

She eyed me levelly, "Countless cultures throughout time have used psychotropic plants for healing psychological wounds and for other reasons, like seeking spiritual or practical guidance, or for the exploration of consciousness. What we're doing here isn't new at all. We just use the substances we have access to. We are growing peyote, ayahuasca and chacruna, some of the plants used traditionally, but we don't have enough to harvest just yet. But we do have a great chemist, so we use pharmaceuticals for now."

I was opening my mouth to ask more questions about their drug rehab program, and what would ultimately happen to the Slavers they had captured, when Frank showed up.

"Hey there," he exclaimed happily. Hugs were exchanged between Frank and me and Victorio. "I was hoping I could find you. It's a pretty big place. I'm glad to see you both looking better. You feeling okay?"

"I'm okay, except for the bruises that'll take a while to heal," answered Victorio.

"Lots better," I replied, nodding.

"Good, good! Let's go talk."

We thanked Nola for her time and headed off to the Common Room with Frank to find out what he, Ching Shih and the others had been planning.

"We should get going pretty soon. Like tomorrow morning. We dealt the Northern Slavers a pretty big blow, taking so many of their people, and releasing so many of their captives. The Makers don't think the Southern Slavers have caught on to what's happened. Apparently they've been keeping to themselves lately. But that could change at any time too. We're going to travel to the university to see the Uvies with some of the Makers, some of their scientists, because there are several scientists at the university too, plus a much bigger, better stocked lab than they have here. They want to see if they can make up a large enough batch of sedative to dose the whole Northern Slaver complex. They've been setting up a giant drug rehab place like they have here, to hold a lot of Slavers."

"What does that have to do with us?" I asked.

"Well nothing, except that we're going to travel together, and soon, so we can get over there safely, and give you a chance to expand your book collection."

24

The next morning our horses were packed and ourselves astride them before the sun had cleared the eastern horizon. The sky was cloudless but that changed by mid-afternoon, when we received our seasonal daily dousing from our modest monsoon. Numerous birds flitted amongst the trees and other plants set around the Maker enclosure. Several of the Makers' scientists and security people accompanied Victorio, Frank, Ching Shih, Tochuku and myself. They were on foot, laden only with backpacks, since the university was little more than a mile away.

Tochuku was loathe to leave the Maker compound, with its huge array of technological wonders, but they had agreed that Tochuku should return once winter had passed.

"There is so much I could learn from them, that would benefit us. We could have an indoor garden like they do, and make so many things...," he commented.

Leaving Robert was hard, but we too promised to reunite in the spring.

If the Maker's plan to eliminate the Slavers by transforming their very characters was successful, then travel in the spring would be much safer and easier than our journey there.

"I'd sure like to come visit," Robert said as he held me long and close in his bear-like embrace.

"That would be great," I said, noncommittally. I wasn't in a position to grant him a unilateral invitation, as much as I would like to. I would have to gain the permission of the rest of our community.

Robert shook Victorio's hand.

"Thank you for taking good care of my friend, my sister, Lakshmi," he said.

"More like the other way around," Victorio commented wryly, "At least lately."

The Uvies had no way of knowing that the Northern Slavers had been temporarily incapacitated so we had to follow the usual routine of approaching the hidden entrance and using the rather complicated secret knock upon the door. I suspected it was Morse Code. The Makers were in somewhat regular contact with the Uvies so they knew the knock. Most of us stayed out of sight while three of the Makers knocked at the reinforced steel door.

It seemed like forever before our Maker emissaries whistled for us to come.

"They thought maybe we were being forced by the Slavers to knock. We had to tell them the whole story about the raid, and about you guys, before they'd open the first door."

As we made our way through the double doorway, horses and all, we found ourselves in a long, dank, cinderblock passage that led to another huge steel door, which required another knock that allowed us into the building itself. That knock was changed frequently, and only given to the Uvie's security people.

Then we were led through another long hallway and out a door that led into a grassy courtyard. The buildings that comprised their whole living space were surrounded by high chain link fences topped with razor wire, much like the Slavers used. Several guards walked the fence perimeter, enough to ensure that they could each see two others at all times, I was told later. The courtyard housed goats, chickens and a few horses.

Once our horses were shown the water trough and a pile of freshly cut grass for eating, we humans were led into the largest building, the "Student Memorial Building" from the lettering on the side. We had hardly passed through one of the long line of doors on the east side, and into a broad tiled hallway, when I saw it.

To our left stood two heavy glass-paned doors with the word "Library" printed above them, formed in thick wooden letters, painted in dark red with fine gold lines that traced the edges. Through the doors I saw an enormous room with stairs that ran up to two more stories. The long rows of books continued too far into the depths of the room for me to be able to see the end of them. Three stories of books. My library wasn't the Library of

Alexandria, this was. Sita's library, as impressive as it was, wasn't any more than a large personal collection in comparison.

Victorio, who had been focused on the introductions being made by our Maker escorts to the Uvies who greeted us, looked at me with a puzzled expression.

"What's going on Lakshmi?" he whispered my direction as I stood slack-jawed, gaping at the informational spectacle before me.

I turned to him, completely mute and eyes wide. He directed his gaze to where I had been looking. His eyes widened too, and a broad smile spread like warm honey across his face.

"You found the motherlode eh?" he said, clearly amused by my astonishment.

"And this is *our* librarian, Lakshmi," Frank was saying to a tall serious looking man in front of him.

I turned at the sound of my name and when the man took in my face his frown melted like summer ice cream and he exclaimed, "Oh my god. Lakshmi! I can't believe it's you."

I was amazed for the second time in a matter of seconds as I found myself confronted with one of my mother's old friends and colleagues, Elphias Dade.

"Doctor Dade!" I exclaimed.

He laughed and shook his head at me. "No need for the 'doctor' anymore my dear, just Elphias is fine, or even 'Elf,' as most around here call me," he added rolling his eyes comically. I couldn't think of anyone who looked less like an elf than Dr. Dade, tall, wiry, beak-nosed and grizzled, but I was so happy to see him I would call him anything he wanted.

I had never known Elphias, Elf, particularly well myself, but my mother often chatted with the university's librarian as I followed her through the stacks as she searched for suitable material for her classes. As a child, Elf had always treated me with a kind formality completely unlike any other adults I knew. Memories of my mother came flooding back to me. I would always associate the smell of books with her, and here I was, with a mountain of books to one side, and her dear librarian friend on the other.

But there was no time to indulge nostalgia now. Our hosts, including Elf, led us away from the library to show us to the rooms where we would stay. First, we descended the stairs, passed the second floor of the building which housed the huge kitchen and dining room, then down to the ground floor which served as a general gathering area. We emerged out the southern doors then headed east towards two enormous buildings which had been the dormitories before the virus.

"This is where we all have our bedrooms and personal living space. Many of the individual dorm rooms have had walls removed and doors installed to connect several together so families can live comfortably in one continuous space. The bathrooms are at either ends of the halls on both floors," said Elf as he guided us to several rooms at the end of the second-floor hallway, the ones so far unoccupied by the permanent residents. "After you've gotten settled here, we'll be happy to show you around our little settlement. I'll be in the library—as usual," he said with a wry grin.

Victorio and I shared a room, while Tochuku, Frank and Ching Shih were assigned separate rooms, all of them in a row.

"Some library, eh?" Victorio asked as we unpacked our belongings.

I shook my head, speechless at first. Victorio grinned.

"I've been so worried about how few books, how little information we had. I forgot how big this library was." I said.

"You can copy a lot of them can't you, on the scanner Tochuku gave you?"

"Yes, and he gave me the one he had, making me promise to include as many of the engineering textbooks as I could. Still, we will only be able to get a fraction of the books here copied."

We lie on the separate twin beds in the room, staring up at the ceiling as we talked.

"How are you doing now, since you bravely rescued me?" he asked, only half teasing.

I guffawed shortly. "Yeah, that was crazy!" Turning serious I rolled onto my side to look at him. He looked back at me.

"You were really brave Lakshmi. I was so glad to see you. I couldn't imagine how you were going to get me out, but you did. You know, I could hear all the stuff you were screaming at them. I was so scared for you. I thought for sure they would kill you the second they got the gate open." Victorio rubbed his still bruised wrists absentmindedly, as if his body suddenly remembered the restraints that had held him.

"Troglodytes? Cockroach spawn?" Victorio was now starting to laugh in earnest. "You...you," gasping between laughs, "you really do have a great vocabulary!"

The memory came back clearly, rattling the fence and shouting insults and soon I was overcome with giggling too. Victorio was hugging his sides and rolling back and forth on the bed, his laughs growing louder as my own rose in volume too.

"Oh my god!" I gasped, "You looked so awful in the stupid stock...."

"And then Ching Shih jumping in like that. I've never really seen what she can do before. Made me feel even more respect for her. Don't want to ever piss her off."

Victorio's mirth started to calm a bit, as I hiccupped a little between my own bouts. He rolled off his little bed and slid onto my own, wrapping his arms around me, face against mine.

"Hey," I said, "when we left, you and Joe exchanged a look. Did he know something was going to happen to you?"

"Yeah. He 'told' me that I'd get into trouble, but I'd probably get out of it too. I forgot all about it until I stupidly went on ahead of Frank and they jumped me."

"Well, I hope you listen to him better next time he gives you a warning like that. I'm may not be around to save you," I teased.

"I always knew you were smart, and a good woods-woman, but I never knew you were so *dangerous*!" He nuzzled my neck in the way he knew I liked and soon my breath became a little ragged and my body pressed into his.

A knock at the door stopped the sensuous motion that had ensued.

"Yes?" I called.

The door popped open and Ching Shih stuck her head in.

"We're ready to take the tour," she said, eyebrows raising at seeing us so entwined. "Do you want to go? Or..."

Victorio and I looked at each other, and with a silent communication both slid off the bed and onto our feet.

"Yeah. We'll go...," I said.

We found Elphias in the library as promised. He and a sturdy looking woman named Alethea took us out the northern doors and down a long staircase to the science building. As we peeked in the doors of the long row of laboratories we saw people in white lab coats looking through microscopes and mixing things in beakers. At first the people inside barely noticed us, until Elf introduced us, and by "us" I mean Tochuku, to someone who recognized his name.

"You're Tochuku Adeyemi? The computer engineer?" the man's eyes widened in disbelief. "Hey! You guys, look who's here!" he called to the others in the room. Soon we, and by "we" I still mean Tochuku, were surrounded by people who were crowding each other for a chance to shake his hand.

"It's unbelievable that you're here!" exclaimed another.

"How on earth did that happen? Didn't you leave to go

to State in Cruces?" asked a skinny, dishwater blond, thirty-ish looking woman.

"Yes, well, I came back to take some friends camping in the Gila, just when the virus struck...." Tochuku barely got that much out before he was bombarded with questions by the crowd that was growing as word spread to the rest of the building.

Then, I recognized the woman, just as her eyes focused on me where I stood behind Tochuku. She was the woman who, with Stinky Boy, had detained me and Burl in Deming. I almost didn't recognize her in her lab coat, cleaned up and hair neatly trimmed.

Eyes wide she whispered in horror, "You're that girl. The one in Deming."

Victorio, shot me a questioning look as Frank raised his eyebrows in surprise. My face grew hot with rising fury.

"Yeah," I said. "That was me." She certainly gave a different impression, dressed in a lab coat, in a university laboratory. Not stealing my food and threatening to kill me.

"Oh my god," she said.

"Yeah." My head spun with the visceral impulse to grab her by the neck and bash her head into the wall behind her. If it weren't for my hunting and gathering skills, I could have died after my encounter with her and her companions.

"I'm so glad you're alive," she said. I stared at her.

Seeing that I wasn't going to hold up my end of the conversation, dumbfounded as I was, she continued in a rush.

"We had escaped from a Slaving compound, one in Cruces. We had barely managed to keep from being caught by the Slavers in Deming, and just holed up in that old bank, waiting until we were sure they were off our trail. Then Darian came to question and threaten us. We were starving."

Finding my voice finally I said, "So you decided it was you or me."

"Look, I'm sorry. And Derek, the boy with the gun. It wasn't even loaded. I mean, he did have to kill some Slavers before, for us to escape, but he wasn't going to kill you. We just needed your food really bad."

"I get it. Tough times." I turned towards the hallway. "Like you say, I made it."

Tochuku was oblivious, chin deep in chattering scientists. My other companions watched the exchange alertly.

"We'll find you later," Frank said to Tochuku as we exited the room to continue on our tour. Tochuku nodded briefly and returned to the conversation with his fans. The woman stared at me as if I *had* struck her.

"Someone you know, I take it?" asked Elf.

"She and some others captured me when I was going through Deming. Took my food. Threatened me."

"She's one of our best scientists, from the New Mexico State agriculture department. She came to us, along with some others, over a year ago. She's helped us improve our crop yields and our livestock practices quite a bit."

"Good for her," I said curtly. Elf said no more about her but sure enough, the areas between the buildings, which had all been lawns Before, were covered in gardens and orchards. There was a large field covered entirely in corn, another in wheat, still another in amaranth. Large patches sported the traditional "three sisters" of corn, beans and squashes of various kinds. Other patches grew tomatoes, onions, potatoes, garlic and numerous varieties of peppers.

"We don't eat a lot of meat here, since we don't have access to hunting and we don't have enough land to grow feed crops. We do have the goats for the milk and some meat, chickens, and some rabbits, but that's it," Alethea explained as we strolled the grounds.

"We do pretty well but we're practically imprisoned here because of the fear of the Slavers. The Maker scientists and ours have figured out how to make large batches of a sedative that we can produce in a liquid form and atomize in misters. Others have been transforming one of the unused buildings into a 'drug rehab' center like the one they have at the Maker compound," added Elf.

"In fact," Elf continued, "we're having a meeting about that very thing at lunch. We've been collaborating with the Makers about neutralizing the Slavers. I understand that you got a head start on that effort already. Because you've already weakened them, it will make our job much easier."

We returned to the Student Memorial building again, this time to the dining hall, for lunch. The Makers we had traveled with were already there, engaged in such focused conversation that they hardly noticed as we served ourselves from the buffet and joined them at their long table.

"We're not sure we have enough security people to go

on the raid and also keep watch here. We have lots of people, but not a lot of well-trained people," said a serious looking woman with the leathery skin and the thick freckles of a fair skinned person who spent a lot of time outdoors.

"We brought everyone we could spare," a rangy looking Maker responded.

Frank chimed in, "Well we brought our whole security team with us," nodding to Ching Shih, "so we'd be happy to come along if that would help."

"I could come," added Victorio. I stayed silent. My job was to collect books, and I was glad I had a valid reason not to round up more Slavers.

The Makers and Uvies looked at each other.

"Yeah," said the leathery woman, looking the trio over, "I think that'd be enough."

The Makers and other Uvies nodded in agreement.

"We should go soon though, while they're still trying to regroup after our last raid," said the rangy Maker.

"We need to head back home within a few days, so if you want our help we need to do it sooner rather than later anyway," said Frank.

"We don't have much more to do," said leather lady. "I think we could get all the sedative spray into the bottles and pack our gear today and tomorrow. Be ready by tomorrow night."

"Sounds good," said the Maker. "Let's have a full briefing tonight after dinner, with all the folks coming."

That evening the rest of the Cavers met with the Uvies and Makers who would make the trip to the Slaver compound, while I went with Elf to get the tour of the library.

"They're all clearly marked, and though we do still have the computers we used to use to search for books, we've also made an old-fashioned card catalog. It wasn't much of a change for me, since I remembered that sort of catalog from when I was young."

Staring at the immense rows of floor-to-ceiling books, the shelves neatly labeled according to the Dewey Decimal system for non-fiction, and alphabetically for fiction, I felt overwhelmed. How on earth was I going to decide which of these books to copy and which to leave? I had a list of books, or subjects, requested by everyone at home but surely there were others that we should have too. I decided to start fresh in the morning, with the lists I had been given, then figure out what else to copy from there.

After the raider's meeting I rendezvoused with Victorio in our room.

"We'll leave tomorrow night, around midnight. The Makers and the Uvie chemists will put the sedative in spray misters. Others will prepare the wagons that will hold all the sleeping Slavers. And trauma specialists will be taking other wagons to help the captives get back where they were taken from. They say that some of them will have been there so long that they won't have any place to go, so they'll get to choose between coming here or going to the Maker place," Victorio explained.

"Does that mean you'll have time to help me copy books tomorrow? I want to get that done as fast as possible so we can get back home soon, and it will take a good couple of days even with your help." I had asked Tochuku if he would help me, but he just made some cryptic comment about important work he would be doing with the other scientists and handed me the big hard drive he brought to store the books that have been scanned.

"Yeah, I can't help the Makers and Uvies much since its their wagons and misters and everything. I'll have to take a nap in the afternoon so I'm not too tired for the night work, but other than that I'm all yours."

After Victorio had gone to sleep, which came after our delayed tryst, I lie on my side in bed and stared at the wall wishing I could sleep, images of books of all sizes, colors and bindings danced in front of me. I wanted to take all the books back with me. I was greedy for knowledge.

The next morning after breakfast, Elf, Victorio and I started our search. I read the first list aloud, the one given to me by Gavin, and Elf dashed off into the stacks while Victorio and I rushed to keep up.

"Let's see, let's see," Elf muttered to himself as he scrutinized the row in front of him. His eyes lit up and he quickly pulled down a mound of books onto the floor. "That should get you started," he said with a nod to me. "What have you got Victorio?"

Victorio read his list, one from Jeanne, and the two shot off while I pressed the knob on the front of the scanner against the first book's cover and clicked a button, as Tochuku had shown me. It would take several minutes per book for the scan to be completed.

Elf bounced back and forth between me and Victorio,

replacing the books he had taken down while Victorio and I did the scanning. Despite the tediousness of the work it was exhilarating to see the counter on the scanner register one book after another so quickly.

We took a short break for lunch, then went back at it. When it came time for Victorio to take a nap I decided to take one with him, though I had to remind him several times that the purpose of our being in bed together was to *sleep.* An hour later we were scanning again. By dinner time we had scanned a hundred books or so.

After dinner I watched as the raiding party packed their bottles of sedatives, blankets, medical supplies and the like. As I saw them head into the tunnel from which we had entered, I felt especially glad for the afternoon nap. I knew I wouldn't sleep until they returned. Hopefully it wouldn't be long.

I spent the time waiting for their return in the lounge area on the bottom floor of the Student Memorial Building with the others who would help get the captive Slavers to their drug rehab center across the lawn in what had once been the gymnasium. Elf came to join me, sitting next to me on the couch.

"Did you happen to pass by the public library on your way here Lakshmi?' Elphias asked.

"No, I didn't. Why?"

"Because it was burnt to the ground soon after the virus. Deliberately. A mob declared that it was the scientists that had made the virus, that all the 'book learning' had poisoned people, figuratively as well as literally. They called it a 'turbo-charged' book burning. They sang hymns, holding hands, then cheered as it collapsed." Elf sat in silence, remembering.

I couldn't imagine such a thing. I wondered where those people were now. I didn't know what to say, so I said nothing at first.

After a few long moments I announced, "We have a library. Much smaller than yours."

Elf turned to me, eyes wide.

"You can't tell anyone though," I continued in a rush, "we've all promised to keep it a secret, to protect it. But I'm telling you because, well, I was thinking of our library as the Library of Alexandria, but now I realize it's really here, with you."

"Yes, yes, I understand. After I saw the public library burned I started rounding up people to live here at the university, to help me protect the library here. I thought of the Library of Alexandria too. That's how it started. Of course most of the professors left alive were thinking along similar lines. Our community is mostly centered around preserving knowledge as best we can."

I felt relieved that the burden of all the knowledge of humanity did not rest on my shoulders after all, but mostly on Elf. Still, as much as it was valued, the Library of Alexandria was destroyed eventually anyway.

"Maybe our library can be kind of a back-up library. I'm going to copy as many of your books as I can. I won't be able to store all the books here electronically, but I can at least get a good sampling of each subject. It'll take a lot of time, but that's okay," I told him.

"That's a great idea," he said, looking at me, a slow smile spreading across his face.

"I've been thinking," he said, "now that I have someone to talk to that understands the problem we have, regarding knowledge retention, it occurs to me that there are other things we can do too."

"What do you mean?"

"Well, if the raid they make tonight is successful, they can probably repeat the process with the other Slaver compound, to the south. If they succeed in that, it will make it much safer for the rest of us to cooperate. In all ways. Especially technologically and in food production. There's no reason that we can't cooperate by sharing knowledge too."

"You mean, like a school?" I asked, my interest peaked.

He smiled, his mouth a cheerful pink slit in a thicket of grey whiskers.

"Exactly like a school, my dear, exactly."

I couldn't believe I hadn't thought of it before. The library of Alexandria hadn't been just a place with books. It had been a place of learning, where teachers lived and students came to stay while they studied. We were in a university. Of course it could be a place of learning again.

"Certainly many people here have taken advantage of the resources, including learning from each other, but it's been completely informal so far. There's no reason it has to stay that way," Elf continued.

My mind raced with the possibilities.

"Maybe we could arrange for people from the other settlements to come, a few at a time, and study. Maybe people could come also to teach the things they're good at. It wouldn't have to be just about reading either. We have some people who are really great hunters and could teach others. And we have an excellent agriculturalist, who could help everyone improve their gardens...."

Elf's smile broadened, his eyes sparkling merrily. "Yes, yes, dear one. There's so much we could do with the Slavers out of the equation."

I pulled my ever-present notebook out of my pack and began to take notes. We had completed a pretty good outline of what our imagined university system could look like when, a couple hours later, the first of the raiders returned with the unconscious Slavers from the compound.

25

I stood with other onlookers to one side of the tunnel doors as pairs of Makers and Uvies appeared, carrying stretchers each laden with the limp, unconscious, body of a man. With a jolt of recognition I spotted Jeff on one of the stretchers, mouth agape. I guess he had only been knocked out by Ching Shih's fancy neck squeeze after all.

The raiders made their way with their unconscious charges, one by one, through the Student Memorial Building, out the south doors, and over to their new drug rehab center. Somehow, they didn't look as scary like that.

I watched anxiously for Victorio, Ching Shih and Frank, until one of the raiders I had met earlier told me that they had stayed behind to help the freed captives. Apparently, a lot of them were not in good enough condition to travel just yet. It made me nervous to think of them staying there through the night, vulnerable. There was nothing I could do to make the night go faster so Elf and I agreed to continue our book scanning the next day, after we had slept, or at least rested.

I tossed fitfully, in and out of sleep, startling suddenly every time I thought I heard the sound of the others returning. By dawn, they still hadn't come back. I dressed myself and made my way to the dining hall to see if anyone there knew anything.

"They're okay, we've got great medics and your own people are helping a lot with security, to keep an eye out for other Slavers, or anyone else who might interfere," reported a tow-headed guy who had helped bring in the unconscious Slavers. "There were some captives who were physically really weak. And some who, I don't know, just cowered in a corner and stared at us. Like they were scared of us, or didn't understand what was happening. We've got some people who are really good at psychological trauma first aid. And they can use a little of the sedative on those people too. They just wanted to all leave there at once, not leave only a few behind. That wouldn't be safe."

I thanked him for the information and went to find Elf again. Might as well start the day's work since I could neither sleep or do anything to speed Victorio and the others return back to me.

It was nearly noon when they finally arrived at the secure entryway, carrying some of the former captives on stretchers, although most of them were able to walk. Some women carried small children. One mother had a thin, listless baby in her equally thin arms, her eyes large and haunted. The former captives were taken to an infirmary that had been set up in a couple of the rooms down the hall from the library.

Victorio, Ching Shih and Frank brought up the rear, the last to come through the doors. I walked quickly up to Victorio as soon as I spotted him coming in behind the last of the stretchers, but stopped short of hugging him as I normally would, startled by the look on his face.

I clasped his shoulders and looked into his eyes. Then I glanced at Frank and Ching Shih, standing on either side of him. He looked like a zombie, just staring into the air, barely seeing me. Frank and Ching Shih looked like they were tired but otherwise okay, but they looked at Victorio with concern.

Scanning him for physical injury but finding none, I asked, "What happened?"

"Frank, can you take Victorio, while I talk to Lakshmi," Ching Shih asked.

"Yup...," said Frank, guiding Victorio down the hall towards the infirmary.

"He's had a shock, Lakshmi," Ching Shih began.

"What happened? What the *hell* happened?" my voice rose as I spoke, "He looks like a ghost. He doesn't look injured, I mean, other than what he already had when he left."

Ching Shih looked me straight in the eye. It was amazing how imposing her presence could be when she wanted it to be. I stopped talking and waited for her to continue.

"He was carrying a child. A little boy, about five years old or so. The boy didn't seem to be with any particular adult when we found him. He had been curled up on a pile of dirty blankets. He was skinny but he didn't look like he had been injured.... Anyway, Victorio carried him because the boy couldn't walk very well. He seemed very tired. But when we had gone just a few blocks. The boy just died. Right in his arms, for no apparent reason. Victorio started shouting, 'he's dead! Oh my god he's dead!' It was all we could do to get him to quiet down. It was very dangerous for him to be yelling. We didn't know who else was around. But then Frank took the boy from Victorio, and set him in one of the wagons. Victorio's been like this ever since."

"Okay, thanks," I said, turning towards the infirmary.

I found him lying on a cot staring at the ceiling. A plump, soft-looking comforter covered everything but his face, tucked in around his feet and along his sides, like a cocoon.

"He's in shock," said a slim blond woman sitting next to him. "We just need to give him a little time to process what's happened some. I'm watching to see when he starts breathing a little more normally, then I can do more with him."

Victorio hardly seemed to be breathing at all. Just shallow little sips of air.

"I can sit with him," I told her.

"Okay, I'll be in the next room, helping with the others. Let me know when his breathing deepens and becomes more regular."

After having seen so much death, it seemed to me we should be used to it, but the truth is that a sudden death is pretty much always a shock. Especially if it's a child. I pulled another cot over next to Victorio's and stretched out on it, wrapping my arms and legs around him, my face at the back of his neck.

I must have fallen asleep because I awoke to find Victorio facing me, arms out of the top of his comforter cocoon and draped over me, asleep himself. The blond medic was collecting some things from a cabinet, which is probably what woke me. She turned from the cabinet and, seeing me awake, walked over.

"It's good he's sleeping. He'll probably be a lot better when he wakes up," she whispered.

"I'm awake," breathed Victorio groggily. He pulled me closer to him, and I could feel his body vibrating a little.

"You're trembling," I said, starting to feel alarmed.

"No, that's perfect," said the medic. "Victorio, that's good that you're trembling. Just let it happen."

The trembling intensified and Victorio released me, rolling onto his back. It was as if little earthquakes were shaking his arms and legs and his breath became ragged, then gradually turned to sobs. I put my arms around him again as he held his face in his hands and cried for several minutes.

"That's good, Victorio, you're doing great," the medic said quietly.

When the crying finally subsided, Victorio looked red-faced and puffy but his body was relaxed and his breathing deep and slow.

"I'm going to leave you two alone. He doesn't need to stay here anymore. Victorio, just be sure to allow yourself to tremble if that comes up again. No work for you today, just be sure to eat something, get plenty of water and rest, okay?" It seemed to me we had been hearing that advice a lot lately.

Victorio nodded.

When the medic had gone he said, "God almighty Lakshmi, a little boy died in my arms. I didn't think he was that sick!" He wept more, wiping the tears away from his face as fast as they came.

"You couldn't have known. You just did what you could. At least he didn't die alone there. Maybe dying in the arms of someone who cared about him was the best thing that could have happened to him at that point." He nodded silently.

Victorio washed his face in the infirmary sink and we made our way to the cafeteria, where we found Frank and Ching Shih.

"You should go work on your books," Victorio said, as he nibbled unenthusiastically on some bread, "I'll go to our room and sleep some more. I'm still really exhausted."

Frank said, "I'm too wound up to sleep now. I can help with the books."

"I'm tired," said Ching Shih, addressing Frank, "I'll go sleep some and take over from you in a little while."

Frank and I found Elf in the library, and we picked up where Victorio and I left off the day before. The Makers we had come with, and many of the Uvies, had migrated to the gym to help get the Slavers situated in the drug rehab center and others had been preoccupied with caring for the people who had been rescued.

That evening at dinner, Victorio looked a lot better. I hadn't spoken to him since the morning. I had brought him some lunch but he had been asleep so I left it on the table for him. I came back later to find the food eaten, and him asleep again. After I finished scanning for the day I found Victorio in the dining room, just sitting down with a plate of food.

Tochuku joined the rest of us and we traded stories about the work we had all been doing. The recounting of the raid on the Slaver compound was definitely way more interesting than my book collecting and Tochuku's description of the genius convention he had been having with all the other scientists.

"Yup. It was pretty bad," commented Frank in his usual, understated manner.

Ching Shih elaborated, "I've never seen anything like it. They were worked so hard and weren't given much food to eat. Or much water to wash in, or clean clothes or blankets. One lady said they were beaten if they were caught eating the food they harvested, but of course they risked it because they were starving. Except the young women they had living with them. They were also knocked out with the sedative when we sprayed the Slaver's rooms, but when they woke up they were just as happy to be free as the others."

"You know, if we can get rid of the other group of Slavers, it'll be a lot easier for the different settlements to cooperate. We could help each other a lot. Learn from each other, trade goods," Frank said.

"Elf and I have been talking about getting some kind of educational system going here, at the university," I said, smiling at how silly that sounded as I said it. "I think I can finish the last bit of scanning tonight if you want to leave in the morning."

Tochuku cleared his throat and we all looked at him.

"I've been asked to stay through the winter. So we can work on our projects. With the knowledge of the scientists here, and the equipment and tools that the Makers have, we could do a lot here."

The rest of us looked at each other.

"Of course that's your choice, Tochuku," said Frank shifting in his seat to look at him.

"Gavin and young Thomas can do all the maintenance on our electrical and water systems. You don't really *need* me." Handing me a cardboard box he added, "This is a little something for Gavin. Some lab equipment that they were willing to part with here. We can always get the Makers to make more for us if we need it."

I laughed out loud at his rationality, "But Tochuku, we'll *miss* you. Even if someone else can do the work you do. Don't you know that?"

Tochuku smiled broadly at me. "Yes, I will miss you too."

The next day we said our goodbyes after breakfast and promised the Uvies and Makers that we would visit again in the spring, after the snow had thawed sufficiently. There were many hugs all around. I had the hardest time saying goodbye to Elf. It was if I was saying goodbye to some part of my mother.

"I'll come get some more books in the spring," I told him.

Elf beamed happily at me. "I'll be thinking about our

school plan, and you can do the same. Just because nearly everybody on Earth is dead, it doesn't mean the rest of us have to wallow in ignorance, now does it?"

26

The four of us headed back into the forest, stopping overnight at the monastery to fill in Matthew and the others there on the events in Silver City. They were thrilled to hear that one of the Slaver compounds had been disabled, and the concept of the drug rehab program had many in stitches, trying to imagine such a manner of transforming hardened, violent criminals into peaceful citizens.

"The Uvies and Makers plan to take down the southern Slaver compound after they have enough of the northern Slavers rehabilitated to make room for more. And to make more of the sedative," Frank explained.

"You know, that could sure change things around here, to be free of those people. Seems to me that we all have a lot to share with each other, especially knowledge. It doesn't make sense for us to be fighting with each other. It makes sense for us to work together. We'd all benefit," Matthew said.

I told the group about the idea for a school.

"But it doesn't have to be just school-school, we can also organize classes, or apprenticeships for anything. Victorio, Beto and I could teach people about hunting. Kate and your livestock people could share ideas. Jeanne is brilliant when it comes to medicinal plants, and other things related to healing. One of the Forest People's women is going to teach some of our people about midwifery. Every settlement needs that." My mind whirled with the possibilities.

That night after dinner I spent until bedtime catching up on my journal entries. There had been so much that had happened on this trip I hadn't been able to keep up along the way. I thought of the generations down the road who would wonder how their forebears had handled the transition from the 8 billion plus, petroleum fueled world, into the one we had now.

The night before we made it home it snowed. Not much, just enough to melt on my hair and trickle down my neck, making it harder to stay warm, much less sleep. Victorio pulled our sleeping tarp over our heads, causing my breath to echo inside the close covering.

It had been nearly three weeks since we had left, and we knew the others would be worried about us. Sure enough, as we rounded the last bend, all of us off our horses and leading them, Gavin came bursting out of the door of his and Tochuku's cave.

Ignoring the rest of us, he went first to Ching Shih, whose eyes lit up. Gavin hugged her tightly. She seemed simultaneously pleased and embarrassed by this display.

Once Gavin had ascertained Ching Shih's health and well-being, he turned to the rest of us. His face fell, eyes wide with fear.

"Where's Tochuku? What happened to him?" he asked in a low voice.

"It's all good, man," said Victorio, "he just decided to stay with the other scientists at the university."

Relief spread across Gavin's face.

"I guess you're the last, lone, science geek," teased Frank.

Ignoring the jibe Gavin said, "Well I'm sure glad you're back. I'm going to round up the others while you take the horses inside the hill. We've all been worried about you, especially Jeanne," he added pointedly to Frank, "and I've got something I need to tell everybody anyway."

Once inside the bowl of the hill we were greeted with hugs, sighs of relief and a scolding from Jeanne and Hallie about taking so long to get back. Food and drinks were brought outside since it was midday and still warm enough to eat at our picnic tables there.

Gavin continued to look anxious, but I couldn't imagine why. I knew he liked being roommates with Tochuku but I didn't think they were so close that he'd have a problem with him staying in town for the winter.

Questions were raining down on us returned travelers, which we were trying to answer, Frank, Victorio and I all talking over one another, when Gavin interrupted us.

"Listen, listen, I have something to tell you!" he looked on the verge of tears. We turned to stare. He was not behaving like himself at all.

"Go on Gavin, we're listening now," encouraged Grandpa Joe.

Gavin took a deep breath before continuing, voice shaking.

"We've been contacted. Just now. Just before these guys showed up. Someone finally answered my call on the radio."

We all stared at him, stunned.

"Well...," stammered Yazmin, "what did they say?"

"We talked for about twenty minutes. It was some guy up near Denver."

The rest of us stood transfixed while Gavin paced back and forth while he spoke.

"Well, you know how we've always figured that after the virus hit, that people all over the world did what we're doing, trying to recover, get back to as normal as they could? And that we lost about 90% of the world's population?"

I couldn't imagine what he might say next but I wished he'd just get to it.

"More happened after the virus. I mean, people started shooting each other, especially in the cities, so of course we lost a lot more people that way, maybe another ten or twenty percent of what was left. But we also figured that. You know, another 150-200 million or so?"

A cold chill rippled up my spine at the sound in his voice. I had the feeling I wasn't going to like what was coming.

"But that's not what happened. And there aren't, you

know, 650 million people on the planet. After the virus came through, about three years later, climate change kicked in big time. He says the Atlantic current shut down. Since then there have been hurricanes constantly along the coasts, tornadoes have gotten many times worse throughout the midwestern US. For hundreds of miles inland from the coasts, the land has been scoured. The Midwest is unlivable. It's literally impossible to grow food there. Their Great Lakes region is in the midst of a five-year long winter."

The joyous feeling from our successful return from our trip evaporated as the image of what he described bloomed in our heads. The rest of us stared mutely at Gavin, transfixed by his account. And he was far from finished.

"Then there are the places that haven't gotten any precipitation to speak of since then, to the west of us. We're living in one of the two only habitable areas on the continent, in a transition zone between the extremes. Here, and in an area east of the Mississippi river that is far enough south to still get some summer, and far enough from the coasts to miss the hurricanes, and far enough east to miss the tornadoes. We're in a zone between the places that have gotten a lot hotter and drier and the places that have gotten a lot wetter and colder."

"Only two places on the continent?" breathed Jeanne in disbelief. Apparently getting the feeling that things weren't going well in the adult world, Rose began to cry, setting off Sid and Uma in the process. Hallie lifted Rosie, whispering assurances into her ear, while Frank and Jeanne pulled the other two close.

"He says that this same thing has happened all over the world. People were reeling so badly after the virus that when the weather change hit, they just couldn't get out fast enough, or adjust. Humanity is just a *fraction* of what it was after the virus had killed most people anyway. We don't have about 650 million people on the planet now. We have about half that. Or a third. We're almost all that's left." Gavin fell silent as we pondered this stunning information.

"How could he know that?" asked Yazmin, "Who was he, how could he have that information?"

"NORAD," said Gavin, "North American Aerospace Defense Command. The facility in the mountain, with the nuclear weapons..."

The older people in the group inhaled sharply. Us younger people looked around in bafflement.

Frank explained, "The American and Canadian governments built a bunker, huge, inside a mountain. Partly to house our nuclear weapons, but also to provide shelter in case of some kind of disaster. Probably they collected people from that area after the virus. They would have all kinds of technology, and energy sources. And communication with other such facilities that other governments set up all over the world. They would be able to communicate with each other about what's been going on. They probably were able to keep some of the satellites up, at least for awhile. They would definitely know."

All this time we had thought there were people in pretty much all the places they had been before, just not so many, like us. Now it seemed otherwise.

"You didn't tell them where we are, did you?" asked Yazmin.

"No, no, of course not," said Gavin, "I told him New Mexico. It's a big state. We're going to try talking again soon."

As we ate lunch together, outside in the cool fall air, we considered this news.

"We're more alone than we thought then. And more isolated," said Hallie.

"Yeah. And if we can't make it work here, in our little zone, then that's it for humanity on this side of the continent," added Beto.

Later, as Victorio and I put away our gear and travel clothes, we talked some more with Grandpa Joe.

"What do you think about the news today?" Victorio asked his grandfather.

Joe sat staring hard at the wall opposite the couch he sat upon.

"You know, we're starting all over, us humans. It has been predicted in many traditions, all over the world. We made a lot of mistakes. The question is, how can we avoid those mistakes from here on out? We've got to think through how to go from here.

"Before the Taker culture came into being there had been thousands of cultures that came, and also went, but none that were so destructive on a world-wide level. But there were countless cultures, all very different from each other, that got along fine, at least before the days of totalitarian agriculture. They kept the peace, most of the time, with their neighbors. They only killed what they needed to live. They may have accidently been responsible for the extinction of other beings but they weren't *trying* to do that.

"So it's pretty simple. All the world's religions, and other spiritual traditions say much the same thing, though they sure as heck didn't always follow their own sayings. They all say, basically, to live and let live. Don't steal. Don't kill. Don't lie. Take care of one another. We don't know what these other folks are up to, here in the southwest, or in the rest of the world. But we've got to try our best to make things good right here in the Gila area. You helped make some progress by getting rid of those Slavers on your trip. Now let's see if we can work together with the other groups, in a good way." Joe got up from the couch and headed to the kitchen to make his evening tea.

After long hot showers and a short nap we all had dinner at Jeanne and Frank's house. The sun had set and the air chilled. I turned the knob for the hot water radiant heating at Grandpa Joe's cave before we left for Jeanne's. The men didn't mind so much but I hated to be cold, especially on my feet.

By now the others had also had time to digest Gavin's astonishing news to hear about our trip to Silver City. So we told them, in our usual, chaotic, forwards then backwards, then forwards again way that all these stories were told. Some were excited about the prospect of more contact, and collaboration with, the Monks, Makers and Uvies, and some were more nervous about it. But it seemed inevitable that we would have some relationship with all these groups, along with the Forest People. Victorio and Beto never did make it out to the forest north and east of where we were, to see if there were other settlements, but they planned to do so in the spring.

The next day Ching Shih and Gavin came to Joe's. Victorio and I were at the corral, me brushing the horses and Victorio hauling water to their trough. Ching Shih and Gavin were holding hands, like two children who were just learning *how* to hold hands. Ching Shih looked at the ground and Gavin beamed.

"Hey," Gavin said, "Is Joe around?"

Victorio tipped his head towards the cave door, "He's inside...."

They made their way, still holding hands.

Victorio raised his eyebrows at me questioningly and I shrugged back at him.

"They want me to marry them," said Joe at dinner that night.

I stared, perplexed, at Joe. Of all the people in our little community I couldn't think of any two that seemed more incompatible. Gavin was warm, friendly, always saw the best in people, and was a genius at teaching the children, all who loved him wholeheartedly. Ching Shih, on the other hand, kept a distance, even from Kate, with whom she lived. She was reserved and private, although she had warmed up to me since our trip to Silver. She was very smart, highly analytical and took nothing for granted, especially when it came to our security. She was a great martial arts and yoga instructor, patient and clear, but all business, leading classes in each twice a week. She took her role as our protector very seriously, which we all appreciated. The children shied away from her and she seemed just fine with that. Ching Shih had said she had never had children because she had never wanted them.

"Well? Are you going to?" asked Victorio, mouth full of rabbit stew.

"Yes. They want to get married as soon as possible, before the first real snow, down by the river."

27

The next few days were one long gossip session and fashion show. Most of us women buzzed around poor Ching Shih like bees around a hive. We all ransacked our clothing and fabric stores to find or construct something nice for her to wear, although she seemed slightly appalled by all the attention.

Kate found a long silky beige dress in her closet. It was a little short for Ching Shih but then I found a long lacey pale blue table runner which Jeanne sewed onto the bottom half to make it long enough. There was even enough left to top the cap sleeves. Hallie found a pretty sash of a slightly darker blue, to tie around the waist of the dress. Hallie pulled a large lace doily from underneath a potted plant at her house, scrubbing it fiercely until it gave up its store of grit and gleamed prettily again. This would go on Ching Shih's head, our best approximation of a veil.

Naturally we all took turns gently prompting Ching Shih to share the story of her romance with Gavin, which had gone completely unnoticed by any of us. It turned out that it came down to bonsais, the trees carefully cultivated to grow in miniature form. Gavin had a penchant for bonsais and had several along a long window sill at his and Tochuku's home. One day, Ching Shih had come by to talk with Tochuku, about how the technology he was working on could be used for security, when she spotted the diminutive trees. Apparently she had grown bonsai trees in Hong Kong as a hobby, giving them away to friends and family when she had too many. She was surprised and delighted to see them, believing that bonsais were only known in the east. After her brief meeting with Tochuku they invited her to dinner and Gavin and Ching Shih talked into the night about bonsais. Then he invited her to come over and start bonsais of her own, since he had all the tools and pots already.

According to Victorio, the men were having similar conversations with Gavin, although they usually involved the imbibing of mugs of Devon's mead too. Gavin said in his warm understated way that Ching Shih softened when working on her bonsais, and he had seen that beneath her business-like manner was a woman who loved beauty and housed an artist's heart. Somehow, he had found his way into that heart, and she into his.

While the rest of us were at least a little intimidated by Ching Shih at the very least, Gavin—gentle, kind Gavin—took on a protective demeanor towards her. Although, not, of course, physically, since she could kick the behind of any three of us at once in her sleep.

No, Gavin stood guard at the doorway to her soul. I did

not know what needed guarding there, but clearly he did. He always had one arm around her now, and she seemed to melt slightly into his side, accepting protection from these unseen elements.

The morning of the wedding dawned crisp and cold. Frost covered the ground in a sparkling latticework, like a bright white crystalline fungus. The fall sky was clear and bright turquoise. There was no wind. A perfect fall day, if chilly.

After gulping down breakfast I rushed over to Kate and Ching Shih's place. Benjamin sat in his favorite chair in the living room, grinning at the women who poured excitedly into the house. I had never been to a wedding before.

"Welcome ladies, welcome ladies," Benjamin said over and over, nodding at each as they entered.

"It's awfully cold out this morning," said Jeanne to Ching Shih, "are you sure you still want to have it outside? I'd be happy to clear out the living room."

"Oh no." said Ching Shih, "It's perfect. It'll be warmer by noon. I want to be married under the sky, next to the river, with the birds watching. The forest will be our cathedral."

I don't think I had ever heard Ching Shih express such a poetic sentiment before. Clearly there was much more to her than I had seen in the few months I had known her.

"You know, I have a lacy ivory colored shawl that will be perfect to wrap around your shoulders," said Jeanne as she disappeared to find it.

Ching Shih patiently endured our attentions while we fussed and clucked about her.

Kate first combed her hair with water then pinned it into a couple of dozen gentle curls at the ends, so as not to shock Gavin with too dramatic a transformation. The desert air would dry the pin curls well before it was time for the wedding.

Hallie had found some makeup and obeyed Ching Shih's admonition not to make her "look like a prostitute." A little rouge, carefully spread so it looked nearly like her natural complexion. Eyeliner and mascara opened her black eyes. A little rosy eyeshadow and subdued lipstick brought color to her naturally pale face. Ching Shih flat out refused the lacy push-up bra that Olga offered her but accepted a more matronly but pretty version that Hallie had.

"I had this when I was a teenager, before the virus, but since I've been nursing I don't think it'll ever fit again," Hallie said.

Ching Shih and Kate disappeared into her room where she slipped into her wedding dress. Then they returned into the living room where Kate took the pins out of her hair, using a few to attach the doily-turned-veil onto the top of her head. The shiny raven curls formed a festive, delicate border around the bottom edge of the doily.

"Whoa...," breathed Hallie, hands to her face in a humorous, classic "wow" expression. "You're SO pretty!" We were used to seeing her in canvas pants and t-shirts.

Jeanne stepped forward with the shawl, wrapping it around Ching Shih's shoulders, then pulling the ends under her arms and tying them behind her back, so that the shawl became a shrug, showing off the sculpted neckline of her dress' bodice while covering her arms. Then, out of her pocket, Jeanne pulled a necklace of tiny gold colored beads that had been strung to form a lacy latticework. Ching Shih's eyes widened at the sight of it, and her mouth dropped open silently as Jeanne draped it around her neckline, fastening it in the back.

I was so used to thinking of Ching Shih as our tough, sometimes scary, security guard and martial arts teacher, I hadn't thought she could look so soft and delicate. When Kate pulled her full-length mirror from her room and held it in front of Ching Shih, it occurred to me that this might be a surprise to her as well, judging from the look on her face.

Jeanne turned to me, "Run find out what the guys are up to...."

I found Victorio entertaining the children in the courtyard, teaching them to juggle.

"Where's Gavin? And the other guys?"

"They're still at Gavin's, but Frank just walked by and said he was all dressed."

"Can you tell them to go to the river? Ching Shih's ready."

"Aw, c'mon, don't stop now," whined Rose, as Victorio set the balls on a table and went to round up the men.

A little later there was a knock on Kate's front door—Frank, letting us know that the men were at the river. Frank would escort Ching Shih down to where her husband-to-be waited, and give her away. The rest of us filtered out the door, down the winding pathway to a place where the river curved dramatically enough to form a pool deep enough to swim in. Cottonwoods, leaves now gold and russet, towered along the bank, forming a decorative, protective canopy over the small clearing where we gathered.

Gavin stood next to Grandpa Joe, with Victorio, Beto and Patricio lined up beside him, all dressed in dark, clean, pants, dress shirts and suit coats that had miraculously been mined from Grandpa Joe's and Frank's closets.

Kate, Hallie and Olga stood on the other side, each clad in a pretty blue dress of some kind. Patricio and Devon carried Benjamin in a sling they had constructed, and set him in a chair with the rest of us. With so many of the parents in the wedding party, the rest of us each held the hands of the younger children, Rose, Obsidian and Uma. The older children, Thomas, Zoe and Walter, elbowed and "shushed" one another as we all took our places.

Yazmin, who had been smudging everyone with a stick of burning sage as we arrived, began to sing a light, lyrical, enchanting song in a language I had never heard before, Mayan perhaps, since that was her ancestry. Ching Shih emerged from a stand of ponderosas, taking slow, measured steps, hand tucked inside the crook of Frank's arm. She looked like a forest goddess out of some mythical past, the cool fall breeze bringing more color to her cheeks than the rouge had. Gavin's face was transfixed as he watched her, his eyes shining with new moisture.

Frank solemnly left Ching Shih next to Gavin, joining the audience and taking Jeanne's hand.

Joe's voice intoned while Yazmin continued her song quietly in the background.

"Friends, family...we're *all* really family now, aren't we? We are gathered here today to celebrate the joining of

Ching Shih Li, and Gavin Thompson, as husband and wife. They have come together under the most unlikely of circumstances, brought together by a fate that none could have guessed. From across the world Ching Shih came and she became one of us, here, Cave People, in the forest and on the banks of a river called Gila. Many have been born, married and died in this place. We are as much a part of this place as the jays and piñons, the trout and the rabbits. All our relations, the winged, the four -legged, the serpents and the two-legged, as well as the plant nations, water nation and the mineral nations, witness this joining.

"Ching Shih and Gavin, do you agree to care for one another, to treat each other with kindness and respect, for the rest of your lives? Do you promise to be truthful with one another and to consider each other's well-being when taking action, big or small?" asked Joe.

Gavin and Ching Shih both said, "Yes," simultaneously.

"Gavin, do you take Ching Shih, to be your blessed, wedded wife, from this day forward?"

"I do," said Gavin, his voice shaking.

"Ching Shih, do you take Gavin, to be your blessed, wedded husband, from this day forward?"

"I do," said Ching Shih with a wet sniff.

Joe's eyes lit up mischievously, "Well then, how about a nice big kiss, to seal the deal?"

We all laughed as Gavin engulfed Ching Shih in his arms and the new spouses kissed for a long time before coming up for air. Ching Shih was laughing and crying at the same time, Gavin's face was red as a beet with happiness, unable to take his eyes from his wife's face. We all lined up to hug them both, then made our way to Jeanne and Frank's place for the celebratory meal.

We had a sumptuous fall feast of baked quail and finely sliced grilled elk, roasted fall vegetables tossed in a raspberry vinaigrette sprinkled with toasted pinon nuts. Fresh sliced apples drizzled with a dressing of honey and sweet herbs. Flat bread made from mesquite and sacaton flours topped with Kate's finest goat cheese. And Jeanne had used some of the precious sugar and wheat flour we had stored to create a three-tiered cake that looked like it had come out of a bride's magazine from Before. White frosting covered with pink buttercream roses and the last of the fall blooms from the south-facing slopes.

I looked around the room at the people gathered. We had people here from various parts of the world and all over our country. We had old people, small children, artists, scientists, and people with countless practical skills and abilities. We were very lucky to have each other.

A week later a blizzard came that continued off and on for three days, reminding me of the big snowstorm that kicked off the winter last year as I huddled in my little shed trying to stay warm and hoping I wouldn't starve before spring. I told Victorio and Joe about my true friend Burl the burro over dinner, the winds howling outside while we sat snug in our warm nest, bellies full. I still felt guilty that I couldn't save him.

Victorio gently took my hands in his as Joe nodded, "It's the worst pain ever, not to be able to save someone you love from harm."

A year earlier I couldn't have imagined I would be where I was now, and with whom. I had the community I had dreamed of on my long journey here, and much more. I had friends, family, as well. We didn't have to worry about starving or freezing, and winter and isolation would protect us from any Slavers that remained.

Most of us slept more once winter settled in, going to bed earlier and waking up later, a semi-hibernation. I relished going to sleep each night with Victorio's arms around me, and waking up with my head on his shoulder, as if we became one being while we slumbered, returning to our independent state only during daylight.

Everyone had stocked up on a whole winter's worth of books so that I wouldn't have to make trips to the library until the spring, and of course everyone traded books as well, interest peaked by the descriptions of other readers.

Gavin continued teaching the older children, but just a couple of hours a day, at Olga's and Patricio's. They devoted themselves to their artwork now that the demands of food production had slackened. Olga delved into a vivid imaginative series of paintings depicting the various communities we had visited that summer— the Forest People, Monks, Makers, Uvies and a particularly grim one of the slaver compound. Since she had not traveled to these places herself, her imagery was based on the accounts of those of us who had visited these places.

Patricio had collected clay from the river using the directions my Forest People clay instructor, Claude, had given me. Thrilled to have clay to work for the first time since Before, he devoted himself to his pottery, alternating between throwing utilitarian pots of various sorts—mugs, bowls, plates and other dishes—and rolling long slabs of clay, cutting them into squares and rectangles, carving their faces with vivid relief images of flowers, trees and local animals, and experimenting with colored slips, and other mixtures for glazes.

When it wasn't snowing we also spent time outside, sledding down the hillsides and throwing snowballs at each other, secure in the knowledge that we had warm homes with hot baths into which we could retreat once we had become too cold or tired. I wondered how the Forest People were fairing in their tipis and yurts. Firewood had already been stacked high throughout the camp when we had left them.

I read and wrote a lot, filling in my notes from the summer's adventures. I knew what my purpose was, my job. I needed to record as much as possible about the virus, and what had happened immediately after it had scoured our land of loved ones, enemies and civilization as it had grown over thousands of years. Now that we knew that there were far fewer people in the world than we previously assumed, it seemed even more important to document our history as well as possible for future generations.

Since Ching Shih was now living with Gavin at the cave he had shared with Tochuku, we all took turns helping Kate with Benjamin. One evening I was helping Kate put him to bed when he made a surprising announcement.

Lying on his back as usual as we tucked the covers in around him he stared up at the ceiling as if watching a movie and said, "They're looking for us."

"Who is?" asked Kate.

"Those people. In the mountain. They want to know where we are. But they can't find us. Not here. Not for a long time." Then he closed his eyes to sleep.

ABOUT THE AUTHOR

Laura Ramnarace lives in southwestern New Mexico near the Gila National Forest where she works as a mediator and educator. She has authored a column on interpersonal relationships for the Silver City Independent and guest hosts for KURU Radio. Ms. Ramnarace believes that humanity could do better and hopes that they do not wait for a catastrophe before doing so.

Made in the USA
Columbia, SC
08 November 2020

24131020R00207